The One I Want

The Rolling Hills Series

Chelle Sloan

Cover Design: Kari March Designs

Cover model: Cole Forsgren

Cover photographer: Katie Cadwallader Photography

Editing: Kiezha Smith Ferrell, Librum Artis Editorial Services

Proofreading: Michele Ficht and Chloe Kill-Trivelpiece

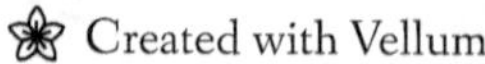 Created with Vellum

To Amanda.
There is no other person I'd want to be on this book journey with (or throw an impromptu Super Bowl party with). Thank you for everything (especially the DoorDash).

Chapter 1
Wes

Suitcases.

I blink a few times because I don't know why I'm walking into my house to see suitcases in the hallway.

Especially today.

I don't know what I expected to walk into. I didn't expect a party. I didn't even really think that Cara would pull the kids out of school to celebrate with me. But, I figured at least I'd come home to a warm welcome from my wife. I mean, it's not every day your husband announces to the world he's retiring from professional football at the end of the season, ending a twelve-year career.

"Cara?" I yell as I drop my duffel bag inside the doorway. I know she hates that, but frankly, I don't care. There are more pressing matters.

Like why she didn't come to the press conference when she said she would.

Why didn't she even send me a "good luck" text, knowing what I was about to do.

Why there are multiple suitcases in our foyer.

"Cara!" I yell again.

She doesn't say anything. Instead I hear her coming down the stairs, her high heels clicking and clacking on the hardwood floor.

"There you are," I say. "What is all this?"

She's still quiet as she makes her way down the stairs. I take a look at her and instantly know something is off. She's carrying her large purse—the exorbitantly expensive one she insisted she needed but only uses when we travel. She's wearing a designer tracksuit. Or as I like to call it, her airport fashion.

"You're home."

I blink a few times, not understanding why this is the first response out of her mouth. "Yes, I'm home. I asked you a question. What is all of this? Where are you going?"

"I didn't want to do it like this," she says, handing me an envelope as she walks past me.

"What's this?" I ask, ripping open the envelope. Though in my head, I already know. "Divorce papers?"

She doesn't say anything, instead tapping something into her phone.

"Were you seriously just going to leave these for me on the table with a note and a see you later?"

She finally looks up from her phone. "That was the plan."

"Are you fucking kidding me?" I yell, which wasn't my intent. But I think I'm justified. I'm just glad the kids aren't home yet. They've heard us fight enough. And I feel like this is about to be a doozy.

"This can't be a surprise," she says. "Can you honestly say that we've been in a happy marriage?"

"We've had fights. Never once have you said the word divorce," I say, because she's right. We've been fighting for a while now. But divorce? I didn't realize we were that far gone. "This morning you were telling me that you were going to meet me at the facility for the press conference. And now you're leaving? So that was a lie? Because these papers didn't magically appear out of thin air."

"I'm sorry," she says, though I don't hear an ounce of sincerity in her voice. "I don't know why I told you that. I had these drawn up last week. Today seemed as good a time as any, since your decision to retire led to this."

I'm stunned. It's not like I sprung this retirement thing on Cara. It's been in the works for two years. Yes, I knew she was opposed to me retiring. She went into great detail about how she had become accustomed to a certain lifestyle, and that lifestyle wouldn't be able to be maintained without my contract. I, in turn, told her that if she paid attention, she'd know that I had money put away knowing retirement was coming. That seemed to have calmed her down.

Or so I thought.

Though now that I think about it, as I kept talking about retirement, she rarely weighed in. This was the last year of my contract. I knew if I signed another, it would be short term. Honestly, going into this season, I was still on the fence. Then I battled through training camp during the hottest summer months on record in Nashville. That was followed by an injury in last week's season opener that has put me out for three games. In my younger days, I would have bounced back after a trip to the trainer's room.

That's when I knew. It was time to hang up the cleats.

So I talked to the coaches and my agent. I talked to my family and, of course, I talked to Cara. They all said that if now was the time I felt sure, then to do it. Well, Cara said to "do whatever I wanted." Maybe I should have read more into her indifference.

"You really think me retiring is a dealbreaker?" I ask. "Is that really the reason?"

She shrugs. "Mostly. I started thinking about life without you playing."

"Do you mean without my contract or with me being home more?"

I want her to say it. Say it's about the money. Because somewhere over the years, my sweet wife became a person obsessed with wealth.

"Both," she admits. "For example, what would you do? Just sit around here all day? You wouldn't work at all?"

Well, that was saying it without saying it.

"I thought I'd take some time off, but eventually I'll do something," I say. "But you know I have plenty of money put away for this exact reason. Plus, now I'll be home during the day. I won't be gone for days at a time in the season. I'll be able to help take the kids to school. I know you hate the carpool line. I'd be glad to do it. We'll travel, we'll take vacations. We can do anything."

"Where would we live?" she asks, crossing her arms like she's throwing a temper tantrum.

"Uh, here?" Why is she asking this? Does she think that when I become a retired player on the Nashville Fury that we have to move out of the state?

"That's a lie," she accuses. "You can't wait to get back to Rolling Hills with your boys. Hell, Oliver is probably planning your welcome home party as we speak."

I blink a few times because I'm totally confused. "When did I ever say that I wanted to move back to Rolling Hills?"

"I heard you talking to Simon last week. I know your plan. I bet you and your little troop can't wait to be reunited. And living next door to your parents? Exactly the life I envisioned."

I don't even acknowledge Cara's sarcasm. It's not worth it right now.

Maybe years ago I would have moved back. Being in the

same town with Oliver, Simon, and Shane was the dream. The four of us reunited. But I knew Cara would never go for it, so I put that thought to the side. Happy wife, happy life, right?

But why now is she thinking that this is happening? I did talk to Simon last week. Yes, he's a real estate agent. If I did want to move back, he's the one I'd call. But it wasn't about...oh.

"You misunderstood," I say. "Yes, Simon and I were talking, like we do regularly. He was asking me if my parents were interested in selling their rental because it's currently between occupants. I made the joke that if my mom had her way, she'd have it set up for us to visit all the time. That's it. I never even considered moving back to Rolling Hills. And do you think I'd just make that decision? That I wouldn't talk to you about that?"

"I don't believe you," she says. The more and more she talks, the more and more she's sounding like a spoiled, petulant child. "But I don't want Rolling Hills. I don't even want Nashville. I've been stuck in this city for twelve years with you. I've been stuck in this house. When I married you, I thought we'd travel the world, or at least the country. But no, you've played for the same team your entire life and vacations are to fucking Disney World."

"I'm sorry for being good at my job and my team wanting to keep me," I say sarcastically. "Are you really mad that we didn't have to move every three years every time I got a new contract?"

"I'm mad that I'm now thirty-five years old and I have nothing to show for my life."

Wow. That fucking stings. And is she even taking into consideration the kids, or is this all just selfishness talking. "Really? Nothing to show for your life? That's really what you think?"

She shakes out her shoulders, trying to put up an air of confidence. "I do."

The more this conversation drags on, the more I'm realizing how many things I had to have overlooked or ignored over the past few years. Yes, I knew retirement was a sticking point for her. But to say that her life—*our* life—was a waste? Wow. I didn't expect that.

Maybe it's because I still think of her as the girl I met at Kentucky our sophomore year of college. That girl who didn't see me as a paycheck. Hell, at that point, I didn't even know if professional football was in my future. I had to redshirt my freshman year due to injury. I wasn't starting. I was just a guy who could say he played on the football team.

But she loved me. She was at every game, my number painted on her face and her smile waiting for me after every game. I loved her. She loved me.

Or at least I thought. Apparently at some point over the years she started loving less of me and more of my salary.

I don't know when that started happening, or when all of a sudden she hated being a mother. We started trying for Emerson, our oldest, within months of being married. I remember her singing to her belly every night. There wasn't even a debate on having Hank and Magnolia. It was just what we wanted.

Wasn't it?

I feel like our entire marriage is now playing back in my head in some sort of sped up slow motion. Though I still don't remember at what point she went from the woman I married to the woman she's become.

I do know that our problems seriously started the first time I mentioned retirement. It was two years ago. If we've had a hundred fights since then, ninety-five of them were about that.

Is this why she stopped coming to games? Or family events? I'd always ask her if she was going to the wives' luncheons, or the family days that the other wives and kids would have, and she'd always have a reason to not go. Though, she always had a reason to go on some sort of shopping splurge. And she had a detailed list of why she needed a fifteen-thousand-dollar Hermes purse.

Damn, was I this blind the whole time? Here I thought it was just a bump in the road. Turns out it was the end of it.

"Your kids aren't something to show for your life? Our marriage? Our life? What happened to you, Cara?"

She shrugs. "I want more."

I didn't know three words could sting like that. "Where are you going?"

She takes the few steps she needs to grab hold of each bag. "California. I have friends out there. I'm going to stay with them until I figure out what my next step is."

I move out of the way as she begins to walk past me.

"What am I supposed to tell the kids? You're just going to leave them without saying goodbye?"

"I think it's better this way. Clean break. It's your turn to parent."

"Are you saying you don't want to even share custody?"

She shrugs as she opens the door and steps out.

"Cara! Wait!"

She stops, and I see her shoulders rise and fall as she takes in a breath. "What?"

I don't know what I want to ask. Hell, I don't even know why I called after her. Clearly she doesn't want to be here. And clearly I'm an idiot for thinking my marriage was still somewhat intact. "This is it. You're done. We're done. Because once you leave, don't think you can come back."

She turns to look back at me. "Goodbye, Wes."

And with that, she shuts the door.

Chapter 2
Betsy

"THAT WAS THE LAST ONE. I THINK. I HOPE. GOOD GOD, I thought Whitley had a lot of shoes."

I look around the bedroom as Jake drops the last box on the floor. I told him and Whitley I'd hire movers. I knew the amount of boxes I had. I watched them being loaded onto the pod when I moved here from Birmingham. But no, Jake is too good of a guy and insisted that he and his friends would help me move my boxes now that I'm in my rental home. My best friend's fiancé is way too sweet.

"Thanks again," I say, trying not to be overwhelmed at what is going to be weeks of unpacking. "For everything."

"It's our pleasure," Whitley says, giving me a side hug. "I'm just glad I could help you out."

"You're more than helping me out. You're saving me. Literally."

One of my bad habits is I say the word "literally" when I should say figuratively. But this time, I'm actually using it in the right context. Whitley McEvoy, soon to be Evans, is saving me.

"You would have figured it out," she says, moving a box from the living room into the kitchen.

"Oh, because I'm so great at figuring things out?" I ask sarcastically. "I'm pretty sure my lack of being able to do that is how I'm in this situation."

"You just haven't found your passion yet," Whitley says as she heads back for another box. Maybe I should help instead of standing here just watching everyone else move my stuff. "But you will. I can feel it."

I wish I was as confident as her. In some ways I am. Before she met Jake, neither of us had problems approaching men at a party or bar. When it came to being the confident leaders of our sorority, we never flinched when a decision needed to be made.

But when it comes to life in general? We couldn't be more opposite. And not in a good way—at least on my part.

There's Whitley, graduating from Alabama with a double degree in business and marketing. She opened her own event planning business when she was twenty-four. By twenty-six, she was turning down events because she was that high in demand. Even after she moved to Rolling Hills, her business expanded to Nashville, and she's killing it in every sense of the word.

Then there's me. I have a degree in general studies and four minors because that's how many times I changed paths, and at the end of the day, that's what my credits all equaled out to. I've never had an "adult" job. Since graduating from college seven years ago, I've been a waitress, worked multiple retail jobs, been a substitute teacher, joined an MLM for a hot minute, and was the worst secretary in the history of secretaries. I also tried my hand at the whole content creator thing. Jake made it look so easy. Granted, I can't do what he does. The man accidentally became a dancing thirst trap. Turns out, being a content creator is harder than it looks. Who knew you actually had to have content to create it?

"Maybe the event business will be your thing too?" Jake says.

"Your faith in me is adorable. You also clearly haven't spent enough time with me."

Whitley comes over and gives me another side hug. "Whether or not this is your dream and I just found my new business partner, or you only work for me for a few months, I'm glad to have you on board. Between the events I have booked, and that little thing called my wedding, I'm overwhelmed. It will be nice having someone here who I can count on."

"You say that now. Remember, I got fired from a Lady Foot Locker because I couldn't organize the shoes properly. And those are shoes. If I can't figure out shoes, I'm screwed."

She waves me off. "No matter. You've never let me down in the past, and I doubt that's going to start now. Plus, I've missed my best friend."

"Hey!" Jake yells. "That hurts."

Whitley rolls her eyes at Jake, who is doing a very convincing fake pout while holding a box of picture frames. "Like you didn't *just* say that about Knox and Trent last week?"

He did. I was there. If people think Whitley and I have a codependent friendship, they should see those three amigos. They take bromance to a whole new level.

"I hate when you're right," he says.

"I'm always right."

Jake shakes his head as he takes a box back to my bedroom. Whitley and I take a seat on the couch, which the bromance helped move in yesterday.

"I'm happy you're here," Whitley says as she gives my hand a squeeze. "I've missed having you minutes away."

"I know. I still can't believe I moved here."

Whitley smiles. "It's a great town. You're going to love it."

I raise my eyebrow. "I don't know about all that. It's very...small."

"It is. But then again, you haven't had the best of luck in the city. Maybe small-town life is what you need?"

I can't argue with her on that, despite it stinging a bit to hear. It's not like I had much in Birmingham. A string of failed relationships—if you can even call them that. Definitely not a career. Yeah, I had a few good friends, but with Whitley here, I was definitely lonely more times than I care to admit.

And then there's my family...

I wasn't surprised when my parents told me they were disappointed I wasn't living up to my full potential by not holding down a job—and also not having a husband. But their decision to "let me figure out things on my own"—aka cutting me off—was a shock. But of course, they were too polite to say those exact words. The Southern passive aggressiveness in them would never allow that.

Not that I ever asked to be on their dime; I just got used to it. It started with them paying for my cell phone—family plans are more economical. Then they said they'd help with my apartment when I graduated and moved out on my own. Yes, I contributed. Yes, I paid my bills. I just didn't tell them to stop paying the other ones.

Sue me. It's not like my parents were hurting in the money department.

Or maybe they are? Either that or they are ready to take the money they were spending on me and use it toward something for them. Like a fifth car.

"You're right. Maybe Rolling Hills is exactly what I need." I think to how happy Whitley has been since she moved here. Then again, she did come into town with a boyfriend. "I must say, the cost of living is way better. I still can't believe we found this place. It's perfect."

"That's one of the benefits of Rolling Hills: when you need something, you're guaranteed to know someone who can help you out."

"I could never afford a rental house in Birmingham," I say, looking around at the cozy ranch that I'm getting for a steal. "And the Taylors seem super nice."

"They are," Whitley says. "It also helps that they own the construction business in town. They did an amazing job when Jake and I renovated the house. So if anything breaks, not only are they next door, they're also quite handy."

"I saw a truck yesterday," I say. "And the guy driving it? If he's their son, I'm going to be breaking a whole lot of shit to make sure he comes over."

Whitley laughs because she knows it's true. If that man is single, I *will* become a one-woman wrecking crew.

"That was probably Luke. Though he's a bit young for you," Whitley says as she pats my leg before standing up.

"Of course he is. Does he have a brother?"

"Two," Jake says as he comes back into the room. "Cade is still in college. Then there's Wes. But he's married with kids. And you don't seem like a homewrecker."

"He's also a player on the Fury, so he's up in Nashville," Whitley explains. The only reason I know what the Fury are is because Whitley's brother is the head coach of the team. That's about the extent of my football knowledge. That and the men look hot as fuck in those pants. "But the whole married thing might not be accurate anymore. I heard his wife asked for a divorce after he announced his retirement last week. He got home and she was waiting for him with papers. Just left him and the kids."

"What?" Damn, that's cold.

"Yup. None of the other wives liked her, so no one is sad to see her go. All of that is coming straight from my sister-in-law, so I know it's the real deal."

Wow. And I think I'm in for a life transition. I can't imagine just being left like that.

"Well, even if the Taylor sons are a no go, I have everything I need right now," I say. "This is the start of my new future."

I head to the kitchen to start putting away dishes. But not before taking one look around my new place. I know it's just a rental, but it feels like home. Maybe because it's the first big thing I've ever written a check for. Maybe because it was the first time I've written a check. Either way, this feels right. This feels like what I'm supposed to be doing.

Then again, I said that about the two months I was a criminal justice major, so who knows.

Chapter 3
Wes

I've always felt a sense of comfort when pulling into the driveway of the home I grew up in. I don't know what it is about seeing my childhood home, where my parents still live, that warms my soul when I need it the most.

Especially now.

It's been a little more than a month since Cara left. She called the first night to tell the kids goodnight. When they asked when she was coming back, she played it off and didn't give them a direct answer. My two youngest bought it. Emerson, my oldest, gave me a look like she knew exactly what her mother was saying without her saying it. Granted, she's eleven going on thirty, so that didn't surprise me.

Before she hung up, she asked to talk to me without the kids in the room. I thought maybe it was because she wanted to talk in a calmer setting. Instead, she wanted to know if I signed and returned the papers acknowledging that I'd received her petition for divorce.

I put them in the mail the next day and immediately called

my lawyer. I told him I wanted the fastest divorce possible in the state of Tennessee.

I can count on one hand how many times the kids have talked to her since she left. Sometimes I don't think they're phased by it. Then there are the nights I hear them crying in their beds. I try to comfort them, but what do you say? How do you tell a child that their mother, who is supposed to love you unconditionally, just didn't want to be a mother anymore?

Luckily, I've had my mom with me for a good part of the past month. Between my football schedule, and just needing help keeping them fed and alive, she has been a God send. It's also how we ended up in Rolling Hills for trick-or-treat. She told them that there was better candy down here. That was all the evidence my kids needed to request Halloween in my hometown.

I didn't protest though. Rolling Hills Halloween is the best. I loved trick-or-treating here as a kid. Every house had good candy—none of that pencil or toothbrush shit. Parents can walk the streets with their friends while their kids run up to the next house.

It's perfect. It's exactly what we need.

All of us.

"I hope I get Reese's," my youngest, Magnolia, says.

"You're allergic to peanuts," Emerson points out. "You can't eat them."

"Ugh," Magnolia groans. "But they look so good!"

"I'll take them from you," Hank says. My middle child is never one to turn down a sweet. "In fact, all the candy you think is gross I'll take."

"Daddy!" Magnolia yells. "Hank is going to take my candy!"

I turn off the car and look back at my son. "Hank. Your

sister gets first dibs on her candy. Magnolia, you can't eat certain candies, so Hank will *only* take those. Is that fair?"

Hank does a whispered "yes" with a fist pump while Magnolia crosses her arms in a pout. I have to hold back a chuckle. She's the cutest damn pouting Rapunzel I've ever seen.

"Now, what's the rules about trick or treating?"

"Say thank you!" Hank yells.

"Very good. Magnolia? What's another rule?"

"To wait our turns."

"You're right. Emerson? Anything else?"

I look at my oldest, who is giving me a devilish smile. She is my kid through and through.

"No house left behind."

I hold out my hand for a fist bump. "That's my girl. Okay! Let's go!"

I get out of the car as each of the kids unbuckles their seatbelts. Emerson opens the door and climbs out before making sure Hank steps down from the SUV safely while I pick up my adorable Rapunzel from her booster seat.

"I love you, Daddy," she says, giving me a kiss on the cheek.

I don't know where it came from, but I'll never get tired of my little girl telling me that. "Thank you, baby."

She scrunches her tiny nose. "I'm not a baby. I'm six. *And* a princess."

I laugh, giving her a kiss on her forehead as I put her down. "My apologies."

"What is all this racket I hear?"

All three kids turn their heads toward the house. "Grandpa!"

My kids make a beeline toward my dad who kneels down and opens his arm as all three run into him. I make my way up the drive, just taking in the moment.

I can't believe Cara is choosing to miss this. To miss any part of this. To miss parts of their lives that are never going to happen again. If she doesn't want to be married, that's fine. I'm not going to hold a gun to her head. After weeks of cycling through the stages of grieving, I've finally ended in acceptance. Well, I skipped denial and bargaining. I did hit depression and stayed on anger for a long time. But I've come to realize that the woman I married doesn't exist anymore. And the woman who left isn't the woman I married.

I have no love for her. She's a stranger.

"How are my favorite grandkids doing?" Dad asks.

"We're your only grandkids," Hank says.

"For now." The words come from my mom, which automatically means the kids leave my dad behind to wrap her in hugs. As if they didn't see her just a few days ago. "Maybe soon enough you'll have some cousins."

"From Luke the bachelor or Cade who has never had a date?" I ask, giving my mom a kiss on the cheek.

"A mother can only hope," she says as she stands up. "Now, who is ready to trick or treat?"

"Me!" All three kids yell in unison.

"Well then, go inside, use the restroom so we don't have to make a stop, and maybe you'll find your first treat on the kitchen table?"

My three munchkins give a wide-eyed look to each other before they full-on sprint into the house. Maybe they will remember to use the bathroom. Probably not. Once they heard the word *treat* I'm pretty sure the rest went out the window.

My dad gives me a pat on the back. "How are you doing, son?"

And there it is. I knew it was coming. Honestly this is probably why my mom sent the kids inside.

"I'm fine."

My mother gives me the side eye. "Really? You know I didn't have to leave this week. I could have stayed."

I let out a deep breath and shake my head. I don't know why I tried to lie to my mom. No one can get anything by Peggy Taylor.

"It's not a complete lie. Right now I'm fine. The kids are, at this moment, happy. They haven't asked a lot of questions recently. Other than that I'm just trying to get used to the fact that I'm about to be a divorced, single dad."

"Has she called recently?"

"Sporadically. We tried to call a few times, but she never picks up. I can't take their faces when that happens, so we've given up. If she wants to call and check in, she will."

"She won't," my dad grumbles with a dark look. "I can't believe it took her this long to show her true colors."

Dad has never been a fan of Cara. Maybe the first few years in college, but definitely not since we got married. He always called her selfish. Told me I was an idiot for buying her expensive purses and presents. I always denied it and told him he was crazy. Looks like I was the crazy one.

Before either of them can ask me anything else, Hank busts through the door, candy bag in hand. "Dad! Look! Gram got us candy bags! And they already have candy in them!"

"Awesome, buddy!" He runs over to show me. And in true Peggy fashion, not only did she get them bags, but she got them ones to coordinate with their costumes: a Harry Potter themed bag for Hank, who is currently obsessed with all things Hogwarts; a *Tangled* bag for Magnolia; and because Emerson is Emerson, an Addams Family bag for Wednesday Addams.

"You ready, kids?"

They don't even answer my dad as they race down the driveway and make a left toward the house my parents own and rent out.

"Kids, keep going. No one is there."

"Yes, there is," Dad says. "Rented it last month."

I look over to mom. "Really? To who? And why didn't you tell me?"

She just shrugs, which is sending up a hundred warning bells. My mother tells me everything. Hell, she's lived with me for the past month. How did this never come up? "Oh. I must have forgotten. Yes, a nice young girl moved in. A friend of Whitley and Jake. She's just the sweetest."

Mom takes a few larger steps to get closer to the kids while Dad and I hang back.

"What's that about?" I ask with suspicion.

He shakes his head. "I quit trying to figure out your mother years ago."

He might say that, but my dad knows my mom better than anyone. They were high school sweethearts. Hell, I've seen my dad still giving my mom an ass slap or a kiss when they think no one is watching.

"So, it's been a big month for you," Dad says.

"You could say that."

"How are you dealing with everything? And none of that *I'm fine* bullshit."

I shrug. "Day by day."

"Can I ask you something?"

"Sure."

"What's the plan?"

I give him a look. "What do you mean, 'what's the plan?'"

"The plan. You being hurt actually helped since it allowed you to not travel in the first few weeks after she left. And then you had the bye week and a home game. Between Peggy and that, you were able to make it work. But in four days you have to leave for an away game. What's your plan?"

Fuck. How did I not think of that? I've been so focused on

just getting through one day at a time that I didn't think of when I was gone.

"Can they stay with you?" I ask. "I can drop them off Saturday morning before we leave."

"Of course. I was hoping you would ask. But just remember, this is a short-term fix. No matter what I think about Cara, she's gone. And with your retirement coming up, the plans you made a few months ago might not be the ones that are going to work now. Think about that. Because you have to assume it's just you and the kids from here on out."

And there they are. The Henry Taylor words of wisdom. I knew I wasn't going to leave here tonight without some sort of life advice.

"Thanks, Dad." He gives me a pat on the back as the kids turn to go up the sidewalk to the rental house. I'm only half paying attention—part of my brain is trying to be in the moment for my kids while the other half is now frantically trying to figure out if I missed any other glaring things I need to take care of. That's why at first I don't notice the woman on the front porch.

"Trick or Treat!"

"A princess, a wizard, and an iconic TV character on my front porch! This is the best Halloween ever!"

I look up to the woman who just made my three kids giggle.

And I can't stop staring at her.

She's gorgeous. Stunning. Her smile is radiating as she talks to each of my kids as she puts candy in their bags. Then there's the all-red outfit that is putting me in some sort of trance. It's hugging every curve of her body, which there are plenty of, in the best way possible.

Yup. She has to be a devil. Because I'm surely going to hell for the thoughts I'm having about her right now.

I know I need to look away, or even blink, but I can't.

Which is how I know when she looks up and locks eyes with me, catching me staring.

But she doesn't shy away. No, she turns her smile from my children to me. And it knocks me on my ass.

"Jaw up, Wes," Dad says, patting me on the back. "No one likes a man who drools."

Chapter 4
Betsy

Halloween used to be one of the nights when I shined. I knew every party to go to. Every club that was going to be packed to the gills. Hell, I could throw a Halloween party with the best of them. And, of course, I always had the best costumes. Unique with the perfect amount of sexy. Nothing over the top, but definitely something that was going to make every man, and sometimes even a few women, look my way.

Oh, if only that Betsy could see me now. She might not believe it.

Not the costume. My red body suit paired with red faux leather leggings and red devil ears is very on brand for me. But the part where I'm choosing to sit on my front porch and pass out candy? Old Betsy would spit out her gin and tonic.

She also wouldn't believe that she's not hitting on the man standing at the bottom of her porch.

Not that I don't want to. In the past I haven't necessarily had a specific type. And if I like it, I go after it. Whitley asked once what my type of man was, and I just replied with "yes."

Tall, short, skinny, big, ethnicity, religion, it hasn't mattered. I have always been an equal opportunity lover.

Apparently now I do have a type—an about-to-be-divorced single dad with the perfect amount of facial hair and gray eyes that feel like they are staring into my soul.

Yes, I might have Googled Wes Taylor. If Whitley didn't want me to internet stalk—I mean, research him—she shouldn't have told me about him. Really, it's her fault.

And yes, I might have stalked—researched—his soon-to-be ex-wife's Instagram. She looks like a real piece of work, and that's an app where everyone is putting their best foot forward. The reality must be a shitshow.

"Can I get another piece of candy?" Rapunzel asks, breaking me of my thoughts. "Gummy worms are my favorite."

"Of course!" I say, digging through my huge bowl of candy to find more gummy worms. I didn't know how much to buy. I've never passed candy out before. But I think I might be set for the next three Halloweens. "You can pick whatever you like."

"Can I pick whatever I like?" Harry Potter asks.

His face is just adorable. He even has the scar drawn on and everything. I might be a Slytherin, but I can never say no to another Potter lover.

"Of course. So can you, Wednesday. Come on over and grab what you want."

The kids look back at their dad, I'm guessing to ask permission.

He gives a nod. "Go ahead. Just don't go crazy."

I don't know how many pieces of candy they grab. They might have taken the whole bowl. I wouldn't know because I'm too busy trying not to drown in the sound of Wes's voice.

Oh God...this is so bad.

I can't find this man attractive. He's going through a

divorce. He's still legally married. He has three kids. He's my landlord's son. He has more baggage than I have shoes. And I have a lot of shoes.

No. Even my barely there moral compass knows that Wes Taylor is on the no-fly list. I can admit he's attractive because I have eyes and a pulse. But that's it. That's where it ends.

"How are you settling in, Betsy?" Peggy asks.

"Just fine," I say, thankful for the conversation distraction. "This house is amazing. Thank you again."

"I'm glad you're liking it." Peggy pauses and turns to Wes. "Wes, this is Betsy, our new tenant. Betsy, this is our son Wes."

"Hello," I say, giving him a small wave. Should I have done that? Should I have offered my hand? No, that would have been weird. Why am I overthinking a wave?

"Hi," he says, keeping his hands firmly in the pockets of his jeans.

Jeans that are clinging to muscled thighs. Jeans that I need to check out more when he turns to walk away, because if his thighs look like that, imagine his ass.

Stop it. Stop it right now.

I need to stop staring at him. Even though I caught him staring at me. Or did I? I'm not sure anymore. I feel like I'm looking at the sun. I know I shouldn't, but I can't help it.

"Congratulations!" I say, doing anything I can think of to break the awkward silence.

He gives me a confused look. "For what?"

"Your retirement announcement?"

"Oh," he says. "Thanks."

He might have said thanks, but his tone clearly doesn't convey that. In fact, between his clipped word and his now-blank stare, I'm pretty sure I hit a sore spot.

Good job, Betsy. Way to go.

Okay then...talking is out.

"Am I your first stop?" I ask the kids. I'm pretty sure they like me better.

"Yup!" Harry Potter chimes in. "And Dad says we can get *all* the candy we want. As long as we say thank you."

Oh my gosh, I love this kid. "That's a very good rule. It's always nice to say thank you."

"Kids, we shouldn't be taking all of Miss Betsy's candy," Wes says, his voice now more even. "We should be going."

Oh the Southern manners...Mama Peggy raised this man right.

"Are we going to more houses?" Rapunzel asks.

He walks to the porch steps, taking the sweet girl by the hand. "We are. And, Uncle Ollie told me earlier that he has special treats for you."

"Woo hoo!" Rapunzel squeals, turning back to me. "Bye, Miss Betsy! Thank you for the candy!"

I can't help but smile as I wave goodbye to this little angel. "Bye! Have an amazing night!"

All three kids wave goodbye to me, and of course say thank you, as Wes leads them away.

Peggy hangs behind, taking a few steps closer to the porch as her group heads toward the next house. "Don't mind him. He's been through a lot lately. I promise you he's usually more talkative."

"Okay?" Why is she telling me this?

"You have a nice night, dear. Don't eat too much candy. Oh, I love the costume. It's very you."

∾

"THESE ARE THE NIGHTS I MISSED," Whitley says as she holds up her wine glass.

I clink mine with hers. "More than you know."

We each take a sip of wine as we watch the kids, along with their parents, finish up the night's trick or treating. This was one of the parts of the house I loved—the two rocking chairs on the front porch.

"So with the move, we haven't talked about the wedding in a while," I say. "What's the update?"

Whitley takes another sip before answering. Actually, it's a full-on gulp. "It's funny I ever thought I could have a small, intimate wedding."

I smirk. "Bless your heart."

She shoots me a look. "That's what we wanted. I wanted my family and Jake's. Our best friends and their significant others."

"But?"

Whitley lets out a sigh. "We sent out *four hundred* Save the Dates. And my mom still sent me a list of people I missed."

"Holy fuck."

She laughs. "Yup. Pretty much. Between our families, friends, extended families, most of the coaching staff and players from the Fury, every player my dad ever stepped on a football field with, and of course the better part of the Rolling Hills population..." She sighs.

The mention of the Fury immediately sends my mind to Wes. Which it shouldn't. Though, I can't even pretend it's the first time I've thought of him since he walked away tonight.

I don't even know why. Yes, he's hot. But it's not like he's the first attractive man I've ever come in contact with. He was abrupt with me, so it's not like I'm clinging on to an interesting conversation.

And yes, I did look as he walked away, and the jeans did exactly what I thought the jeans would do. Those were some good jeans...

There's something about him that intrigues me. Maybe it's

how he was short with me, but when he talked to his kids, I could see the tender side of him. Maybe it was the way he held his daughter's hand as they walked away. The man is a mystery. And I love a good mystery.

"Yo! Earth to Betsy!" Whitley yells, snapping her fingers in front of my face.

"Sorry," I say, taking a quick sip of wine.

"What was that? And don't tell me it was nothing, because I just said that I was going to change your bridesmaid dresses to swamp green, and you didn't say a word."

Wow, I must have really been out of it. Green is not in my color wheel.

"I was just thinking."

"About?"

Before I can say anything, I hear an already-familiar voice calling my name.

"Miss Betsy!" Rapunzel yells, running up my porch steps. "Look at all the candy I got!"

"Wow!" I say, looking inside the bulging bag that my new little best friend is holding up for me. "That's so much candy!"

"I know!" Her grin fades slightly. "But Daddy said I can't eat it all tonight."

"That's probably smart."

"Magnolia! What did I say about running off?" Wes says, stepping up on my porch.

Magnolia. What a great name for a great kid. It fits her perfectly, with her blonde hair and rosy cheeks.

"I'm sorry. But I wanted to show Miss Betsy my candy!"

He crouches down so he's eye level with her. "That's fine. Just next time, don't run off, okay?"

She nods. "Okay, Daddy."

He gives her a kiss on the forehead. Fuck, why is a sexy

man doting on a child so damn attractive? "Go over to Gram's house. I'll be over in a second."

"Okay. Bye, Miss Betsy!"

"Bye, sweetheart!"

Magnolia bounces down the stairs while Wes stands up. Instead of turning to follow her, he faces me. Neither of us say anything for a few beats. He's staring at me again, only this time I can actually feel it. It's like his gaze is burning through my body. Men have made eye contact with me before, but it's never hit like this.

And there's no second guessing it this time. Hell, I'm staring at him, too. I just can't seem to break away from his eyes. They struck me earlier from far away. But now, up close? I'm getting lost in them.

"I'm sorry." he says, breaking the moment.

"Oh," I say too quickly. "It's no problem. She's adorable. I'll never say no to a visit from her."

"Thanks. She seems to have taken a liking to you," Wes says, his hands going back into his pockets. "But what I meant was that I'm sorry about earlier."

"Oh?" I wasn't expecting that.

"I was short with you. And it wasn't against you. It's just... it's been a rough few weeks, and I had things on my mind. But that's no excuse."

"Thank you," I say. "But really, don't worry about it."

Our eyes lock again as a wave of heat runs through me. Did it suddenly become a Southern summer in October? That's the only logical reason as to why I suddenly feel overheated and overcome. It has nothing to do with how Wes is looking at me right now.

"Well then," he says, breaking the silence. "I'll see you around, I'm sure."

"I'm sure you will."

"Goodnight."

He turns to walk away and does a double take. "Oh, hey there, Whitley. I didn't see you there."

Oh shit. Whitley's still here. Forgot about that.

"Hi Wes. Goodnight, Wes."

He nods his head toward her, and I stand in shock as I watch him walk away for the second time tonight.

"Ah, so that was it," Whitley says.

I turn to look at her. "What is it?"

She laughs. "He was what had you spaced out earlier. I wondered which guy it was. And here it's the guy you said not that long ago that you were going to stay far away from."

I sit back down, picking up my wine glass. "I am," I say with as much gusto as I can muster. "That was nothing. He was just apologizing for an awkward moment earlier. Nothing more. Nothing less."

"Mmmhmm," Whitley says, rocking on the chair. "Because it didn't seem like nothing to me."

Chapter 5
Wes

"The sweet sound of silence."

I don't even know why I said that out loud, because I don't want to even hear *myself* talk. All I want to do is exactly what I'm about to do—toss down my bag, kick off my shoes, and lay down in this bed.

In silence.

I love my kids. I would die for them without a thought. Every day they make me more proud to be their dad than the day before.

But holy fuck are they loud. And exhausting.

I knew Cara did a lot. It wasn't like I was on the road every day for the entire year. I helped when I was home or on light days during the season. But even with my mom helping out, I've barely been able to keep up.

That's why I needed this weekend. Yes, I'm away for a game, but that's fine. The kids are at my parents. They love staying in Rolling Hills, so they didn't give me any complaints when I dropped them off this morning. Now I have a hotel room to myself where I can fall asleep watching anything I want and no one will wake me up in the middle of the night.

Just as I'm about to fall into the pillow and pass out for the night, my phone rings. Worried it might be one of the kids, I hurry and grab it, only to see the name Oliver popping up.

"Are you trying to ruin my night of peace?" I ask, making myself comfortable on the bed.

"Not on purpose. But I did figure that for the first time since the incident, you were going to be alone, so if you needed to vent and call your soon-to-be-ex-wife a bunch of names out of earshot of your kids, I'd be the willing ear."

You don't get a much better friend than Oliver Price. In our friend group, every person has their role. We didn't assign them to each other; it just kind of happened that way. I'm the sensible one. Shane is the muscle. Simon has the business mind. And Oliver? He's our caretaker.

"I'm good," I say, mostly believing it.

"Don't lie to me. Your wife leaves you and your three kids with a half-ass goodbye and an envelope of divorce papers? No man is good after that."

"What do you want me to say?"

"I want you to get it out. I know you, and you've been keeping it inside."

"What have I been keeping inside?"

"Your feelings. Your anger. Let it fucking out."

"I haven't seen you since she left. How do you know I haven't already?"

"Because I'm the only one you would have voiced this to, and since you haven't, I'm assuming you're a bottle about to explode. I know for a damn fact you didn't have a bleeding heart session with Shane or Simon."

He's right. If I had tried to have this talk with Shane, he just would have grunted a lot. Simon would have listened in theory, but he also would have been researching a property at the same time. So yes, I might have been looking forward to a nice night of peace and quiet, but maybe talking is what I need. At least now I can say what I want and not have to hide it from the kids.

"Magnolia asked when I dropped them off when mommy was coming home. She hadn't asked that since she left."

"Fuck," Oliver says. "What did you say?"

"I told her the truth," I say. "I said that mommy wasn't going to be living with us anymore and was on a trip. I didn't give her a 'she will come home soon' excuse because when she doesn't, I'm not interested in cleaning up that heartbreak. Was that the right thing? I mean, she's six, for God's sake. How would you have explained it?"

Oliver is a kid whisperer. Always has been. He's one of the best youth football coaches I've ever seen in action. It's also why parents try to request to get their kids into his first-grade class. The man just connects with them in ways that leave me in awe.

"I think being honest with them is exactly what you need to do," Oliver says. "Kids are smarter than we give them credit for. I guarantee they knew things weren't right. They might not have realized it, but kids are perceptive. And your kids are great. Be there for them. Love them. That's all you can do."

I let out a breath, because that's what I've been doing. Or at least trying to. When Magnolia asked me that, my heart broke into pieces. How could Cara leave this precious girl? How could she leave *any* of them?

"I'm just mad," I say, allowing the anger to bubble over. I might be accepting of this, but that doesn't mean I still can't be angry. "I'm fucking mad, Oliver."

"As you should be."

"If she didn't want to be married to me, fine. I'm a man. I can take it. Did she hurt me when she left? Yes. I'm not going to lie and say she didn't. I'll heal. I'll get over it. Especially since she showed her ass in how she left. But to do that to the kids? Her own fucking children? The three best things that happened to us? How could she do that, man? How could she just say that she wanted more and that they weren't enough? *They are everything.* I'm not mad anymore that she left me. Fine. Ask me for a ridiculous alimony? Whatever. It's just money. But to leave our kids and call just enough to not let them heal or get a sense of reality? That's just fucking cruel. And I never in a million years thought Cara could be that."

I let out a few breaths. Damn, that did feel good. Oliver was right. I have been holding it in. But when was I supposed to let it out? When I got home from the facility and in three seconds had to snap into dad mode and make sure they were showered, fed, and homework done? Or maybe during story time, the one moment of peace we've had each night that has kept all of us balanced? Or maybe it was in the middle of the night when Hank would climb into bed with me because he had a bad dream. Little did he know that I needed his comfort as much as he needed mine.

"Feel better?" Oliver asks.

"Much. Thank you."

"No need to thank me. I'm just an ear."

I let the pause sit for a second, because I know he isn't done. "I feel like there's a 'but' coming."

"You know me so well. What I was going to say was, yes, I'm an ear to vent to, but you're going to need more than a few minute vent sessions with me when you're on the road. Wes, you need help, both physically and emotionally. The kids are going to need help. You need friends and family around you. And we will help you. You know I will. Your parents are foaming at the mouth to have their grandchildren closer to them. Hell, I bet we could even get Simon to babysit a day or two."

"I don't need my kids trading stocks at recess."

"You know what I mean," he continues. "Move back to Rolling Hills. You have no one in Nashville besides your teammates. Down here you have free childcare, friends who miss the hell out of you, and a support system that is unmatched."

"I can't," I say, though not really thinking about it. "Remember, I'm still playing football. I can't just up and move."

"I timed it, it will take you an hour, even in traffic, to get to the Fury facilities. It's not ideal, but your kids will be safe and with family—blood and extended."

"Okay, fine. But what about school? I can't rip the kids out of school halfway through the year."

"Oh but you can," he says. "Yes, you need to talk to them first and make sure they know what's going on. But you see, as a teacher, I know for a fact that kids enroll in new schools at all times of the year. And, if the kids are in school here, I can look out for them. I'll be their own personal tour guide and make sure they get settled in."

I open my mouth to give another rebuttal, but I can't think of anything. If I was going to send my kids to any school, it would be in Rolling Hills. One, I know they have a great school system. Oliver teaching there is a bonus. Two, yes, the commute wouldn't be ideal, but hell, it's Nashville. Sometimes it takes an hour just to get four miles. And it's only for a few more months. Even if we make the playoffs—I don't say 'when' because I don't want to jinx anything, despite the fact we have the best record in the league so far—that is three months, tops.

"That sounds great and all," I say, still trying to work this out in my head. "But where would I live? It's not exactly like the real estate market down there is booming."

"Funny you should ask that," Oliver says. "Check your email."

I put him on speaker and navigate to the email app on my phone. I open it and the first name I see in my inbox is from Simon Banks Real Estate.

"Really?" I say, clicking the email. "You talked to Simon already about this?"

"He happened to mention he got a new listing. He also might have mentioned that it's a five-bedroom house, with an in-ground pool and hot tub, that's two miles from your parents."

"Why do I feel like there's more to the story?"

"You don't need to worry about that part," Oliver says. "Just look at it. Think about it. Talk it over with your parents and the kids. But I think this could be exactly what you guys need."

We say our goodbyes, and I toss the phone down on the bed. I need to FaceTime the kids before bed, but I need a second to process all of what Oliver just suggested.

If we were going to move, now would be the time. Maybe do it around Thanksgiving? I'd have to talk to my lawyer about selling the house, in terms of assets, but frankly, I would be fine to get out of there. This house is all Cara, from choosing it to every piece of furniture and trinket. It was my home because it was where my family was. But it's a lot of house, and I know for damn sure I would need to hire a housekeeper, on top of a nanny, if we were to stay there.

I let the thought of living in Rolling Hills sink in. It's funny because that's what Cara assumed I wanted. I swear I had never thought of it before now. But being back in the town I grew up would have its perks.

There's my family, who I know would not only help but would support us with anything. There are my friends, who it would be nice to see more than the few times a year I get down there, despite it only being an hour away. It would be nice to have a drink at The Joint and just relax. Or take the kids for breakfast at Mona's Diner on a Saturday morning.

I don't know why, but a thought of a certain blonde-haired beauty flashes in my mind. But I squash that feeling down quickly. I can't be having thoughts of Betsy. I have my kids to think about. They come first. That's why I'm moving to Rolling Hills.

I'm moving back to Rolling Hills.

I feel the smile forming on my face. Yes, it feels weird because I haven't smiled much recently. But it doesn't feel forced or fake. No, it feels right.

Rolling Hills feels right.

Chapter 6
Betsy

I REALLY DIDN'T KNOW I COULD LOVE SOMETHING AS MUCH as I love my front porch.

This has become my every night routine. After the day is over, and I'm winding down for the night, I pour myself a glass of wine and just come out here and sit. Sometimes I read. Sometimes I scroll through my phone. But most nights I just relax and let the crisp air of fall in Tennessee and the sounds of a small town relax me.

It's perfect.

"Hank! You threw it too far!"

I look over to my left and see Magnolia running to my yard to get what looks like to be a neon ball of some sort. I'm glad I turned my porch light on, which gives her some light to see where she's going.

"Hi, Miss Betsy!" she says, grabbing the ball and running to my porch steps.

"Well hello, Miss Mags," I say as I get up from my chair. "What'cha got there?"

She holds it out for me. "It's a neon ball. Gram says it's for dogs, but that's okay, we like playing with it. What are you doing?"

I take a seat on the porch step. "I'm just relaxing. Hoping a cute visitor would come over and show me her glow-in-the-dark ball."

This makes her giggle. "Do you want to play with us?"

Now I'm the one laughing. "I don't think you'd want me to. I'm not very good at throwing balls."

She reaches for my hand, which I give her as she does her best to pull me up. "Neither am I. I can't catch either. That's why I had to run over here. Come on! You can come play with us!"

How can I say no to this sweet child? So despite the fact that the only reason I passed gym class being because I somehow was a decent enough runner, I walk over to the Taylors' front yard.

"Miss Betsy is going to play with us!" Magnolia announces.

"Sweet!" the little boy, who I think I heard Magnolia call Hank, says. I look over to the porch where the older daughter, whose name I still didn't get, is sitting on the porch reading.

"I should warn you. I'm not very good," I say.

"It's okay," Hank says. "We just like to have fun. It's fun getting to play in the yard at night!"

I laugh as the three of us start tossing around the ball, more times than not missing our targets completely. But no one seems to mind, based on their little laughs and happy dances when one of us actually catches the ball.

"Hey, you two," I say, feeling a little winded, which is kind of depressing but I'm not going to think about that right now. "I'm going to go take a break."

"Will you watch us?" Magnolia asks, her little puppy dog face too precious to refuse.

"Of course," I say, walking toward the porch. "I'll watch right here."

I take a few steps toward where Wednesday is sitting, her nose still in a book. I really should figure out her name.

"Mind if I sit down?" I ask.

"Sure," she says, not letting her eyes divert from the page.

"I'm Betsy, by the way."

"I'm Emerson." Still no eye contact. This girl is invested in this book.

"What'cha reading?"

She doesn't answer right away, instead finishing the page, or so I'd assume, before she puts a bookmark in her spot. "It's a story of two best friends who are trying to hunt down a person who just stole diamonds from a museum."

My eyes grow wide. "Really? How old are these best friends?"

"Twelve."

"Impressive. When I was twelve, I was failing horribly at learning how to put on makeup."

"Dad says I'm not allowed to wear makeup until I'm a teenager. Which technically would be in one year and three months. Though I have no desire to. It feels like a lot of work, and I just don't have time for that."

"You're not wrong," I say with a chuckle.

"Plus, beauty standards are getting out of hand in the days of social media. Why do I need the newest eyeshadow palette from a woman who is famous for doing nothing except having rich parents? Hard pass."

I look over to this girl, wondering if I'm talking to a kid or a middle-aged woman. "How old are you again?"

"Eleven. I'll be twelve in February."

"Are you sure you're not in your thirties? Because you sound more put together than I am."

She shrugs. "It's an older sister thing. Comes with the territory."

I have known this girl for five minutes, and I want her to be my life coach.

I'm about to ask her how I can get my life together when I see a pair of headlights turning into the driveway.

"Daddy!" Magnolia yells, dropping the ball and racing toward the SUV. I can't help but panic as she takes off to the driveway. Luckily, she stops at the edge of the grass and waits not so patiently for Wes to get out of the car and wrap her in a hug.

"She missed him," Emerson says as she stands up. "She asked Gram if Dad was leaving forever too."

I feel my heart break as Emerson walks over to her dad, where Hank has now latched on to Wes's leg. It's now the worst-kept secret in Rolling Hills that Wes's wife left him and the kids. I don't know her, but fuck her. I'm not a mother, but how could she do that? How could anyone? I've known these kids for literally forty-two seconds, and I don't know how I'm going to say goodbye to them tonight.

I stand up from my seat on the porch as Wes and the kids walk toward me.

"Daddy! Look who's here!"

"I see," Wes says. "Nice to see you, Betsy."

"Hi there," I say, suddenly feeling like an intruder. "I was just hanging out with the kids. I hope that's okay."

"She was playing catch with us!" Hank chimes in. "She wasn't very good."

"Hank," Wes says, just firm enough to know he means business. "Was that very nice?"

His face drops. "I'm sorry, Miss Betsy."

I crouch down so I'm eye level with him. "Thank you, but you were right. I wasn't very good. I'll keep practicing, though. That way next time you won't have to chase the ball as much."

"You'll play with us again?"

"Absolutely! Next time you're over at your grandma's, you just come knock on my door."

Hank looks up at his dad. "Did you hear that, Dad? Miss Betsy wants to play with us!"

He smiles and gives Hank a quick mussing of his light brown hair. "I did. That's pretty cool. How about you guys go inside and start getting your stuff so we can get home?"

The three groan for a second before Emerson takes charge and starts herding them in the house.

"You don't have to do that," Wes says.

"I don't have to do what?"

"Hang out with them. Play. If it's not your thing, you can tell them no."

"What if I want to?"

He tilts his head, as if we aren't on the same wavelength. "You really want to play catch in the dark, which will one day lead to tag in the dark, and hide and seek in the dark, and anything else they can think of to play in the dark? I can understand if that's not your thing."

"Why wouldn't it be my thing?"

"Is it your thing?"

"We've said 'thing' a lot in the last ten seconds."

"Yes, we have."

We stare at each other for a second. I don't think either of us know what we were talking about.

"Back on the subject," he says. "I know Magnolia probably gave you the sad eyes that are nearly impossible to say no to. But don't feel like you have to say yes. I can understand if a twenty-six—"

I laugh. "Twenty-nine, but I appreciate that."

This gets me a small smile. "I can understand if a twenty-nine-year-old single woman doesn't want to play catch with kids she barely knows."

"And I said..." I pause for dramatic effect. "What if I want to?"

This throws him. "You want to?"

"That's what I've been saying," I shake my head, giving him a smile to lighten the mood.

"I was just sitting on my porch. They looked like they were having fun. And they didn't make fun of me for how I threw a ball, which, Hank was right, was not good. Then I talked to Emerson and had more of an adult conversation than I have with most adults. I got some exercise and might have found a new life coach. It was a great night."

Wes doesn't say anything. He just stares at me like I have a second head. At least, that's what I'd guess because confusion is written all over his face.

"What?" I ask. All this staring is making me self-conscious.

This causes him to break the stare. "I...You just didn't strike me as someone who'd be interested in hanging out with three kids."

I shrug. "Don't judge a book by its cover, Wes. You might miss a great story inside."

He opens his mouth to reply, but nothing comes out. And he doesn't get a chance to continue because Hank comes barreling out of the door, backpack in tow. Magnolia, Emerson, and Peggy follow behind.

"I thought I heard you out here," Peggy says.

"Yup. They were having so much fun I just had to join in," I say. "But I should be going."

"Do you have to?" Magnolia asks.

I crouch down to her eye level. "I do. It's my bedtime. And I'm pretty sure it's yours too."

"You have a bedtime?" I think this child's head just exploded by that thought.

"Yup. Bedtimes are important. You need your beauty rest! But you better come find me next time you're at your Grandma's."

She nods before slamming her little body into me for a hug. "I will. And don't worry. You'll get better at throwing the ball."

"Thanks, sweetie." I give her one more squeeze before letting go.

"All right kids, into the car," Wes says, shooing them toward the driveway. "I'll be there in a second."

I start to walk back to my house as the kids make their way to the car, but I'm stopped by Wes's hand on my arm. He's not gripping tight. I'm not sure why I felt like I was electrocuted. He might only be lightly holding my forearm, but I swear I can feel his touch all over my body.

"Thank you," he says, his voice low and sincere.

"You never need to thank me for hanging out with those kids."

He shakes his head. "I do. I'm sure I'm going to get the full play-by-play in the car, but I can already tell you made their year. So thank you."

"Anytime."

We stare at each other for more than a few seconds, his hand still touching me. I don't know what I'm supposed to do right now. Do I say something? Do I move? Do I breathe? I'm not sure of the protocol.

"Excuse me!" Magnolia yells as she runs through us, breaking our connection. "Gotta pee!"

"I'll go make sure she's okay," Peggy says, turning to go inside—but not before giving us a wink.

Shit. Peggy was here the whole time. How do I keep forgetting that people are around me when this man is near me?

"Like I said, I should be going."

I start walking down the stairs of the porch and turn toward my house.

"Betsy."

I turn to look over at Wes, and I don't know if it's how the porch light is shining on him, or because I can still feel the lingering of his touch, but at this moment, he might be the most handsome man I have ever seen in real life.

"Yeah?"

"Thanks again."

I can't help but smile, because I can feel how much those two little words really mean right now.

"Anytime. See you around?"

He nods as he slowly slides his hands into the pockets of his joggers. Gray joggers. Gray, very fitting, very not hiding anything, joggers. Those things should be illegal.

"Yeah. See you around."

I turn and quickly make my way back to my house and slam the door shut. It takes me a second to catch my breath, even though I wasn't running. I feel like it, though. Between his touch, his words, and those criminal sweatpants, I feel like I'm breathless.

Which is a very, very, bad thing.

I can't be having these thoughts about Wes. Well, I can, but I shouldn't. Or can I? I'm single. He's about to be single. I overheard Peggy the other day saying that the lawyers have started doing their thing. So between that and the light stalking sessions I've done, it's safe to say they are just waiting for a judge to sign off.

Shit. No. I can't let myself think like this. I'm just going to pour myself another glass of wine, get into the bathtub, and push away all thoughts of Wes Taylor.

And those damn gray sweatpants.

Chapter 7
Wes

"First round's on Taylor!"

I shoot a look over to Shane as we walk into The Joint. "The fuck, man? I bought a house today. Don't you think someone else can pick up the tab?"

"Oh come on, you can afford it Mr. Ten Million a Year," Oliver says. "I bet we could even splurge and get some jalapeño poppers."

He and Shane laugh as we head to our normal table. At least, I think it's our normal table. It's where I've always sat when I've been here with the guys. Yes, Nashville is only an hour away, but I didn't make it down here as much as I should have. When I did make it to Rolling Hills, it was for a visit with my parents. If I could see the guys, I would. But Cara always made sure the visits were few and far between, and when we were there, she didn't want me leaving her alone with my parents.

But those days are behind me. And today made that a little more official.

"Here you guys go," Porter, my cousin and the owner of

The Joint says as he brings us over our three beers. What I wasn't expecting was a tray with four shots. "Congratulations, Wes. Welcome back."

The four of us grab a shot glass and give them a clink before we throw them back. I pull my wallet out of my pocket but notice Porter waving me off.

"You sure, man?" I ask.

He nods. "My favorite cousin is moving back to town. Now I can quit pretending it's Luke."

That makes everyone laugh. "I appreciate it."

Porter gives me a slap on the back as he picks back up the tray. "I mean it, it's good to see you back here. Back where you're supposed to be."

I don't say anything for a second as Porter's words sink in.

I've loved every minute of my twelve years in Nashville. I played my entire career there. It's where I got married and started a family.

But once Oliver put the bug in my ear to move back to Rolling Hills, it's all I could think about. Being here with my family and my best friends since elementary school was just too good of a chance to pass up.

If I'm about to start a new chapter in my life then I'm going to be happy doing it. And nothing makes me happier than my family and friends.

"So, has it hit you yet?" Oliver asks.

"Not yet," I say, setting down my beer. "It probably won't until we move in. Or start packing. Then again, Emerson started packing the day I told her I was thinking about moving."

"I take it the kids are on board, then?"

I nod. "Their only question was if they could pick out how they wanted to decorate their rooms. Shockingly, they weren't fans of the all-white and chrome decor that Cara had picked out for them."

"Okay, I've bit my tongue for long enough," Shane says. "Why did you marry a bitch, Wes? Was there no other girl on Kentucky's campus?"

"Oh, thank God you said it," Oliver says, almost as if he's relieved to get a weight off his chest. "We bit our tongues because we knew you loved her. But we've never forgiven her for not letting us wear our fun socks in the wedding. They were just socks!"

I laugh, because at this point, that's all I can do. "I promise you guys, I never saw that side of her. And you should have told me about the socks."

"Forget about the socks, though they were fun," Shane says. "She was horrible over the years, Wes. No person should keep their partner from their family and friends. And she did that. You know she did. How many times have you been here in the past decade? How many holidays were short visits because she couldn't stand to be here more than she had to? She wouldn't even let you come to our ten-year reunion. How much did you sacrifice to keep her happy?"

Fuck, he's right. They all are. Shane, Oliver, I'm sure Simon too, if he was here. He, like my dad, openly disliked her.

I feel like an idiot. A fucking idiot.

"Why didn't I fucking see it?" I say through clenched teeth. "I know I was on the road and away with football, but how could I not see it? How could I be so blind?"

Oliver puts his hand on my arm. "Because you loved her. But people change, Wes. She's different. You're different. Now, it's time to move on."

Shane holds up his glass. "To moving on."

We clink our glasses, but the conversation falls silent. All I keep thinking of is how as each day goes by, the more I'm seeing the real picture.

I married the fake Cara. She fooled me for years. But not anymore.

"What's the status of the divorce?" Shane asks.

"My lawyer called me yesterday. She doesn't want any more than a visitation schedule with the kids in the summer and some holidays. What she really wants is money."

"No prenup?"

I shake my head. "It never even came across my mind back then. The ink was barely dry on my contract, which was barely above league minimum. I didn't think I needed one."

"But now you wish you did?" Oliver says.

"Yup," I say, taking a pull of my beer. "But money is money. I saved and have investments, so I'm fine. The kids will be fine. I'll pay whatever is needed so we can move on and the kids can have some sort of stability. We've both agreed with our lawyers to just sell and split the house and everything in it. Hopefully, it's done before Christmas."

"Who knew Cara could be so...agreeable?" Shane says.

"Apparently she is when the price is right," I say. "But enough about that. No more divorce talk. I feel like that's all we talk about. Tell me what's been going on with you guys. Oliver? Still seeing Rachel?"

Shane nearly chokes on his beer as Oliver's face turns red.

"What?" I ask. "Oh, now you have to tell me."

Oliver looks down, suddenly too shy to talk. Which means this is about to be good. And by good I mean really, really terrible.

"The short answer to your question is no," Shane begins. "The long story is that he might have set a new record on how fast he proposed to her."

I snap my head in his direction, which he can't see. His face is currently buried in his hands.

"Oliver, we've talked about this," I say, patting him on the back. "We wait at least a year until we propose marriage. And even then, you run it past us first."

"I know," he groans, his face still buried. "But I thought she was the one! I felt so right about it."

"I'm surprised he didn't call you," Shane says to me. "He took her to Nashville and did it overlooking the river."

"He knows I would have tried to talk him out of it," I say.

They both laugh, and Oliver just points at me because I hit the nail on the head.

Oliver is one of the best guys I know. He always has a smile on his face and can find a silver lining in a shit storm. And all the man has ever wanted is to get married and start a family.

However, instead of waiting until he finds the woman who truly deserves him, he proposes to anyone who makes it past the six-month mark.

Or sometimes sooner. I believe he's up to twelve proposals with no marriages. Or yeses.

"New subject," I say, turning to Shane. "How about you?"

Shane takes a sip of beer, which I know means he's trying to figure out how he can say the least amount possible. Shane isn't exactly the sharing type.

"Oh no, who made Ollie cry? Taylor? Did you do this?"

I turn over my shoulder to see Amelia Evans giving me a look I know all too well. The one she used to give all the time growing up when I, or the four of us, did something she didn't approve of. Which was a lot.

"In my defense, I didn't know what I was asking when I asked it."

I stand and open my arms, which Amelia steps into. Apparently, Shane sees this as an opportunity to avoid this conversation and heads toward the bathroom.

When I think of my best friends in Rolling Hills, I'm immediately referring to the three guys who have been with me through it all. The very next person I think of is Amelia. She was the sister I never had. She was the sister *none* of us had, and that includes Simon, who has four sisters.

Amelia was one of us. She still is. When girls were getting ready to try out for cheerleading, she was asking if she could be on the football team. She wore eye black instead of eye shadow. She was the best softball player to ever come out of Rolling Hills High School. To this day, I've never seen her in a dress.

She's tough. Not afraid to speak her mind. But at the same time, she's nurturing, and the person you can always go to if you just need an ear to listen. I think every one of us had some sort of memorable heart-to-heart with Amelia at some point in our lives. For me it was the night before my wedding.

I wasn't having cold feet, but I was nervous as hell. I was just out of college. I had been drafted a few weeks before. And then I was getting married. It felt like a lot all at once. And hell, I didn't know that we'd get pregnant with Emerson a month later.

I was freaking out. But Amelia was there like she always has been, telling me that everything was going to be okay.

Maybe I need to yell at her for not having a crystal ball.

"Good to see you, Wes," she says, patting my chest. "But seriously, what's up with Oliver? Oh no. Did you propose again?"

We laugh as Amelia walks over and gives Oliver a hug from behind. We might all be in our mid-thirties, but some things will never change. Case in point—Amelia comforting Oliver after a woman has left him broken-hearted. She's been doing this since we were ten.

"What brings you here on a Tuesday?" I ask.

"Meeting my brother and Whitley for dinner. My kids are at practices, and I gave them money for dinner because there is no cooking happening in my house tonight. Speaking of..."

We turn to look at the door and see Jake and Whitley walking through hand-in-hand. I know they're heading our way, but I'm not paying a lick of attention to them.

Betsy had sauntered in right behind Whitley, and as soon as I saw her, it was like everyone else in the bar disappeared.

Chapter 8
Wes

I grab the back of my head where Shane just hit it. That fucking hurt.

"Just snapping you back to reality," he says with a smug smirk on his face.

"What's that supposed to mean?"

"It means since the new girl in town walked in the bar tonight you've been...well, I don't know where, but it's definitely not here."

I don't respond to Shane but instead take another glance over at Betsy. For some reason I can't take my eyes off of her. Yes, she's beautiful. Any man in here, and probably most of the women, would admit that. Her dark blonde hair is the perfect complement for her tanned skin. The bar is dark, but I swear when she smiles it lights up the room.

My mind drifts back to the night when she was playing with the kids. When I pulled in, I immediately saw her on the porch with Emerson. It struck me as odd because Emerson isn't my most social kid. That distinction goes to Magnolia. But for those few seconds, I watched the two of them talk like they were best friends. I don't know what Emerson was saying, but the way Betsy was smiling at her was not only beautiful but genuine. On the drive home that night, I was expecting Magnolia, and even Hank, to go on and on about Betsy. To my surprise it was Emerson. She just kept talking about how Betsy wanted to learn things from her and wondered if she'd like to borrow one of her favorite books.

The younger kids have taken the split as well as they could. They ask for their mom. Each has spent a few nights in bed with me, wondering why Mommy left. I was ready for that. I knew it was going to come. But Emerson? She's my little steel trap. Hell, the nurses had to force her to cry when she was born. I know she's been trying to be strong for me and her siblings. That's just who she is. One day, and I don't know when, she's going to snap, and the tears are going to flow. But until then, I'm just excited she's showing some personality. Because she doesn't let many people see it, but those she lets in get to know the best kid in the world.

"There he goes again."

This time I hear Shane and don't need a slap on the head to break my gaze. "Fine. You caught me. Happy?"

Shane's smug smirk is still there. "I never pegged you as one to go for the younger women. Especially before the divorce is even finalized. But hey, good for you, man."

"I'm not going after her," I defend. "She's renting the house next to my parents. We've met a few times. She's been nice to the kids. That's it."

"Really?" Oliver asks. "That's it? Nothing else?"

"Really," I say as firmly as possible.

"Prove it," Shane says, nodding toward the bar. "Go talk to her. Let Oliver and I be the judge if she's really just your parents' tenant who is nice to your kids. Or if you, Mr. Taylor, are floating on a river called denial."

"Fine," I say, standing up, grabbing my beer. I think I hear the two of them mumble something about how I have no clue, but I choose to ignore them.

They have no idea what they're talking about.

I'm not interested in Betsy. A man can think a woman is attractive without immediately wanting to take her to bed. I've been a professional football player for twelve years. I've spent plenty of nights in bars and clubs where many beautiful women tried to hit on me. Some didn't know I was married. Some didn't care. The result was all the same—I could appreciate their beauty while also rejecting their advances.

Was I looking at her tonight? Yes. But it didn't mean anything. I looked at a lot of people tonight. Hell, I hugged Amelia. That doesn't mean I want to sleep with her. And even if I was ready to date—which I'm absolutely not—Betsy would be the last person I'd go after. For one, she's my parents' tenant and neighbor. That would just be awkward. And second, she's six years younger than me. When I was in college she was still in middle school. No thank you.

So if these two assholes want to see how unaffected I am by her, let them. Hell, I wish I could put money on this.

As I approach the bar, I see that she has taken up a conversation with Porter. But not just any conversation. I don't know if Betsy realizes this, but Porter is about to turn on the charm. He's already done his signature lean against the bar, throw a towel over his shoulder move. Even without living here for years I know that's step one for him.

Sorry, cousin, I'm going to have to cock block you this time. I have a point to prove.

"Don't believe a word he says."

Porter shoots me a look as Betsy slowly turns her head toward me. "Oh really?"

"Really," I say, taking a final swig of my beer and putting it on the bar. "I've known this man my whole life. He has stories for days. Some of them are even true."

I look at Porter, who is shooting daggers at me right now. Oh well. I'm sure he'll get over it. "Can I get another beer, and whatever the lady wants?"

"Gin and tonic."

Porter sends me another "fuck you" look before going to make our drinks.

"I didn't take you for a gin girl," I say.

She shrugs. "What did I say about assuming? Have you learned nothing?"

I take a seat on the barstool. "My apologies. I promise to never do it again."

She tilts her head, as if she's trying to decide whether or not to believe me. "Promises are a big deal."

"Oh, I know. My youngest is very big into pinky promises these days."

Betsy holds up her pinky. "Well then, you should be used to it."

I look down at her finger then back up to her. Am I really about to do this? I'm thirty-five years old, for fuck's sake. It's one thing to do it with Magnolia...

"I'm not going to pinky promise you."

"Well then you must not intend on keeping your promise. Just wait until I see Magnolia and tell her. What would she think of that?"

"Using my kid against me? That's playing dirty."

She leans in slightly, her pinky still in the air. "I never said I played nice."

"Fine," I groan, holding up my pinky and linking it with Betsy's. "But only because my daughter is relentless."

Neither of us let go, though I have to think that we have gone past the standard time for a pinky promise. This is taking me back to the night I picked up the kids and Betsy was there. When I grabbed her arm, it really was just to tell her thank you. But once I made contact with her, I didn't want to let her go.

Now? I know I need to. I just can't seem to do it. I might not be looking at them, but I know for a fucking fact that Oliver and Shane are watching every moment of this, and they are going to have some smartass remark.

"Gin and tonic and another beer," Porter announces as he puts down our drinks slightly harder than necessary. That breaks the spell as we both drop our hands.

"Thank you," Betsy says to Porter, standing up from her barstool. "And thank you for the drink."

"My pleasure," I say. "See you around?"

She smiles, holding up her pinky again. This time, I don't fight it.

"It's a promise."

She lets go much quicker this time and makes her way back to her table. I take a big pull of my beer before I get up and head back to mine.

I sit down, mentally preparing for the shit I'm about to get from my two best friends. They're both looking at me, but neither are saying anything. For Shane, that's not uncommon. But Oliver? The man loses to his first graders when they play the quiet game.

"Nothing? That's it? You guys aren't going to say anything?"

Shane smiles, holding up his beer and tipping it toward me. "I don't think we need to say anything. In fact, I promise you we won't."

"Yup," Oliver chimes in. "We *pinky swear* we won't."

The two dramatically link pinkies as I roll my eyes.

"It was nothing," I say. "You don't even know the conversation behind it."

Oliver shakes his head. "Don't need to. We saw everything we needed to see."

"You have no idea what you saw."

Shane finishes his beer and stands up, giving me a slap on my back. "You keep on believing that, buddy."

Chapter 9
Betsy

WHEN WHITLEY OFFERED ME A JOB WITH HER EVENT planning business, I thought I'd be doing a lot of office work. Emails. Calling vendors. Ordering invitations. That kind of thing. I have training in all those things. From multiple past jobs.

If I would have known that my job description would include tying one thousand balloons to an arch, I would have told her thanks—but no thanks. Being unemployed has to be better than this.

"Shit!" I yell as another balloon slips through my fingers and blows away. It's not an overly windy day, but man, those suckers take off.

"Miss Betsy, I think these are yours."

I look up to see Hank, his arms filled with four of the twenty balloons that got away from me.

"Thank you," I say. "Can you hold them for a second until I'm ready for them?"

"Yup!" He sits down on the grass across from me. "What are you making?"

"A balloon arch for a party."

"Do you have to tie all of these to it?"

"Yup."

"Are the balloons supposed to fly away?"

As if on cue, another one gets through my fingers.

"Shit!" I yell.

Hank's eyes go wide. "You said a bad word."

Crap. I forgot I'm around a kid. "I'm sorry."

"That's okay. Dad swears a lot. He just has to put money in the swear jar."

For some reason, this makes me smile. I can see Wes dropping an f-bomb and Hank instructing him to add money to a jar. Or Emerson. She probably has a spreadsheet with the deposits. "Does your dad have to put money in a lot?"

Hank nods as I take one of the balloons from him. "Yeah. Especially since Mom left. He really can't get the hang of braiding Magnolia's hair. He's good for a few bucks every morning."

My heart simultaneously fills and breaks thinking of that. On one hand, kudos to Wes for trying. But on the other hand, fuck the woman who would leave him to do that.

And I'd say that out loud and put a twenty in the jar for emphasis. That would be money well spent.

"Are you guys here for the weekend again?"

Hank shakes his head. "Nope. Dad's game was on Thursday this week. But he and Uncle Shane and Uncle Oliver are moving our stuff into our new house."

New house? Did I know this? I feel like I should have heard this through the town grapevine. I might still be new to Rolling Hills, but I have found all of the hot places to get the latest tea. So either my skills are way off, or somehow, this has stayed out of the Rolling Hills gossip mill.

"Where are you guys moving?"

Hank nods down the road. "That way. It's a really nice house. And Dad says we can decorate our rooms however we want."

"That's cool," I say. "How are you going to decorate yours?"

"Hogwarts," he says matter of factly. "All Gryffindor."

"I should have guessed. You know, I'm a Potterhead too."

This stuns him. How do I know? His eyes are wide, his jaw is dropped, and he just let go of the remaining balloons he was holding.

"You? You like Harry Potter?"

"Of course. I even took the sorting test."

"What house are you? Are you with me in Gryffindor?"

"Nope," I smile, shaking my head. "I'm a Slytherin."

"What!" He stands up like he's about to run away. "You can't be!"

I shrug. "I am what I am."

"I don't know if I can handle this."

I laugh at his dramatics as Emerson, Magnolia, and Peggy come walking over.

"What's the matter with him?" Peggy asks as Hank starts pacing the yard.

"Hogwarts drama," I say. "How are you?"

She just shakes her head. I have a feeling this isn't the first time Hank has been crippled by fictitious ethical decisions.

"Oh, just fine, my dear. Just getting another day with my grandkids. I would ask you how you're doing, but I feel like I already know the answer."

We both turn our gazes to my shoddy-looking balloon arch as the kids start running around the yard, chasing all of the ones that have floated away. "You would be right."

I walk up the stairs to my porch and take a seat on one of

the chairs. "Whitley asked me to do this for her. It seemed easy enough when she told me how to do it. And I'm a pretty crafty person. But this? I can't handle it. What kind of event planner am I if I can't even tie balloons?"

Peggy pats my hand as she takes a seat next to me. "The kind that maybe isn't meant to arrange large balloon arches."

As soon as the words leave her mouth, three balloons that I thought I had secured somehow get loose and fly away.

"Fuck me."

I slap my hand over my mouth. That has to be worth at least ten dollars in the jar.

"I'm so sorry."

Peggy waves me off. "I raised three boys, and my husband owns a construction firm. It's nothing that I haven't heard before. Plus, judging by the amount of balloons the kids are carrying back, I probably would have said it too."

The more and more I talk to Peggy Taylor, the more and more I love her. She's just so...motherly. She always asks how I'm doing or is making sure that I've eaten. Once a week she stops over just to talk. In fact, I think I've talked to her more since I moved here than my own mother. The few phone calls we've had have all gone the same way—her making me feel like a disappointment. So I quit calling. I'll answer when she calls, but I do my best to make the conversations as short as possible. Because despite her passive aggressive digs, I am loving this town.

The job? Not so much.

"What's the matter with me, Peggy?"

She looks at me curiously. "What do you mean, my dear?"

I nod down to the balloon arch. "This balloon arch is symbolic to my life. Every time I think I have it down, something happens and it ends up a disaster. I really hoped moving here and working for Whitley would help me find my path, but maybe this isn't it either."

That feels good to say out loud. I've been thinking about it for weeks. Yes, the balloon arch is the first major thing I've messed up. But even if I had done that to perfection today, I still don't know if I would have felt any sort of excitement or sense of accomplishment. Being Whitley's assistant is fine. She pays me well and working with your best friend is the best. But from the moment I start until the minute I leave, I'm watching the clock. I literally can't get out of there fast enough.

If I can't even work for my best friend and be happy, then maybe I'm doomed.

"Growing up, my mom swore by Julia Child's cookbooks," Peggy says. "I actually still have them."

This is such a random comment in the middle of my confession that I pause to wonder if she's older than she looks and is having cognition issues. But I play along. "My Meemaw had Julia's cookbooks," I say. "That's how I learned to cook."

"Well then, one day we are going to have to tackle a recipe together," she says. "But did you know that she didn't write her first cookbook until she was fifty?"

"Oh, wow."

"Wow is right. Do you know what she did before that?"

I shake my head. "Was it assemble balloon arches? That would make me feel a lot better."

This makes her laugh. "She was a spy."

"Really? That's actually a job I haven't had. Though I am a social media detective. I can find anyone—just give me a phone, a first name, and a glass of wine."

"That's good to know," she says. "My point is, some people don't know their paths right away. And some paths diverge. Don't let the pace of others dictate your race. You're the only one who knows your destination. So you should be the only one who decides how fast you get there."

I let that sink in. Damn, this woman is good. And, I'm happy to say, her cheese is not slipping off her cracker like I feared.

"You should take up motivational speaking," I say.

She gives me another pat on the hand as she stands up. "Maybe one day. But, can I now ask you a favor?"

"Anything."

"Can you watch the kids for a little bit? Wes is moving the big things into the house today, and everyone is there helping out. I wanted to take them some lunch, but he wants a few things to be surprises for the kids. Do you mind?"

I blink a few times. Did she just ask what I think she just asked?

"Um, sure? Though you do see how I handled balloons, right?"

She waves me off. "You'll be fine. I'll leave my door open so they can go in and out. They've had lunch. Plus, Emerson's here. I let her do the heavy lifting."

That's true. "Okay then. Sure. I'm happy to help."

"Oh, thank you. I'll be back in an hour or so." She walks down the front porch and turns toward the kids, who are now playing some game in the yard. "Kids! I'm going to the new house for a bit. Betsy's going to watch you."

"Woo hoo!"

I don't know who yelled it, but before I know it, all three of them are running toward me. Well, Hank and Magnolia are. Emerson is walking behind them, picking up the shoes that Magnolia kicked off mid-run.

"Can we play dress up?" Magnolia asks.

"No!" Hank yells. "I want to play Wizards and Witches!"

"We always play that. I want to play dress up. I bet Betsy can actually braid my hair like a princess!"

"But she's a Slytherin! I need her to get her to the good side."

The two continue arguing as Emerson slides next to me.

"You ready for this?"

No. No I am not.

Chapter 10
Wes

"Please explain something to me."

I look up to my brother, Luke, who is helping me carry Emerson's bed frame up to her new room.

"What's that baby brother?"

"Please tell me why you, as a man who is not hurting in the money department, is making his family and his friends move him into his new home instead of paying a moving company?"

"Because," I say as I take the last step and turn into Emerson's room. "Why hire people when I have plenty of able-bodied friends and family who would love to help?"

Simon snorts and mutters something rude as he walks past the door. He's complained the most today. Probably because he had to put on clothing that wasn't a business suit.

"Could I have paid movers? Yes. But then we wouldn't have had this chance to catch up."

"We could have caught up over a beer. That would have been better."

We set the bed frame down so we can start moving the

mattress and headboard onto it. "So what's new? You know, since we're catching up."

I see him try to hold back a smile, poorly.

"What's her name?"

"What do you mean, what's her name?"

"Oh little brother," I say as I connect the headboard to the frame. "I might have been out of the dating game for the past fifteen years, but I don't think the look a man gets when a woman is kicking his ass ever changes."

Luke shakes his head. "It's nothing."

His mouth is saying one thing, but his smile is saying something else. Which is interesting. Luke has never been shy about his exploits.

"Fine. Let me know when that changes. I'd like to meet the woman who has my brother smiling like that."

I hear a gasp behind us. I turn to see my mother standing in the doorway, holding one hand over her heart, and the other over her mouth.

"There's a woman? Luke Michael! Why didn't you tell me?"

I hold in a laugh as my brother whips around to stare at me with bugged out eyes. "Take it easy on him, Mom. He's had a rough day moving furniture."

Luke walks past me and slaps me on the back. "Thanks, man."

I laugh as Luke walks out. "Hey Mom," I say, walking over to give her a kiss on the cheek. "What are you doing here? Kids downstairs?"

If I were to tell you a million things about my mother, all but one of them would be how and why she's the best person in the world. The one thing that isn't positive? She can't lie for anything. Some say that's a good thing. The problem is that you can read it on her face, so when she's trying to be sneaky, you know immediately something's up.

And right now? Something is very up.

"Where are the kids, Ma?"

"They aren't here."

"What? Where are they? How could you leave them alone?"

She crosses her arms. "Do you really think I would leave my grandbabies alone?"

"Well, they aren't here! Everyone who could watch them is here. And despite the fact that she runs the household, Emerson cannot watch both kids alone. So tell me, Ma, where are my children?"

"With Betsy."

I feel my eyes start to pop out of my head. "Betsy?"

Betsy? I know I should be thinking about if she's able to handle the three kids, but for some reason, all I can think about is her damn smile. The smile that kept me up too many nights for my liking.

I start to storm out of the room, but Mom steps in front of me.

"Don't go flyin' off the handle and stomping out of here like you have a rocket up your behind. They're just fine."

"How do you know?"

"Because I have a sense about these things. Plus, Emerson's there."

"That's all well and good, but Mom, still, you can't leave the kids with her."

"And why not? What's the matter with Betsy? Or my judgment, for that matter?"

"She's..." I trail off because I don't know the answer. It's not like she's ever done anything that would make me concerned that she can't watch my kids for a little bit. And Lord knows my kids are obsessed with her. Magnolia has even gone as far as saying that she's prettier than any princess she knows. Which is a high compliment from a princess expert.

"She's what?" Mom asks. "Come on, you must have a reason for wanting to stomp out of here."

I still don't have anything. In fact, the only thing I can think of right now is that damn pinky promise to not assume or judge. That and Betsy's face when I gave in. That knowing smile she gave when she knew she had me. I haven't told anyone, but I've thought about it more times than I should have.

And she's right. I do assume. I assumed she didn't want to hang out with them. I assumed her drink order. And I'm assuming right now that she can't handle my kids.

I broke the damn pinky promise. But I'm not telling Betsy. I'll never hear the end of it.

"Exactly," Mom says, sitting on Emerson's bed and patting the spot next to her. "Wes, have you thought about how you're going to navigate things now that you and the kids are here full time?"

"Some," I admit. "It's just been so much, Mom. The divorce. The kids. Moving. And, oh yeah, I'm still playing football. We're in the playoffs. I have at least two more months. Three if we make it to the championship. I don't know if I'm going to be able to do it."

I haven't said any of this out loud. But it feels good to get it off my chest. Because every night before I pass out from exhaustion, I wonder how I'm going to be able to do it all again the next day. Then, somehow, I do.

I just don't know how much longer I'm going to be able to keep going.

"You know you have us, Wes. And the boys, of course," she says. "But you need help after school. And before school. I love you. You're who made me a mama. But you're just bad at doing little girls' hair, and my grandbaby can't be going to school looking like she stuck her finger in a light socket."

"It's not that bad."

She shoots me a look. "Emerson sends me daily pictures. Trust me, Wes. It is."

Figures. And apparently I need to have the *snitches get stitches* conversation with Emerson.

"Besides that," Mom continues. "The kids need a routine. And while I love them and I will watch them anytime you ask me to, they need structure. You need to hire a full-time nanny."

I let my head fall back, letting my mom's words sink in. She's right. I mean, she's always right. But she's really right on this one.

I'm struggling, and while it's going to get easier on the kids now that we're here, it's going to get harder on me. I have an extra commute into Nashville. By the time I get back each night, it will be nearly their bedtime. I don't have time to help them with homework, or to make sure they have what they need ready for school the next day. And Mom is right. Shuttling them back and forth between our house and theirs isn't going to help, even though we are now only two miles away.

But who? Is there a nanny service in Rolling Hills? Who could I trust enough to basically help me raise the kids while also getting along with them well enough that I don't have to worry about things when I'm away?

Then it hits me. My conniving mother and her shitty poker face. I look over to her, only to see her trying, yet failing, to look innocent.

"Really, Mom?"

"What?"

"Don't play innocent. This is why you left the kids with Betsy today, isn't it?"

"I don't know what you're—"

"Don't play coy with me, woman."

She shrugs. "I've talked with Betsy a lot since she moved in. She's good people, Wes. She has a good heart, and you know the kids love her. Plus, I think she's a little lost. Trying to find her way. I think this could be good for her. It will be good for *both* of you."

So she thinks. I don't think it's good for me to be around a woman everyday who has taken up more brain space than I have to spare. Her and her damn smile.

"You want me to hire your neighbor because she's good people? I love you, Ma, but you don't have a bad word to say about anyone."

"That's not true. I think Gladys Mackey is an awful woman. She stole my cobbler recipe and tried to pass it off as hers. And I heard she asks to speak to managers a lot. I don't have time for her kind of people."

"Good to know," I say with a slight laugh.

She pats my knee. "All I'm saying is talk to Betsy about it. You need help, and she does too. But don't go into it already assuming what she's going to say. You have a bad habit of that. Did you know that?"

I smile. "Matter of fact, Mom, I was recently told that."

"Good. Work on that. And hire that girl. You need help. And so does Magnolia's hair."

Chapter 11
Betsy

I watched the kids yesterday for exactly two hours and twelve minutes.

It wore me out so much that I went to bed at eight-thirty.

Kids are exhausting. I mean, I had heard that from others. I had a glimpse of it for the two weeks I was a substitute teacher.

But that was nothing compared to this. And yet, it was the most fun I've had in a very long time.

Yes, my nights and time with Whitley are great. She's been my best friend since our pageant days on the Southern beauty queen circuit, which continued through our college days in Tuscaloosa. But yesterday? It might have started with a shit show of a balloon arch, but it turned into a day that filled my heart. We played wizards and witches and princess dress-up. Hank worked on my throwing ability while Emerson told me about the latest mystery book she was reading. She even gave me a copy of one she had already read so I could check it out.

I might have been scared when Peggy left them with me, but the day turned out to be exactly what I needed.

I let out one more yawn before I check my phone. That's

when I realize I've been in bed for twelve hours. Yet, somehow, I'm still exhausted. The benefit of working for your best friend, who lets you work from your home or hers, is that there's usually not a firm start time. Which is good. I'm going to need a bit to get going today.

I roll out of bed, slide into my slippers and put on my robe as I make my way to the bathroom. I'm finishing brushing my teeth when I hear a knock on the door. Weird. No one should be knocking on a door this early. Maybe it's Whitley? But even if it was, she would have texted me, right? Or just let herself in.

Toothbrush still in my mouth, I head out to the living room and unlock the front door. When I open it I immediately regret the decision to still have the toothbrush in my mouth.

And more so for not getting dressed yet.

"Hey, Betsy," Wes says as he does a shit job of keeping the smile off his face. "Am I interrupting?"

"No." I don't know if that came out clear since I have a mouth full of toothpaste, so I shake my head for emphasis. "One minute."

Wes laughs as I swiftly walk back to the bathroom. I hurry and spit out the toothpaste and do a quick rinse of my mouth. I glance in the mirror and do my best to not let out a scream of horror. I didn't look earlier. I didn't think I needed to. I should have.

My hair is a mess and I have pillow marks on one side of my face. Oh, and my robe just covers my sleep shorts, making me look like I'm basically naked underneath.

What a way to start the morning.

I quickly throw on a bra, T-shirt, and sweats and make my way back to the living room, only to see Wes still standing in the doorway.

"You could have come in," I say.

He does, closing the door behind him. "I didn't want to assume."

We share a knowing smile. "Have a seat. Want anything to drink?"

"No, thank you," he says. "I actually wanted to talk to you about something, if you have a few minutes?"

"Okay," I say, my curiosity spiking. "What's up? Is this about yesterday? Are the kids okay? I swear when they left me they had all their fingers and toes and nothing was broken. Except my pride, because I still can't throw a ball despite Hank's best coaching effort."

Wes laughs. "Yes, this has to do with yesterday, and yes, the kids are fine. Nothing to worry about there. I did want to ask you, though, how did it go?"

Oh, I wasn't expecting that. "It went great."

"No problems?"

I shake my head. "Surprisingly, no."

"Why do you say 'surprisingly'?"

"You don't know this about me, but I've had many jobs over my lifetime. None have ended well. Maybe because that wasn't a job, so the fates decided not to screw with me."

Wes starts smiling. I didn't realize that overshare was smile worthy.

"Want to make it your job?"

"Excuse me, what?"

He laughs. "I asked you if you wanted to make watching my kids your job?"

Now I just stare at him. He's said it twice now, yet I don't think he's really saying it.

Me? Watch the kids? As a job?

"Betsy?"

"Yeah," I say, blinking myself back to reality. "I'm, uh, I didn't expect this today."

"Sorry about that," he says. "I wanted to talk to you about it without the kids around, because if they knew I was here asking you to do this they wouldn't leave either of us alone about it."

"I can see Magnolia's sad puppy face now. I'd be a goner."

"Exactly."

I take a second and think about this. Could I do it? I mean, if I were to ever watch a set of kids full time, it would be Wes's three. I know them. They know me. And best yet? They are all potty trained.

"I mean, I'm flattered," I say. "But can I ask you a question?"

"Sure."

"Why me?"

I'm not asking this for him to pump up my ego. I'm genuinely curious. In my history, I've never been the one to be sought after for employment. Yes, Whitley asked me to come work for her, but I doubt she would have if I hadn't been freshly cut off and about to be kicked out of my lease.

Wes lets out a breath and clasps his hands, letting his elbows rest on his legs. "I'm guessing you know by now that my wife and I are getting a divorce."

I nod. "Yeah, I'm sorry about that."

He shakes his head. "Don't be. I was shocked when it first happened, but the more I've thought of it, the more I know it's going to be the best for everyone. We weren't happy. And I don't want the kids growing up in a house where their parents always fight and only stay together for them."

"That's a good way to think about it."

"It's the best I can do with the cards I've been dealt. But with that comes the fact that I'm now going to be a single father. She's made it clear she only wants set, sporadic visitation. I'd rather her admit up front that she only wants to be a barely part-time mother instead of promising them the world only to let them down."

I swear the day I meet this woman I'm going to ask her what the hell her problem is. That is, of course, after I make a not-so-thinly-veiled insult on her dupe Hermes bag. Which I know it probably isn't a dupe but calling it that would piss her off.

"Anyway," Wes continues. "I love my kids. I'm happy to have them, and I want to give them as normal and best a life as I can. But for the immediate future, at least until I'm done with football season, I need help. I barely got them to school today, and I woke up at four so we wouldn't be late."

"Wow," I say. "You got them there, right?"

He nods. "Thank goodness we had gone last week so they could get registered and a tour of the building. Otherwise we would have been fucked."

This makes me laugh. "I'm also guessing Emerson made a map?"

"Close," he says. "She did type out time schedules for everyone and exact locations for pick up."

"That girl is going to run the world one day," I say.

"That's the plan," he says. "But until then, she needs someone to help her out. They all do. Honestly, so do I. I don't know if you could tell, but I'm not the best at the girl stuff. Hell, I'm barely adequate with any of it. I can cook three things. Breakfast is always cereal. Luckily, the kids have some sense of style so they can pick out what they wear, otherwise I'd just be getting them Fury shirts in every fit and color, and they'd just wear those every day."

"You mean, like you're wearing?" I nod to him as he sits there in a Fury hoodie and gray joggers.

I snap my eyes back up because...*fuck*...Does this man own any other kind of pants? The answer is yes. Jeans. Jeans that hug his legs so well you'd think they were made specifically for him.

Stop. Stop this. These thoughts are not allowed, especially if I'm going to be working for him.

Shit, am I going to do this? Apparently according to the little voice in my head, I am.

But can I? I don't think Whitley would really be losing any business if I stepped away. Hell, it might make her more productive not having to redo what I've screwed up. But can I do this? Some days I'm lucky if I take care of myself.

"What exactly would you need me to do?" I ask. Which I must say, is a very adult-like question to ask to a prospective employer. If I would have asked this question to about six other jobs I probably would have avoided them altogether.

"I'm still figuring that out," he says, sitting back against the couch. "I thought I could do this alone, but I was very, very wrong about that. This morning proved that fact for me. I do know I'd need you to help me in the mornings. And when they get home from school. My practices usually go until the early evening, so I'm generally not home until after dinner. You'd be in charge of dinner, homework, any activities, those kinds of things."

"So I need to learn how to cook?"

He snaps his eyes to mine and blinks a few times. "You can't cook?"

Oh, this is too much fun. "Now, Wes. Did you go just assuming again that because I'm a woman, I know how to cook?"

I see him swallow what looks to be a huge lump in his throat. "I mean...well, I was hoping...but..."

I laugh. "Yes, Wes, I can cook. It's one of the few things I'm good at. Luckily, I had a Meemaw who knew her way around a kitchen. But we really need to work on you making assumptions. And breaking pinky promises."

This makes him smile. "Make it my free pass?"

"Sure."

We sit and smile at each other for a few seconds, which gives me time to think. Oh, who am I kidding? I don't need to think. In fact, the only thing I need to think about is how to tell Whitley I'm quitting.

"When do you want me to start?"

I don't know how, but I can literally see the weight being lifted off his shoulders. It's accompanied with a smile I don't think I've ever seen on him. I do know it makes him even more handsome than he already is.

"How about now?"

Chapter 12
Betsy

In the approximately thirty-two jobs I have had in my adult life, not once have I ever been nervous for the first day.

So why am I sitting in my car in Wes's driveway, my hand on the door, but unable to open it?

"Get it together, Betsy," I say to myself, trying my best to give myself a pep talk. "Wes is here this morning. Peggy is a phone call away. And if all else fails, just ask "What Would Emerson Do?"

With one last deep breath, and a big swig of the coffee I made at home, I get out of the car and walk up to the front door. With each step I take, I can hear a little more of the chaos that is already ensuing at seven in the morning.

Here we go...

I knock on the door and only have to wait a few seconds before Wes flings it open.

I quickly cover my mouth with my hand. It's the only way to stop myself from laughing at the scene in front of me.

Wes is holding Magnolia, who looks like she just rolled out

of bed. I don't know what he was trying to cook, but there is flour all over his T-shirt. And from what I can tell behind him, Hank is running around in his underwear with a wand stuck in his "pocket." There's no sign of Emerson, but I don't really blame her. I'd be hiding too if I wasn't being paid.

"Good morning, Taylor family," I say, doing my best to put on a super positive and peppy exterior, despite the fact that my coffee is still twenty minutes away from kicking in.

"I'm not a very religious person, but thank God you're here," Wes says.

"Is this a normal morning?" I ask as I set down my bag and coffee.

"It has been since we moved here. I just don't think we've found our new rhythm in the new house."

"Well never fear, your backup is here," I say as I hold out my arms for the sweet, sleepy princess. "How about I take this one and you go get our favorite wizard dressed?"

Wes quickly passes Magnolia to me, who immediately wraps her arms around my neck. "And then can you start breakfast? I tried to change it up from cereal, as you can see, but it didn't go well."

"That's what I'm here for," I say. "Now go. I got this."

I see the sigh of relief from Wes as he wrangles Hank up the stairs. I follow behind him and go to Magnolia's room, which I only know is hers because she insisted on giving me a full tour last night. Wes and I thought it would be best to talk to them and tell them how things were going to go now that I was going to be helping out. Before I knew it, I was getting a full house tour from all three kids—each making sure to tell me which room was theirs. Needless to say, they were excited.

Honestly, so am I.

Am I nervous? Absolutely. I might be putting on a confident front, but I don't want to mess this up. For the first time maybe ever, this is a job I want to do well. These kids have so quickly become important people in my life.

And so has their dad.

Until last night, I had only caught glimpses of Wes as a father. I knew the kids adored him. I knew he was doing his best to adjust to being a single dad. But seeing them together in their house? I saw Wes in a whole new light.

This man is the whole package. He's an amazing father who would move mountains for his kids. He's trying to balance his final days as a football player while doing his best to give his kids everything they need in what is the most tumultuous time of their lives.

Oh, and add on the fact that he's sexy, has manners, and loves his family? You don't find men like that every day.

And of course he's now even more off limits than he was before. I might have had questionable morals and taste in men in my past, but even I know you don't go after the man who writes your paychecks.

"All right Miss Mags," I say, setting her down on the bed. "What do we feel like wearing today?"

"Dress," she says, slowly but surely starting to wake up.

"I can do that," I say as I dive into her closet, which might have more options than mine. Which is saying something.

I grab a cute tan and maroon dress, which must make her happy because she immediately perks up as she puts it on.

"Beautiful," I say. "How about we do your hair?"

The way her face lights up when I say this will forever be etched into my heart. "Can you do bunnies?"

Um...what the fuck is a bunny?

"Sure," I say, because there is no way on this green earth I am letting this child down. "But you have to tell me exactly what you want."

Magnolia grabs my hand and pulls me toward the Jack-and-

Jill bathroom she shares with Emerson, who I can see through the other door sprawled on her bed, reading. And because Magnolia is a strong, independent woman who don't need no man, she grabs the stool and climbs up to sit on the counter.

"The brush is in the drawer with the ties," she says, sitting up nice and tall.

"So, Magnolia," I say as I slowly get everything ready. "Because everyone does bunnies different, can you tell me what exactly you want?"

"She wants pigtails but don't pull them all the way through," Emerson says as she walks in, phone in hand. "A mom on the *ForU* app does this with her daughter. Magnolia thinks they are awesome."

"Thank you," I say, giving the video a quick watch before spraying Magnolia's hair with water so I can pull it into the two high pigtails. "How are you this morning, Em?"

She gives me a funny look. "No one calls me Em."

"Oh," I say, not even thinking about that. "I don't have to call you that if you don't want."

"It's okay," she says. "Mom didn't like us having nicknames."

"I'm sure she had a good reason," I say, not wanting to bash their mom on my first day. I can also tell by Emerson's expression this is not a road of conversation she wants to go down.

"How is your new school?"

"Great!" Magnolia says, nearly bouncing off the counter. "My teacher is nice, and I made three new friends yesterday. And Uncle Ollie came and saw me at lunch."

"That's great. How about you Em? Settling in?"

She shrugs. "It's okay."

"Just okay?"

She doesn't say anything for a second, and I don't press her. Between the divorce, the move, a new school, and just being a preteen, I can't imagine everything going on in that amazing brain of hers.

"In my old school, we had uniforms," she says. "I never had to pick out what to wear."

"That would have made my mornings easy," I say. "I used to have to pick out an outfit the night before or I would have been late every day."

"That's my problem," she says. "I don't know what to wear. I've never had to make this kind of decision before."

"Girl. I got you," I say, pulling through my first bunny. Based on Magnolia's smile that is brighter than every bulb in this vanity, I'm doing it right. "How about this? Go pick out three tops and three bottoms you think you might want to wear. As soon as I'm done here, I'll come in and help you."

I've learned that Emerson's smiles are guarded. She doesn't give them out freely. So when I see a small one shine through, I take it as the biggest win of the morning.

"Thanks, Betsy," she says and walks back into her room.

"Okay Miss Mags," I say. "Now close your eyes so I can put the finishing touches on it."

She quickly puts her hands over her eyes as I pull through the last bunny and give her hair a quick spray. I might not dress children a lot, but I do know no proper girl is set for the day without accessories. Luckily, I find them quickly, grab two bows, and clip them in.

"All right...open!"

She uncovers her eyes, and I wish I had my camera with me. Her face is priceless. Is this why parents video every single thing their kids do?

"Do you like?" I ask, giving her one last pass with the hairspray.

She doesn't say anything, instead just turning around and

jumping into my arms in the biggest hug her six-year-old self can give.

"I love them," she says.

Fuck. I think I'm going to cry.

"I'm so glad you do."

I give her one more squeeze and set her down. She barely has her two feet on the ground before she goes running off across the hall.

"Daddy! Daddy! Look at my hair! Betsy gave me bunnies!"

I lean against the door as I watch Wes kneel to Magnolia, who does a little turn for him to show off her dress and hair.

He listens to every word coming out of her sweet mouth as she tells him about our getting ready process and how I surprised her with the bows. He makes all the correct facial expressions and reactions as she talks about the past twenty minutes as it's the most important thing of her life. He then tells her how beautiful she looks and how she's going to have an amazing day at school.

And, there go my ovaries.

Chapter 13
Wes

There have been times this season when I wondered whether or not it was the right choice to retire. Every once in a while, I have those really good days where I start thinking I have another season in me. One game this season I scored three touchdowns and seriously thought about rolling back the retirement plans.

Then there are days like today, where everything hurts and I limp out of practice. These are the days that confirm I made the right decision. Not even an hour session with the trainer and a good ice bath could do the trick.

"Just a few more months," I say to myself as I turn off the highway toward Rolling Hills. We have seven regular season games left, and unless we decide to implode, we are headed to the playoffs. If you listen to the talking heads, we're the favorite to win the championship this year.

If we do that, then I know I'll be meant to retire. I don't think you can have a better end of a career than going out on top. Even if we don't win, this is it. My body can't do this anymore. And to be honest, I don't know if I can do it mentally.

Moving to Rolling Hills and relying on my family, and now Betsy, to help with the kids is good for the short term. It's the best situation to have as I finish out the year. But I don't want to be an absentee parent. I want to be there for them. I don't want to be gone for weeks at a time, or even nights like tonight, when the day went long and I'm not there to tuck them into bed.

Nope, this is it. At this time next year, I'll be spending Thanksgiving with my family, not eating my football season macros then packing a bag for wherever we have to travel to that weekend.

I can't help but look at everything as I make my way to the new house. As I drive past the high school football stadium, I see the lights on. I smile, remembering night practices that Coach Lockwood used to have. From the looks of it, he still does. Every Tuesday night, we'd have practice under the lights. I don't even remember how it started. But I am glad to see it still going on.

We loved Tuesday night practices. More specifically, we loved *after* Tuesday practices. We'd all hop in Shane's truck and drive to The Joint. We couldn't go in because we were under eighteen, but since my uncle owned the place, he'd bring us out wings and burgers and we'd eat in the bed of the truck. The four of us would shoot the shit, complain about school and girls, and just...be.

Those were the days. Fuck if I don't miss them.

Before I know it, I'm turning into my driveway and pulling into the garage. I don't get out for a second, needing one more minute to myself.

I didn't know how I was going to handle today. Do I trust Betsy? Yes. I wouldn't have offered her the job if I didn't. But there's always that worry lodged in your brain that today would be the day that something would happen. And somehow, Betsy knew that. Throughout the day I got updates, setting my mind at ease. First one came from the drop-off line, where each of the kids were making faces. The second came from pickup. Again with the faces, only these ones looked like they had just had the longest, most exhausted day of their lives. I also got a video after school of the three of them doing homework. I know Hank is convinced Betsy has magical powers, and I must say I have to agree, because that's the only way I can figure out how she got them all to sit and quietly work.

Which means if they were quiet for her, I'm going to get absolute chaos.

I'm just about to get out of the truck when my phone notifies me of a text. I grab it but don't leave the truck, snatching up the excuse to stay in here for just another minute.

> Oliver: Just so you know, Betsy was at the school in plenty of time for pickup and everything went off without a hitch.

> Wes: Thanks, man. And thanks for helping the kids get adjusted. I appreciate it.

> Oliver: No need to thank me. I meant to tell you, I'm glad you hired Betsy. I can tell she's going to be good for you guys.

> Wes: You mean the kids.

> Oliver: Sure, we'll go with that.

I navigate away from the messages, grab my bag, and start heading inside. At first, I wonder if they are hiding from me because I don't hear a sound. It isn't until I'm a few feet from the living room that I hear anything, and that's the sound of credits from one of their favorite movies.

"What—"

I start to say something but snap my mouth shut when I see them. I don't want to ruin this moment.

There, on my oversized couch, is Betsy, with all of my kids snuggled around her, everyone sound asleep. It looks like Magnolia nodded off as Betsy was holding her. Hank has decided to use her leg as a pillow. And then there's Emerson. Her head is on Betsy's shoulder.

I slowly pull my phone out of my pocket, needing to take a picture of this. I have never been the picture taker of the family. That was all Cara, and while I love the photos and the memories captured, she took them to mostly keep up her social media persona as Mom of the Year. But since she's been gone, I've been trying to remind myself to capture the moments. Even if they are little things. Because once they are gone, they are gone for good.

And I have a feeling I'll want to remember this moment for a long time.

As soon as I snap the picture, Betsy's eyes slowly start to blink open. I take a few steps toward the couch, sitting on the edge of ottoman where Betsy's legs are currently sprawled.

"Hey," she says quietly.

"Hey to you," I say. "Rough first day?"

She smiles. Not the full and bright one I have seen many times. No, this is a soft and subdued one. Two words I never thought I'd use to describe Betsy.

"Yeah, I guess," she says, trying to move but realizing that all of her limbs are currently being used by my children. "We put on a movie after dinner. Guess we fell asleep."

"What movie did you pick?"

"They found out I had never seen *Cars*. And since I think we fell asleep twenty minutes in, I can still say I haven't."

I smile, gently stroking Emerson's hair off her face.

"You guys can try again tomorrow," I say. "Let me get these guys to bed so you can free yourself."

"Thanks," she says, hugging Magnolia a little closer to her.

I ignore the rush of warmth that goes through my body at seeing Betsy with my youngest. But I can't ignore the fact that for the first time in months, things just feel right. My kids don't look stressed. They don't look tired or confused or worried. They look relaxed. Comfortable.

Loved.

That must be the effect Betsy Sullivan has on my kids.

I gently tap Emerson to wake her up, and to my complete shock, when she slowly wakes up, she holds her arms out for me to carry her. I push down the wave of emotion as I pick her up. She hasn't had me carry her since she was Magnolia's age. My girl was independent out of the womb. Once she realized that she could walk to bed on her own, my days of daddy duty were done. Sometimes I forget that she's still a little girl, one who at first grew up fast because she wanted to. And now I'm scared she thinks she has to.

"Daddy?" she whispers as I enter her bedroom. I do my best to pull back her covers while still holding her. It's not as easy as it used to be. Once I do, I gently place her down and bring the blankets back up.

"Yeah, baby?"

"I really like Betsy."

I smile, because the Emerson seal of approval is the real deal.

"I do too." I smile as I brush her hair back from her head and kiss her forehead. "Sweet dreams."

I exit the room, slowly closing the door behind me. I quickly go to Hank and Magnolia's room to pull down their blankets so it won't be as hard to put them to bed.

When I make my way back down the stairs, I stop again at the sight in front of me. Betsy has fallen back asleep. Hank and Magnolia haven't moved an inch.

I don't take a picture this time. No, this time I take it in. But I'm not looking at my kids.

No, I'm looking at the woman who came into our lives when we were least expecting it. The one who is quickly making all of us forget the hurt. Who is reminding us what it's like to be happy.

The one who is making it harder and harder for me as the days go by to not feel some sort of way about her.

Chapter 14
Betsy

I've been known to make some pretty dumb decisions in my life.

There were the plethora of jobs that I took, most of them with me knowing they weren't going to pan out. There were, of course, the men I've dated and/or slept with. I'd like to forget about most of those. Except a few. When I'm old and gray I'll still—hopefully—have the memory of the male stripper from spring break in Vegas.

And still, even with all of those questionable decisions on my resume, today might take the cake. Because I came home to Birmingham for Thanksgiving with my parents.

It's everything I hoped it wouldn't be.

"So Betsy," my mother begins. "Did you hear about your cousin Ingrid?"

I let out a breath as I set down my fork. "No, Mom. I haven't."

"I'm surprised, I know she put it on social media. She got engaged."

I try not to roll my eyes at the news. My cousin Ingrid has

been trying to get her M.R.S. degree since the day she stepped foot onto campus at Alabama.

I have a lot of other things I want to say. Like asking if she's going to drop out so she can start popping out kids now, since she only went to college to find a husband. Or I could ask how many fraternities she had to go through before she found him.

But I don't. Because I'm a polite fucking Southern lady.

"Good for her," I choke out, quickly taking a bite of turkey so I have a reason to not talk.

"It is," Mom continues. "The wedding will be this spring."

"She pregnant or something?"

"Betsy Ann!" she yells. Oops. Apparently I didn't say it as under my breath as I would have liked.

"What? Come on, you had to think it too."

"I would never," she huffs, digging back into the three bite-sized portions of food she allowed for herself today.

"So Betsy," Dad says. "How is your new town? Things still going well with Whitley?"

I reach for my glass of water, needing to take a few drinks to figure out exactly how I'm going to answer this.

Because I haven't told my parents that I'm now working for Wes.

In my defense, the only time I've talked to either of them in the past week was when Mom texted me that she was hoping I could make it for Thanksgiving. I know my mom well enough to know that was more than a request.

I want to tell them. I know I need to. But all I can hear right now is my mom's sigh of disappointment and my dad going into simultaneous lectures about how I can't keep a job and also how this job is going to be another dead end.

So I do the only thing that I think will benefit all parties at the moment—I lie.

"It's going great," I say. "She's keeping me plenty busy."

Dad smiles. "That's good. Any events coming up in Birmingham we can attend?"

"Nope," I say, hopefully not too quickly. "Plus, I'm more behind the scenes. Making sure the machine stays running."

"I get it," Dad says with a nod. "Those behind-the-scene workers are the backbone of a good company."

Yup. I made the right decision.

Luckily, the conversation drifts off to where my mom and dad are doing a lot of talking and I just have to sit here and listen. Good. I'm one more round of mashed potatoes and a piece of pie away from getting out of here.

Just when I hear my dad say something about a nice young man he works with that he'd like to introduce me to, I hear my cell phone buzz next to me on the table. I turn it over to see a FaceTime request from Wes.

"I have to take this," I say, grabbing my phone and standing up.

"It is very rude to leave during dinner," Mom says tartly.

"I'll just be a few minutes."

I quickly walk out of the dining room and across the hall to my dad's study.

"Hello?"

"Betsy!"

I laugh as all three kids are yelling my name and frantically waving to me through the screen.

"Hey, you guys," I say, the smile on my face the first genuine one I've had today. "How is your day so far?"

"Great!" Hank says. "We watched Dad and Uncle Oliver and Uncle Shane run a turkey trot."

"Wow," I say, not realizing that Wes was a runner. "Did they win?"

"No," Emerson says with a snort. "They're old."

"Hey now!" Wes says. "I think I did pretty good. I beat Uncle Ollie."

Hank turns and gives his dad the most serious look his eight-year-old self can give. "Dad. You're a professional athlete. Uncle Ollie is a teacher. Of course you're going to beat him."

I laugh, loving the banter between the four of them. That is one of the things that I've noticed the most this past week, how much of a special, and unique, bond he has with each of the kids.

Hank might be a cool kid who loves his Potter, but he's also a football junkie. I think the two of them talked football for an hour last night while we finished up dinner. With Emerson, he knows she's a little more reserved, so he lets her bring the conversation to him. And more times than not she does. It's like she knows he's there when she's ready.

Then there is Magnolia. Good Lord, that child will give you a run for your money. And it's impossible to say no to her. Hence the pink nail polish on Wes's fingers today.

"Why do you look sad, Betsy?" Magnolia asks. "It's Thanksgiving. You should be happy."

I don't know whether to smile or cry at her sweet words. "I am happy, sweet girl. I'm happy now that I'm talking to you guys. I miss you!"

"You just saw us yesterday," Hank says.

"I know, but that's how much I like spending time with you."

"Hey, kids," Wes chimes in. "How about you go get your shoes and jackets on so we can go to Gram and Grandpa's house. I need to ask Betsy something."

They all tell me goodbye and exit the room like he asks.

"What's wrong?"

"What?" I ask, wondering how he knows. I thought I was playing off this wonderful display of family quite well.

"There's something off."

I let out a sigh. No use in hiding it. "It's just my parents. No big deal."

"It is a big deal," he says.

"I swear, it's not Wes," I say. "We just...our relationship right now is a bit strained since they shared their disappointment with my life choices and cut me off, which led me to Rolling Hills. I hoped today might be a little better, but it's not. Not even a little bit. And I haven't even told them I'm working for you now and not Whitley. I just can't muster up the courage."

Wes doesn't say anything, and I don't know if it's the lighting in the room or what, but I think his face is turning red. "That's how you ended up in Rolling Hills? Because your parents cut you off?"

"Yeah," I say. "Now before you think anything, yes, they were helping me pay for things, but I had jobs. Just not good ones. Or ones they approved of. Or, if none of that were to work, a husband. So I was told to do it on my own. I doubt being a nanny is going to be to their idea of a promotion."

"You are a what?"

I snap my head around and drop my phone in the process. My mother is standing at the door, looking utterly horrified.

"Did you just say that you are a nanny? What happened to your job with Whitley?"

Well, glad to see that the lie I told earlier is now biting me in the ass.

"I was working for Whitley, but it wasn't panning out. And a new opportunity came up."

"A new opportunity? Betsy Sullivan, you are not the help. We did not raise you to take a service job. My goodness, where did we go wrong with you? Why can't you just—"

"Why can't I what, Mom? Why can't I get a job that you

would approve of? That's rich coming from a woman who never worked a day in her life. Or maybe I'll be like Ingrid and fuck my way through Fraternity Row before convincing some finance bro to marry me."

"Watch your tongue, young lady," Dad says, suddenly appearing behind Mom. "You do not speak to your mother like that."

That's it. I've had it.

"Or what, Dad? Are you going to cut me off? Take away my credit cards? Oh wait, you already did that. And—I'm sure to your complete shock—I'm doing just fine."

I switch my glare to my mother, because she needs to hear this next part loud and clear. "You think that being a nanny is slumming it, Mom? Well, I have news for you. That family is the best thing in my life right now. It's rewarding being a part of their lives. And you know what? They appreciate me. The Dad? He has put more trust in me in a week than you two ever have. So you know what? I'm not ashamed. I'm proud. They are more of a family to me than either of you two are."

I lean down to snatch up my phone and storm out of the study. Luckily, my purse and keys are at the entryway.

"Betsy!"

I stop and consider turning around. I don't know what they want to say, but frankly, right now, I don't want to hear it. So I make a good decision for once and walk out.

I don't look back. I just keep on trekking forward until I'm in my car. Luckily enough, the driveway is so long that neither of them will be able to see me sitting in the driver's seat, catching my breath.

"That was a hell of a speech."

Wes's voice scares the living crap out of me. I forgot we were talking. I can't believe he stayed on the line.

Oh shit, he stayed on the line...

"You're still there?'

"Yeah," he says with a smile. "I'm still here."

I let my head hit the back of the driver's seat. "I'm so sorry. You shouldn't have had to hear all of that, and on Thanksgiving Day."

God, he heard everything. He had to have.

And he's not saying anything. Which is scaring me. Does he think I'm a spoiled rich kid? A flake? I know it comes off that way, but I hope he knows I'm none of those things. Or did my speech change his mind about that? Or am I too much of a hot mess for him to even want to bother with me anymore?

Oh God, is he going to fire me? After my epic monologue he's going to fire me. I'm going to set the world record for most jobs in a ten-day timespan.

"Betsy."

I let out a breath, bracing myself for the worst. "Yeah?"

"Come home."

He has to see the shock on my face, judging by how he's trying, but failing, to hold back his smirk.

"You want me to come home?"

"Well, home as in Rolling Hills. We're on my way to my mom's, and you know she's going to have cooked enough for an army. Plus, the kids would be thrilled if they got to see you today. Either way. Get on the road. Get here. Be with us tonight."

I feel the tears starting to leak from my eyes. "Okay. But for the record, that is not what I thought you were going to say."

He laughs. "What did you think I was going to say?"

"I thought you were going to fire me."

He shakes his head as he gives me a knowing smile. "Now, I heard from someone, I forget who it was, about not judging a book? Or making assumptions. Do you know who that came from?"

This makes me laugh. "That person sounds amazing."

"She is."

The conversation stops as we just look at each other through the phones. I don't know what he meant by that, and if I were in any other mental state I'd be dissecting it six ways from Sunday, but right now I'm just going to focus on the fact that there *is* a family out there that wants me to be a part of it.

And I want to be a part of theirs.

"I'll see you in a few hours."

He nods. "Drive safe. I'll save you a slice of pie."

Chapter 15
Wes

In most towns, Thanksgiving Eve is the biggest bar night of the year. Not in Rolling Hills. We do our partying on Thanksgiving night.

Because after a day spent with family, running a stupid race, and eating your weight in carbs, it's only right to finish the night with good drinks, good friends, and good tunes.

And after today, a night at The Joint is exactly what is needed. Especially for Betsy.

"Are you sure it's okay if I tag along?" she asks for the fiftieth time.

"Do you think this time I'm going to say no?"

"I don't know," she says with a shrug. "You're meeting your friends. I've never really met your friends. Whitley and Jake won't be here because she has family in Birmingham she actually likes. You know, in contrast to my situation. And I don't want to be in the way. I've hung out with groups of guys before. I know a woman in the mix is an immediate cock block."

I blink a few times, because she didn't honestly just say that. "What did you just say?"

"Cock block," she says matter-of-factly. "You do know what a cock block is, right?"

"I do, but—and I'm probably going to regret asking this—but why do you think you'll be one?"

"Because, I'm going to be sitting there, and maybe a woman wants to come talk to one of you. But she sees me and she says to herself, 'oh crap, which one is she with?' So she doesn't come over. And just like that, I cock block you guys by just existing."

"You think just your presence is going to keep women away?"

"It will," she says. "And if a woman comes up and starts talking, that means she doesn't care who I'm with. And that means she's level eight crazy and, unless you're into that kind of thing, you need to run."

"That would only be Oliver," I say, turning off the truck. "Maybe Simon if he's feeling a certain kind of way. But believe me, if that's the case, then please come with us. I can't have Oliver proposing to someone else."

"Proposing? As in marriage?"

I laugh. "Yes. Ask him about the ring he always has in his pocket."

"You're not serious."

"As a heart attack."

I exit the truck and walk around to open Betsy's door, only to see that she's getting out of the SUV on her own.

"What are you doing?" I ask, my voice deeper than I mean for it to be.

She gives me a confused look. "Getting out of the car? Or was your plan just to crack a window and come give me water every hour?"

I pull her toward me so I can shut the door. What I wasn't planning on was for her to end up just inches away from me, giving me no choice but to inhale her sweet perfume.

"I was trying to be nice."

She looks up at me, sass filled in her eyes. "My apologies. I'll remember for next time."

I don't know how it's humanly possible for one woman to bring out a full spectrum of emotions and feelings when it comes to her. This week with the kids, I've been nothing but thankful for her. I was worried about the transition the kids were going to make moving down here, but with the help of Betsy, she's made it seamless.

Today when I heard the way her parents spoke to her, it ignited a rage in me that I normally only feel when I'm playing football. And even that's only when we're playing teams I have a bad history with. But when I heard the way they talked to her, and how they clearly don't know what kind of wonderful woman she is, I wanted to punch a wall.

Then there's right now. This is the most confusing feeling of them all. Whenever I touch her, I never want to let her go. It's weird. It's like she's a magnet I can't break away from. Even though I know I need to.

"We should probably go inside," I say.

"As long as you're sure I'm not going to cock block."

I laugh. "You're ridiculous."

I take my hand and put it on the small of her back, just for a second, as we start walking toward The Joint. I have only experienced a handful of Thanksgiving nights here in recent memory. Usually, Cara would insist on returning to Nashville, and that's only if we made it down here in the first place. But from what I remember, this is the night Porter goes all out.

And by the looks of the crowd as we walk in, he hasn't held back this year.

There isn't an open seat or barstool that I can see. Groups of people are taking up all available square footage to gather. The dance floor is already packed, which makes sense as this is the one night a year Porter will splurge on a DJ. This is also the only night where someone can order a drink called the "Thanksgiving Dream," which is a Porter concoction that will get you real fucked up and put you to sleep before you know it.

"Hey! Over here!"

Somehow I hear Oliver's voice over the crowd, waving us down to our normal table where he, Simon, and Shane are already seated.

"Sorry we're late," I say, pulling out Betsy's chair for her. "We had to go get the kids' bags so they could spend the night at my mom's."

"Yes, this is a 'we' situation," Simon says, reaching over the table and extending his hand for Betsy. "Simon Banks. You must be the famous Betsy I've heard so much about."

Instead of shaking her hand, he brings it to his mouth and kisses it.

What the fuck was that?

"I am," she says. She also doesn't pull back her hand.

"I thought Wes was going to hide you forever."

This makes her laugh as she and Simon finally let go. "He allows me out from time to time."

I shoot Simon a look, who is giving me a fucking smirk as he takes a sip of his whiskey. I have no idea what Oliver and Shane have told him. But it has to be something because this man is intentionally trying to push my buttons. And he's not even letting me get a drink in before he starts his shit.

"Well, we're glad you're here," Oliver says as he extends his hand. But in the correct way. Because he's not an asshole. "And we haven't formally met. I'm Oliver. Or Uncle Ollie as the kids call me. The quiet one here is Shane. He would introduce himself, but that would require words."

She returns Oliver's shake. "Nice to officially meet both of you. And I must say Oliver, you run the smoothest pickup line. The other teachers should take notes."

"I take that as the highest compliment," he says. "Can I get you a drink?"

"Sure. Gin and tonic?"

"Oh, I should have clarified. Tonight we only drink Thanksgiving Dreams. Except Simon. He doesn't know how to have fun."

"What's in it?"

"That's the beauty of it. No one knows."

Betsy gives me a worried look as Oliver walks away.

"Don't worry," I say. "It's safe. It will just make your worries of today a thing of the past."

"Then go tell him to get me two," she says.

"Rough day?" Simon asks.

"Something like that."

And just like that, her mood changes. I can't even blame Simon; he didn't know what she went through today. It's my fault for bringing it up.

When she walked into my mom's house tonight, I had to pull the kids off her leg so she could have a minute to herself. I could tell she had been crying. When I asked her if she was okay, she put on a brave front. But I heard that conversation, and no one could have walked away from it unscathed.

What she doesn't know is that this holiday was hell on me and the kids as well. I didn't know how the kids would take the first Thanksgiving without their mom. The kids asked to call her during the parade. They watched it together every year. Luckily, Cara remembered the part of her that actually liked being a mother and picked up the phone. Hard to say if that did more harm than good. When they hung up, their mood was very subdued. Which I get, but I didn't know what to do. It took all I had not to scream into the abyss in frustration and anger at what Cara's doing to them.

As we were getting ready to go to my parents, and I was fumbling all over the place with Magnolia's hair, it hit me. The kids needed their sunshine.

They needed Betsy.

And so did I.

As soon as I called her, the air in the room shifted. Their smiles came back. And so did mine. That's just what she does. Even when she was in a toxic place, belittled by her parents just minutes before, she was still able to pull us out of the dark.

It's what I want to do for her now. Bring her to the light. I hate what happened to her today, but I can't change it. Just like I can't change what Cara did. But just as she's making us see the sunshine through the clouds, I want to do that for her. Betsy deserves that.

She deserves everything.

"Well, we can't be having any doom and gloom on the day we give thanks," Oliver says as he stands back up. "Betsy, you seem like a girl who is no stranger to a dance floor."

"I am not."

Oliver extends his hand. "Then grab your drink and get out there. Give the people something to stare at so they can quit pretending that they aren't checking out the new girl."

She turns to look at me and I nod. "Go on. Have fun. He's the best dancer out of all of us anyway. Just make sure he doesn't propose to you."

"Got it."

With a wink to me and a drink in her hand, Betsy and Oliver head out to the dance floor. I watch the two of them walking away, Betsy laughing at something Oliver said. When I turn back around I see Shane and Simon staring at me.

"What?"

Neither of them say anything, but the look is not hard to decipher. It's definitely a silent "What the fuck?"

"Just say it. I'm not up to mind reading today."

I take a sip of my drink, forgetting that Porter's specialty drink goes down as smooth as iced tea on a summer's day.

Simon sets down his drink. "I just think it's funny that you shot me a death glare when I kissed Betsy's hand, but you have no problem letting her go dance with Oliver."

"Maybe that's because I know you will try to get her into bed in five seconds, and Oliver isn't an asshole."

"Why would you care?" Shane asks. "If I remember correctly, you told Oliver and me there was nothing between you two. So, if that stands true, and she really is *just the nanny*, then why would you have a problem with one of your best friends pursuing her?"

"I don't," I say through clenched teeth. "She's a grown woman. She can do whatever she wants."

"Or whomever she wants."

Simon lifts an eyebrow at me, practically daring me to say something. That motherfucker knows exactly what he's doing. He's always been the instigator of our group. I swear the man gets off on how far he can push someone before making them snap.

"Yes, or whomever she wants."

I barely move my lips as I say those words, because they taste like poison on my tongue.

"You're going to go down swinging, aren't you? I mean, bravo to you, friend. If that woman was in my house all day, every day, I know for a damn fact I would have punched me about five minutes ago for making a move. But hey, to each their own."

I don't answer him, instead changing my focus to Betsy and Oliver on the dance floor. As I predicted, nothing is happening between them. It's just two people enjoying the night dancing to a song I only know because the younger guys play it in the locker room.

For a brief moment, I imagine another random guy out there with her and not Oliver. My temperature immediately spikes at just the thought of it.

Which is ridiculous. Betsy is a grown woman. I know she's going to eventually date. She might even be dating now. Hell, there's a good chance at this time next year she will be on the dance floor with a guy who isn't Oliver. He'll be holding her close as a ballad is played. She'll be giving him that smile that will make him feel like a million bucks. They'll kiss, pretending that there isn't another person in this place.

And I'll be here, divorced and retired, fighting off the urge not to beat that guy's ass.

Fuck. This is bad. So fucking bad.

Chapter 16
Betsy

"THAT MIGHT HAVE BEEN THE MOST EXHAUSTING NIGHT OF my entire life."

I drop down onto Wes's couch, which I have to say is literally the most comfortable piece of furniture I've ever experienced. That could also be because this day felt like it was never going to end. After five hours of Christmas decorating and a very argumentative bedtime, the kids are asleep and it's just Wes and me now.

"If you think this is exhausting, just wait until actual Christmas Day."

Wes hands me a glass of wine as he sits down next to me on the couch with his beer. The crispness of the moscato was exactly what I needed after tonight.

Today was Christmas tree decorating at the Taylor house. And despite my best attempts to leave and tell them that it was a family thing, they insisted I stay to help.

One of these days I'm going to figure out how to tell those kids no.

"Speaking of Christmas, have you started shopping yet?"

He lets out a groan, followed by a big pull of his beer. "I haven't. Honestly, the only reason I knew it was December first is because Emerson reminded me this morning. I hate thinking about getting old, but I feel better knowing she's going to be the one to decide what nursing home I go into."

"She really is something. But why did she need to remind you about December first?"

He sighs as he sets down his beer bottle on the end table. "December first is when the tree goes up and the decorations come out. Every year since they were kids, December first has been tree day. Even if it fell on a Sunday and I had a game, that's when it happened."

"That's sweet," I say. "Kind of like the kickoff to Christmas."

"Exactly." He lays his head back against the sofa and stares at the ceiling. "I think they look forward to this more than Christmas. And I almost forgot it."

"But you didn't. Well, Emerson didn't," I say. "Don't beat yourself up. It's done. The tree is up and decorated. The holiday décor is displayed. Christmas kickoff went off without a hitch."

I take a second and look at the multicolored lights slowly flashing on the tree. There is something really comforting about the ambiance.

"You know, I never got to have a fun tree like this," I say.

"A fun tree?"

"Yeah," I say, looking at the Rapunzel ornament that Magnolia wanted to make sure had a prime spot in the front of the tree. "My parents are old Southern money. Which means 'proper' Christmas trees with white lights and the same red bulbs all around. When I was in first grade, I made ornaments in art class and other kids were talking about how their parents hung them on their trees. I remember running home and showing my mom, asking if she could hang this one I made out of Popsicle sticks."

"Do I even want to know what she said?"

I shake my head. "Let's just say it was made very clear that my work was not good enough for the family tree. I remember crying for hours that night."

I haven't thought about this in forever. I can still remember the excitement I had coming home from school. I also distinctly remember the look on her face when she told me no. Now that I think about it, I believe this was the first time I knew I had disappointed my mother.

"Cara wanted fancy trees too," Wes says. I don't dare say a word. It isn't often he brings her up, and I'm not about to be the one who interrupts whatever he's choosing now to get off his chest.

"I didn't buy the house we moved from until Hank was born. By then, I had a sizeable contract that could allow us to have a bigger home. Anyway, I remember that first Christmas, right on December first, I was getting out the ornaments. They were a hodgepodge of ornaments that we had before we were married, ones we got for the kids, and other random ones we acquired along the way. I remember she looked at them like they had mold on them. She said that now that we were in a better house, we needed a better tree. She showed me one, I swear to God it was twelve feet tall, and she wanted it deco-rated in red and gold ribbon with soft white lights. I said that was fine, but that we were still having a tree with these on them. She agreed, but it had to go upstairs in the kid's play-room. I didn't think anything of it, really. Then over the years it slowly became the tree for me and the kids. I bought them a new ornament every year for us to put on it. They'd make me ornaments at school, probably the same one you made, and we'd hang it up. It was our tree. I'm just glad we can have this one now. I think it meant a lot to them to have this down here. To have our tree."

"Your fun tree."

He smiles at me. "Our fun tree."

I wipe away a tear that sprang loose. I've thought this many times since I met Wes, but how do you walk away from a man like him? He's clearly an amazing father. He's sweet and kind. He listens when you talk and always seems to know what you need at that moment. And then there's the whole handsome as hell thing. I have to smack myself sometimes because I catch myself staring. I can't help myself.

Like now. I take the chance to look at him as he stares into the lights of the tree. His brown hair is a little wild from the day. His jawline is covered in that perfect length of beard. And yes, I will admit I have thought about that beard a few times and wondered what it would feel like against my cheek. Or my thighs.

I'm a woman who is in a bit of a dry spell. Sue me.

Plainly said, the man is beautiful, inside and out. When the day comes that he's ready to date again, that woman is going to be the luckiest one on the planet. Because once you get a Wes Taylor in your life, you don't let him go.

"Well, I think your tree is beautiful," I say. "It's the perfect tree."

"Just wait until you see it on Christmas morning."

Now this gets me excited. "Please tell me you go completely overboard at Christmas and buy them a ton of stuff and it looks like presents are exploding from the bottom."

"Of course," he says. "Though I don't know what the actual presents will look like. I can buy a present like no other. I'm the king of gift giving. Gift wrapping, though? Not a strength of mine."

"Well then, you're in luck," I say. "Give me the paper and some scissors. I got you."

"Weren't you the woman who couldn't tie balloons to an arch?"

"Listen. That's completely different. Balloons have a mind of their own. And there were environmental factors."

"Whatever you say," he teases. "Either way, I'll take you up on it. It can't be worse than what I'd do."

"I'm sure you aren't that bad."

"Oh, just you wait."

We share a smile as each of us reach for our drinks, taking another sip. This is nice. In the three weeks I've been working here, we haven't had many nights where it's just the two of us. Not that we're supposed to. I'm here for the kids. There have been a few nights where the kids are either doing homework or getting ready for bed, and we've had a few moments while I'm finishing up. But nothing like this.

It's nice. Comfortable. I like talking to Wes. He knows the hot mess I am. I know the struggles he's going through. There are no fronts or facades. I don't know if I've ever been able to talk to anyone besides Whitley like this. Yes, I had other friends in college and when I was in Birmingham, but those were all friends due to circumstance and social status. Those conversations and friendships were surface level at best. And the men I've dated? Ha. They never saw the real me. Mostly by design. My thought then was the situationships didn't need to know and men I really wanted to get serious with needed to be eased into knowing the real me.

But not Wes. The man knows me, warts and all. Which is why I have given myself a pass when I think about him and the gray sweatpants. Or now in the white T-shirt that is clinging to his biceps. We're never going to happen. Between me being me, him being him, and the fact that I'm now the nanny, I have a better chance of winning the lottery.

"So these presents," I say, needing to get back to the conversation so I quit staring at him. "When you buy them, do you just want to bring them to my house? That way I can wrap them away from the kids and you don't have to worry about a hiding spot."

He looks at me with a sense of relief on his face. "That would be great. Then again, that would require me actually going to buy the gifts."

"That would help."

"I just," he begins then stops, frustration now overtaking the relief. "This is the first Christmas, you know? It's the first Christmas that their mom and dad won't be waiting for them at the bottom of the steps. I want it to be perfect."

"It will be," I say.

"I'm trying. I just need to figure out how the hell I'm going to get that new gaming system that just came out. That's all Hank has asked for, and I didn't realize it was going to be sold out in five minutes."

"You know, if you don't get it, he'll understand," I say, patting Wes's hand.

He lets out a sigh. "I know. But the kid has been through a lot. They all have, but I think Hank is taking it the hardest. He was a mama's boy. He's trying to hold it in, because I think he thinks he has to, but I know it's just a matter of time before he blows."

"Listen," I say, letting my hand rest on his. "I know you think Christmas is riding on this. Will you be disappointed if you don't find it? I'm sure you will be. And Hank might be a little sad. But in twenty years, he's not going to remember that he didn't get the gaming system. He's going to remember that in what could have been the worst Christmas ever, his Dad went above and beyond to make sure it was the best."

"Do you really think that?" Wes asks. "Because I remember when I was ten and I didn't get the bike I asked for. It's still a sore subject with my dad."

"Hmm," I say, all of a sudden remembering back many years ago. "I didn't get the Bratz doll I asked for. It's all I wanted. But of course, my mother didn't think children should have toys, or fun, so I didn't get it. But that's my screwed-up childhood. Not Hank's."

I go to pull my hand back, only I can't. I look down to see that Wes has taken a hold of it and isn't letting go. When I look back up, I'm taken aback by the look in his eye.

Want. That's the only word that comes to mind. Like the first night we met, my body is coming alive because of his touch.

Does Wes want me? He can't, can he? Again, let's list out the reasons why I can't want him and why he shouldn't want me.

But there's no denying the look in his eye right now.

Wes wants me.

And I can't deny it either. I want him.

"Wes."

My word comes out as a whisper as we slowly lean into each other. We're like magnets right now, unable to pull away even if we want to. Even though we should. I know this is a bad idea, and it's going to change everything, but I can't stop this.

I don't want to.

I see his eyes look down at my lips, which might be the sexiest thing he's ever done. I come in a little closer, wanting to be as close as I can. His hand is slowly sliding up my arm, giving me goosebumps all over. I can feel his breath on me. I close my eyes, wanting to revel in the moment.

"Daddy, I don't feel good."

The sound of Magnolia's voice is an instant ice bucket dumped over us. We jump back from each other before we snap our heads to the stairs, where Magnolia is standing, baby doll in her arms.

"I'll be right there, baby," he says.

He looks back down at me, regret written all over his face.

"I should go," I say, hurrying up from the couch. Just as I'm about to make a beeline for the door, he stops me, grabbing me much like he did the first night we met.

"What?" I ask.

"I'm sorry."

I shake my head, which is really just me trying to hold back the tears that are forming. "Nothing to apologize for. Take care of Mags. I'll see you in the morning."

And before he can say anything else—or see me cry—I walk away.

Chapter 17
Wes

"Does anyone have any questions before we move on?"

Coach McAvoy looks around the room to his team. No one raises their hand or even breathes what could be misunderstood for a question. One, because at this point in the season, we've become a well-oiled machine when it comes to the playbook. Two, because no one is going to be the guy who keeps the meeting going longer than it has to. Team meetings and review sessions are an important part of football, especially the night before a game. They are also the most tedious part of the job, and no one wants it to go longer than it needs to.

"All right, moving on. Defense..."

I let myself zone out for a second, which I normally don't do. I haven't played defense since high school, but it's still important to know what's going on. But tonight I have barely listened to a word Coach has said.

It's been two days since I've talked to Betsy, and it's been eating me up inside. God, I almost fucked everything up. I don't know what came over me. But at that moment, the only thing I could think of doing, the only thing that felt right, was to kiss her. And I was close. So fucking close. I could nearly feel her lips on mine before Magnolia came down the stairs.

I couldn't sleep that night, and that wasn't because Magnolia insisted on sleeping in my bed after she claimed she had a fever, which she didn't. All I could think of is what a huge mistake I almost made. Because it would have been a mistake. As much as I'm attracted to Betsy, and no matter how much I care about her, I can't cross that line. I can't risk the kids losing her because I decided to have an impulsive moment of weakness.

I was ready to talk to her on Friday until I remembered that she had the day off. When she came over this morning, I was running late to get to the airport for the team plane. But even if I had time to talk to her, I don't know how I would have since she could barely look at me.

And it fucking killed me inside.

How could I be so dumb? I mean, I know why. As much as I want to deny it, or tell myself that it's wrong, the more time I spend with Betsy, the more I want her. Yes, it started with just a pure attraction. I could fight off attraction. But it's more than that. It's her smile. It's her laugh. It's how she has made my kids, who are going through the roughest time of their lives, seemingly forget the bad stuff. It's the way she looks at me when I tell a dad joke. It's the way she makes me calm and balanced with just a simple touch.

I fucking want her. I know I shouldn't. I need to get over it.

But I don't know how.

Just as I hear the coaches move on to special teams, my phone vibrates in my pocket. I pull it out to see a FaceTime request from Betsy. I quickly look at the clock in the hotel meeting room that we're currently gathered in to see that it's eight o'clock.

I signal to Coach McAvoy, pointing to my phone. He nods his head in the direction of the door. I don't know many coaches who would be as accommodating as he has over the past few months. I asked him the first weekend we traveled if it would be okay if I ducked out if my kids called. He didn't even hesitate. He told me the kids and family came first, especially now.

I close the door behind me and open FaceTime to see three smiling faces looking back at me.

"Hey, you guys," I say as I sit on a bench in the hotel hallway. "How was your day?"

"Great!" Magnolia says. "I made rings!"

I look over at Emerson. "Translation?"

"Betsy had us each pick out Christmas craft projects today. Magnolia made a Christmas countdown of red and green rings."

"That's fun," I say. "What did you make?"

She holds up an ornament. "I made ornaments with beads. I've already hung two on the tree. I'm giving two to Betsy because she says she doesn't have ornaments yet for her tree and she needs some."

"That's nice of you," I say. "What about you, buddy? What did you make?"

"I made a Grinch! He looks so good. Just like the cartoon one. Not the real life one. But he's drying right now, so I'll show you when you get back."

His enthusiasm is contagious. "Sounds good."

The kids continue to go on and on about their craft day, which also included a taco bar for dinner.

"Sounds like you guys had a packed day."

"We did," Hank said. "Betsy says we can watch a movie and make hot chocolate with marshmallows, but she knows we're going to fall asleep, so she said to call you before we started."

I laugh. "Well, I'm glad you did. I love you guys."

"We love you too, Daddy." That comes from Magnolia, but they all say it in their own way.

"Hank, Magnolia, how about you two go help Betsy with the hot chocolate? I need to talk to Emerson."

The two don't think anything of it, leaving me alone with my oldest as they tell me goodbye one more time.

"You guys had a big day."

"It was. I used a hot glue gun, which I'm probably too young to use, but Betsy said that if she could handle it, so could I."

"I'm just glad you didn't burn yourself."

"Dad? Did you really tell me to stay on to talk about crafts?"

This kid is too smart. "What if I did?"

"Then I'd say we need new things to talk about."

I don't say anything, wondering how I'm going to ask my eleven-year-old the thing I'm about to ask her.

"Dad, if you're going to ask about Betsy, then just ask."

"Why do you think I'm going to ask about Betsy?"

She gives me a look that screams "Are you kidding me?"

"I noticed this morning that you two didn't really talk before you left. And tonight she just handed me her phone to FaceTime. She usually hangs out with us and will say hi to you. Did you make her mad? You better not have. There are very few people that all three of us are going to like and if you mess this up—"

"Whoa, there," I say, trying to calm her down. "We had...a misunderstanding."

It's the only thing I can think of to call it. I don't know if that's the best word, but I can't think of a better one.

"Are you two fighting?"

I shake my head. "No, sweetie. We just need to talk when I get back. I promise. Everything will be fine soon."

"Okay," she says, her voice clearly worried. "Should I put in a good word for you?"

I laugh. "Can't hurt."

"I love you, Dad."

"Love you too, Emerson."

We hang up the phone and I take a second before I head back into the room. Except when I open the door, everyone is starting to stand and gather their things.

"Taylor," Coach McAvoy calls out. "Come see me before you leave."

I go and gather my things and wait as my team files out of the conference room. When it's clear, I head up to the front, where Coach McAvoy, along with Coach Davis, are waiting. If you were to look at our team and didn't know one from the other, you'd probably think they were players. They could be if they wanted. Hell, Coach McAvoy is two years younger than me. Davis, I believe, is right there with him. But not once since the moment the two of them took over have I felt like they were unqualified.

Nope, they are innovators. Hunter McAvoy is the youngest head coach in the league for a good reason. The man's football mind is brilliant. And with Davis as his offensive coordinator, our team has rewritten how you score points in the league. I've been proud to be a part of it.

"How are things?" Hunter asks. "Everything okay?"

I nod. "Yeah. The kids just like to tell me goodnight before they head to bed. If I can give them that little bit of comfort, I'll do it."

"Absolutely," Davis says. "I'm expecting a call from my little one at any minute. She gets very sassy if I don't answer."

"Being a girl dad is something," I say. "Too bad this guy won't get to know that."

Hunter holds up his hands. "Not my fault. Though I do think the universe knew that the combination of my wife and I did not equal parents who would know how the hell to raise daughters."

We share the laugh as Davis's phone rings. "That's my cue. See you guys later."

We nod to him, but Hunter doesn't move. I had a feeling he wasn't done talking to me.

"You didn't answer me before," Hunter says.

"Which question was that?"

"How things were. I haven't had a chance to talk to you in a minute. You think the move was the right choice?"

We each take a seat. I've been in this situation before. When Coach McAvoy wants to catch up with you, it's not a short conversation. It's one of the reasons his players love him so much.

"Honestly? I can't imagine it going better."

"That's great."

"I'll admit, I was worried at first, wondering how I was going to do it all myself. I know I had my family and friends, but you can only ask them to do so much, you know?"

He laughs. "Unfortunately, I don't. Between my in-laws and my parents now living here, we are never wanting for childcare."

I laugh. "Well, that's good. And I'm sure my parents would have done if it, but I didn't want to ask them to. Bringing Betsy on to be the full-time nanny was the best thing I could have done. She's been a savior."

Hunter's eyes grow wide. "Betsy? As in Whitley's friend, Betsy?"

"The very one," I say. "I sometimes forget that you know her."

"Oh yes," Hunter says. "Did Betsy ever tell you how they met?"

"No."

"They were both competing to be Miss Teen Alabama."

Good thing I'm not taking a drink, or I might have choked on it. "Betsy was in pageants?"

Hunter laughs. "Oh yes. Whitley won, and Betsy came in second. I think the other girls thought Betsy was going to push her off the stage. Instead, Betsy made sure her tiara was on just right. They've been inseparable ever since."

Now I really need for things to be right again. I'm going to need proof of this era of Betsy's life.

"Betsy was always my favorite of Whitley's friends," Hunter continues. "She had every chance to be a spoiled rich kid from the old money part of Birmingham. But she wasn't. Did she have her fun? She absolutely did. One weekend they visited me at Alabama when they were in high school, and I was pretty sure I was going to have to beat up about six guys she was hitting on."

I swallow the lump in my throat, refusing to even picture the scene Hunter just painted.

"So yes, was she a bit crazy? Sure. What teenage girl isn't? But at the end of the day, she's had my sister's back at every step, and that's who you want in your corner. And she's the one who made sure that Whitley and Jake got their shot. Those are the kind of people you want in your circle."

I let Hunter's words sink in. He's right. She's the kind of people you want around. Yes, she has her quirks. Yes, I think, at least according to her stories, I might almost be the longest job she's had. But at the end of the day, like my mom said, she's good people. She's the kind of people you want in your life. In your kids' lives.

I already knew what I was going to tell her, but this conversation seals it. I'm going to make sure she knows that what almost happened the other night was a mistake. As much as I wanted it to happen then, and I know she did too, we can't take the chance. It's too risky. Because having Betsy in my life platonically and professionally is better than not having her at all.

Chapter 18
Betsy

"Betsy? Betsy, wake up."

I jerk awake, needing a second to remember where I am. The lights of the Christmas tree remind me that I'm at Wes's house. And it's Wes who just shook me awake.

"Sorry," I say, looking at the clock to see that it's after midnight. "I didn't mean to fall asleep."

"You're fine," he says, sitting down next to me. "Everything okay with the kids?"

I nod as I let out a yawn. "Yup. Homework is done. Book bags are packed for the morning and so are the lunches. They went to bed without a fight, and I haven't heard a peep from them since. Or maybe they threw a very quiet house party and were successful in not waking me up. Your guess is as good as mine."

He laughs softly, which is good. Helps make this less awkward. This is the first time I've talked to Wes since the almost kiss. Last night when the kids FaceTimed him, I hid like a coward. I have a feeling he was asking about me, though. I find it more than a coincidence that after Emerson talked to him alone she suddenly started asking me questions about how I'm doing and if I'm still liking my "employment" here. She also opted to ask specific questions about me getting along with her dad. Emerson is a lot of things, but being sneaky is not her forte.

"I heard something about you this weekend."

I tilt my head, wondering what on earth he is talking about. "From who?"

"Hunter."

Oh shit. What did he say? "Did he tell you about the Alabama visit? In my defense, I was eighteen and stupid and at the time didn't realize that I get even more bold when I drink whiskey."

"He mentioned a visit but not that. And sometime I'm going to have to see you drink whiskey." Wes stops for a second, a devilish smile appearing on his face. "You, Betsy Sullivan, did not tell me that we were in the presence of beauty pageant royalty."

I feel my face heat as I take a pillow and immediately bury myself under it.

"Why would he tell you that?"

Wes leans over and pulls the pillow from my head. "I don't know, but I'm glad he did."

"I'm going to kill him," I say, sitting back up. "At least he didn't show you pictures."

"Oh no, but you will," he says. "I think it's only fair."

"Fair? Why is it fair? I have seen no incriminating photos of you. But I can. Who has them? Your mom? Oliver? I bet it's Oliver. You think he'd give them to me? He would. We're tight now. Please tell me you went through a mullet phase before they became cool again."

We both start laughing, each shushing each other as we were probably getting too loud.

"This," he says.

"This what?"

"This...this is what I don't want to lose," he says.

Oh, we're having the conversation now. I knew it was coming. I just didn't expect it to segue like this.

"I don't want to lose it either," I say. "I like what we have going on here."

"I do, too."

The relief on his face is clear. So yes, I do like what we have. But that's the last truth I'm going to say tonight. Because I know what he's about to say. And it's going to hurt like hell when he does. It's going to hurt even more when I say that I agree.

"That night," he begins. "I think I just got caught up in the moment. We got caught up in the moment."

"You're right," I say. Okay, one more truth. Because if this is the last time we have this kind of talk, I want him to know exactly where I stand. "I want you to know, I wanted to kiss you. I wanted you to kiss me. If Magnolia wouldn't have come downstairs, I wouldn't have stopped you."

He lets out a breath. "I wouldn't have stopped either."

We sit in silence for a second, our eyes locked onto each other. I think we're both wondering what would have happened. What would it have felt like to feel his lips against mine? How far would it have gone? One kiss? A couch make-out session like we were in high school? I don't think we would have slept together, but how close would we have gotten? Because I don't know if you can just kiss a man like Wes Taylor.

"But we did stop," I say. "And you're right. The kiss would have changed everything. And probably not in a good way."

There's lie number one. Because I think in a different situation, and a different time, that kiss could have been everything. And maybe the old Betsy would be saying "fuck it" right now and just let the cards fall where they may. But I can't do that now. I won't. He means too much to me. This *family* means too much to me.

"It would have," he says. "I know we wouldn't have told the kids, but I'm sure they would have picked up on something. Emerson would have noticed in a day. Magnolia would just ask us questions until we cracked. Stopping was for the best."

An awkward silence falls between us, which hasn't happened since the first night we met. I know he's right. I might not like it, but he is. I love this job. For the first time in my life, I feel like I'm making a difference. I feel like I'm helping these three amazing kids, and their equally amazing dad. I might not be their teacher or a coach, or even a parent, but I feel like I'm helping them navigate life, and that's a damn good feeling. So he's right, we can't risk ruining this just for a kiss.

Even though I've never wanted to kiss someone so badly in my entire life.

"I do need you to know something," Wes says, breaking the silence.

"Please tell me the next words out of your mouth was that you were in an all-boys hip-hop troop when you were younger and there's video evidence."

That lightens the mood. "Not even a little bit."

"Too bad. That was the only thing I could think of that was going to top my beauty queen days."

He has to take a second to catch his breath from laughing. "What I was going to say was, I hope you know that me thinking that we shouldn't kiss has nothing to do with you and everything to do with me."

That takes me back. "I mean, doesn't me being the nanny have something to do with it?"

"Well, yes," he says. "That's part of it. You've become invaluable to me. My kids think you walk on water. And as

Emerson told me in not so many words yesterday, I better not do anything to make you leave us."

I smile and shake my head. "I'm not leaving until you kick me out."

"She'll be glad to know that. But what I was going to say," he stops and takes a breath, grabbing my hand. I wish he wouldn't do that. I wish he'd quit being so damn sweet. And also making me feel things that I don't want to feel anymore but have no control on how to turn it on and off. "I was going to say that I'm a mess, Betsy. In two weeks I'm going to be finalizing my divorce. I'm about to retire from football, which means I have no idea what I'm about to do with my life. I'm living back in my hometown. The only reason my kids are alive, bathed, and fed is because of you. You should be with someone who doesn't have more baggage than an airport. A kiss is all I could have given you, and you deserve a man who can give you the world. Not a guy who doesn't know what day of the week it is."

I feel my heart breaking as Wes talks. I hate that's how he sees himself. Because that's not the man I see. And he needs to know that.

You know, from a friend.

"Well, I don't see that," I say, not removing my hand from his. Because apparently I'm a glutton for punishment. "I see a man who is getting a fresh start. I see a man who could have crumbled at his situation, but instead he picked himself up and did what was needed for his family. I see a man who is thinking about everyone but himself to make sure they are getting what they need. And, I see a man who deserves to be loved. Who shouldn't settle for anything less than epic, once in a lifetime, can't write it in a movie, kind of love. That's what you deserve, Wes. Nothing less than that."

I start to stand up, because I'm three seconds away from crying. But Wes's hand pulls me back down to the couch.

"I wish I could be what you see me as."

I give his hand a squeeze and pull it away. "You are. One day you'll realize it. And the woman that gets to be on the receiving end of it, she's going to be the luckiest woman in the world."

Chapter 19
Wes

I PULL INTO THE MEDIATOR'S OFFICE AND JUST SIT AND stare. Today is the day. Today I'm going to be officially a divorced man.

I've said that phrase to myself over and over all morning, and while I have no problem with that being one of my new titles, I also still can't believe I'm here. Don't get me wrong, Cara has shown her true colors over the past few months in how she has acted and treated the kids, and if this is who she's choosing to be, I don't want to be married to her.

I check my phone before I go in and see a bunch of messages I missed in the drive up to Nashville. The first is from my mom, telling me good luck. The second is the group chat with the guys, each of them giving words of encouragement. Except Simon. He just texted the champagne bottle emoji.

Then there's one from Betsy.

Betsy: Thinking of you today. Be strong and
know this is the first step to moving forward.

Betsy: Oh, and later there is a surprise for
you. Don't worry about the kids. I got them.

The last one gives me pause, but I don't have a chance to think about it as I see my lawyer getting out of his car. I shut mine off, grab my suit jacket from the back seat, and start making my way inside. Just as I approach the front of the building, bleached blonde hair that you can see from a mile away grabs my attention.

I turn to see Cara, who I can now only recognize because of her hair. She was always blonde, but as the years went along, it became lighter and lighter to where it's now almost white. The biggest shock to me is how thin she is. Cara was never traditionally skinny. Her curves were there in college and only became more pronounced after the kids. I tried to tell her over and over throughout the years how much I loved her body. And it wasn't a lie. But now? She has to have dropped at least fifty pounds.

"Wes," she says, her oversized sunglasses still on her face.

"Cara," I say, holding the door open for her. Both of our lawyers walk through as we follow silently and get on the elevators.

I take another look at her. The clothing doesn't shock me. I knew she'd come in wearing her most expensive dress, while simultaneously asking me for a shit ton of money. Which, shocking no one, is the only thing left we have to hash out today. Once that's finalized, we're each going to sign and this is going to be over.

We all exit the elevator as it opens, and just as I'm about to pass through, Cara stops me.

"What?"

She takes the sunglasses off her face. I have to school myself not to recoil when I see dark circles around her eyes.

"I was just going to say that you look good."

What is her game? Is she fishing for a compliment? From me? The man she left?

"I don't think it's a good idea if we talk."

She looks at me like I'm crazy. "Why are you being like this?"

"Being like what?"

"Short. Abrupt. That's not like you."

I laugh, because I can't believe her right now. "Are you serious? You're going to be the one talking about how I've changed?"

"What's that supposed to mean?"

"It means I don't know you, Cara. Maybe I never did. But the woman I married, who I thought I married, wouldn't have decided to spring a divorce on me. She wouldn't have just up and moved without warning. And she definitely wouldn't have abandoned her kids. So you know what? Think I'm being short, or mean, or rude? Fine. Because however I act is nothing like how you have."

She looks at me in disbelief. Again, I don't know why. If she really doesn't think she's acted like this, maybe she's more delusional than I thought.

"I told you I wanted something new. I wanted a chance to not be a mother and a wife."

I nod. "You did. And you're getting it. Now let's get this over with. That way we can both get what we want."

"I NEED both of you to sign here."

I hurriedly scribble my signature for what feels like for the fiftieth time today. But it's the last one.

I'm now divorced.

"And that should do it," the mediator says. "We'll make sure to get these filed."

I look up at Cara, who is nothing short of pissed off about how today went. She thought she was walking out of here set for life. If she wanted that, she should have divorced me years ago, not the year before my ten million a year salary was about to end.

We had already agreed before today to sell and split the assets—the house and everything in it. The only thing I took to the new house was stuff the kids wanted. Even she wasn't going to fight that. I asked to keep the SUV, but we agreed to sell the sports car.

Then it came to custody and alimony, which is where Cara didn't see what was about to hit her.

She said she only wanted one month a summer and a visit around Christmas based on the kids' school schedules. Her reasoning being that she wanted to see the kids, but also wanted to live on the west coast, and any more visitations wouldn't be feasible. Though, I have a feeling her lawyer told her to say that.

Because of her visitation demands, I was granted sole physical custody. Which then meant I didn't have to pay child support.

She didn't see that coming. Though by the look on her lawyer's face, he did and she didn't believe him. Also, because my financial situation will be changing drastically in the coming months, the mediator, and both lawyers, agreed that it would be best for all parties if I paid a lump sum of alimony in installments. I flinched at the number, but in the end, she's not getting as much as she thought, and I'm not going to be stuck paying her for the rest of my life.

She wanted to fight it. She actually said the words, "Well then we'll go to court." I don't know what her lawyer said to her when he pulled her aside, but when they came back, he said the terms were fine and she looked pissed.

That made me smile for the first time today.

"Thank you all," the mediator says as we all stand to leave. "And everyone have a Merry Christmas."

I shake my lawyer's hand, who promises to update me if he needs anything else. I notice Cara hasn't left. In fact, she hasn't even stood up.

"I guess we'll be in touch," I say. "I'll let you know when the kids' summer vacation ends. We'll figure out when they can come out."

She nods, her demeanor a complete shift from earlier. She looks sad, which I can say is the first time I've seen her look like this all day. "I know I don't have any right to ask this, but can I see the kids?"

This shocks me. "You want to see the kids?"

"Yeah," she says. "I have their Christmas presents. I thought since I was here we could do a visit."

I take in a deep breath because, fuck, am I conflicted. On one hand, she is their mother. I don't want to be the parent that keeps their kids away from the other just because we aren't together. But on the other hand, she's done less than the bare minimum since she left. Why should she get to see them?

"I'm going to say yes." She smiles, so I hurry up and finish. "But! Please be careful. They are just starting to figure out their new normal. Please be respectful of that."

She nods. "I will. I just want to spend the day with them. Exchange Christmas presents. Have a night in with takeout and movies."

"I think they'd like that a lot. They each got you a Christmas present we were going to send to you. Let me text Betsy. She'll get them ready."

The mere sound of Betsy's name completely changes her demeanor. "Who's Betsy?"

"She's the nanny."

"You hired a nanny?"

"I did," I say. "I'm surprised you care."

"They are my kids. Of course I care."

Oh, that fucking does it. "If you cared you wouldn't have left the way you did. That's what has fucking pissed me off this whole time. You didn't want to be married to me? Fine. But not saying goodbye to them? That was fucking low, Cara. And you better fucking apologize to them tonight for that."

"I didn't know what to say."

"Well, you better figure it out, because in a few hours they are going to ask. And you better have a fucking answer."

I storm out of the conference room and hit the elevator button. Of course, it takes its sweet ass time getting here, which allows Cara to ride down with me.

"I'd like the kids to come here. To my hotel room," she says without looking at me.

"That's fine," I grit through my teeth. "I'll drive them up. Do you want them to spend the night? They're on Christmas break."

"Yes," she says shortly. "I have a suite. There will be plenty of room."

I bark out a bitter laugh, knowing that somehow I'm paying for that. "Just text me the address and I'll have them here in a few hours."

We don't say anything else as we exit the building. I turn to head toward my car, when all I see are balloons waving in the air, and my three best friends standing around a huge, propped-up sign that says "Congratulations! You're free!"

"What the fuck are they doing here?"

I can't help but hysterically laugh as I see Oliver, Shane,

and Simon standing around my SUV, each holding up what looks to be champagne flutes. Every window is painted "Honk! I just got divorced!" They also tied balloons and streamers to every place they could.

They are idiots. But man, I fucking love them.

"Real mature, guys," Cara says, now stomping to her car. "You got your wish. He's back with you."

"Nah," Simon says. "The real wish was granted the second you asked for a divorce. We won't miss you. Oh, and the tuxes you made us wear for your wedding were ugly. Kind of like the knockoff designer shoes you're wearing now."

"Fuck you, Simon."

"Not even with my worst enemy's dick."

I swear at that point I see smoke come out of her ears, which of course makes them start laughing even harder. I do my best to put a neutral expression on, but it takes everything I have in me.

"Oh, come on!" he yells as she gets in the car. "Be sure to call me if you want to buy a house in Tennessee!"

She slams the door and speeds away.

Simon looks at us, wearing the best fake confused face I've ever seen.

"Was it something I said?"

That sends me over the edge and sputtering with laughter. I don't know if you could have three better friends than these guys right here.

"You didn't have to do this," I say as I look at Shane. "They even got you in on this?"

He nods. "The balloons were my idea."

"Thanks, guys," I say. "I don't know what else to say."

"You can thank us later," Oliver says, opening the door to my car. "Now, we need to get you back to Rolling Hills. Amelia is setting up as we speak."

"For what?"

"My friend, you just got divorced," Simon says. "We would be shit friends if we didn't properly get you drunk tonight. It's the rule."

"I don't know," I say. "I really don't want to be around people. And I just told Cara the kids could come visit tonight so she could have her Christmas with them."

"We thought you might have objections," Oliver says as he finishes typing something on his phone. "We have set up coolers, a grill, and a bonfire in your parent's field. And as for the kids, Betsy's on top of it."

I smile. This must have been what Betsy was referring to earlier.

"I guess I can't say no."

"You can't," Shane says, patting me on the back as I get in my car. "Now get in the car. You, my friend, are officially a single man."

Chapter 20
Betsy

When Wes first told me what he was going to pay me to be the nanny, my jaw literally dropped. And that's not me using literally wrong. It did. It did again when I found my first direct deposit amount.

However, I think I'm going to need to ask for a raise after what I'm about to do.

"Kids, we're here."

I pull up to the Four Seasons and put the car in park. It's only a minute before a valet comes around and helps us unload our bags and presents that we wrapped after I got the text from Wes.

When he told me what the new plan was, I didn't say anything, because it's not my place. But I'll admit I was nervous about how this would go. Luckily, Wes was back at the house before we left. He assured the kids—and me—that tonight was just a night with their mom. That it was going to be presents and movies and a big slumber party.

That seemed to help the kids relax. Not so much for me.

"You ready?"

"Yes!" Magnolia says, running toward the rotating door. "We're going to see Mommy!"

Emerson and Hank don't share her enthusiasm, instead walking next to me, each carrying their overnight bags and presents.

"Are you guys okay?" I ask as we step onto the elevator.

Emerson just shrugs. "Yeah. I mean, she's our mom. We should see her. I just don't know how to act."

The kids don't talk about Cara a lot. I don't know if it's because they don't think they can talk to me about her, or if they just don't want to talk. What I really think is happening is that they don't want to talk about her around Wes—especially Emerson.

"You act like yourself," I say. "She's still your mom. You're still her kids. Yes, things are different now. But those two things will never change. So just talk. Tell her about your new school and friends. Tell her about that new book series we found. Tell her anything you want to talk about."

Emerson nods. "She's going to flip when she sees how I'm dressed."

I check out her outfit. Today it's a Nirvana T-shirt and a pair of ripped, wide leg jeans. After that first day when she asked me to help her pick out an outfit, she told me how she didn't like a lot of her clothes. That her mom bought them, so she wore them. Slowly but surely, we've been turning over her closet from skirts and a lot of pastels to a more Emerson-appropriate style, which consists of T-shirts, jeans, and not an ounce of the color pink.

"She might," I say, suspecting she will and not wanting to lie to the girl. "And if she does, just say that you like it."

Emerson nods. "Thanks, Betsy. Can I text you if I need anything?"

"You better," I say, wrapping my arm around her shoulder.

"And if she says anything bad about that T-shirt, you better tell me. I have one at home, and I'll make sure to wear it tomorrow when I come get you guys."

She starts laughing as the elevator door opens. Magnolia immediately sprints out of the elevator and goes the wrong way.

"Miss Mags! Over here!"

She stops and turns, somehow losing no momentum as she races back toward us. The poor girl is out of breath by the time we reach the room.

And just as I'm about to knock I feel a tug on my shirt.

"Betsy?"

I look down at Hank, who is almost white in the face. "Yeah?"

"I'm nervous."

"Oh buddy," I say, wrapping him in a hug. "You have nothing to be nervous about. It's your mom. It was her idea to have you come for a sleepover. She missed you and wanted to give you guys an early Christmas."

"I know," he says. "It's just weird."

"It is," I say, giving him a kiss on the forehead. "But like I told Emerson, if you need me, or don't feel comfortable, call me. I'll be in the car so fast Uncle Shane might have to give me a speeding ticket."

This makes him smile. "Okay."

Magnolia starts knocking on the door as hard as her little six-year-old self can do. It takes a minute, but the door finally opens and I'm face to face with the woman I've been social media stalking—*researching*—for weeks.

"Mommy!" Magnolia yells, racing into the room and wrapping her arms around Cara's legs.

"Hey, sweet pea," she says, leaning down and hugging her. "Emerson, Hank, come on. Give mommy a hug?"

I give the two a little light pat on the back as they make their way to their mom. They each give her a hug around her waist, but I can tell it's guarded.

Cara looks up at me as the kids let go and go take their bags into the room. "You must be Betsy."

She looks me up and down as if she's checking me out. She's trying to make me feel self-conscious. Jokes on her. I know exactly how I look. Hot without trying. Put together. Hair perfect. Makeup on point. I had a feeling just based on my stalking—*researching*—that she'd be checking me out. So when Wes told me he needed me to bring the kids to Cara's, I did what anyone would do—I called Whitley to bring me over an outfit and my emergency hair and makeup bag. I wasn't about to give Cara ammo. I've been around way too many Southern beauty queen bitches in my day to not know how this game is played.

So I do what I know will enrage her. I'm nice to her. I reach out my hand, but she doesn't return it. Because of course she doesn't.

"I am. Nice to meet you."

"I thought Wes would be bringing them?"

"Sorry to disappoint," I say with mock sincerity. "He had plans."

She rolls her eyes. "Let me guess. The four musketeers at it again? That stunt they pulled today was just tacky."

I laugh. "I saw pictures. They really did go all out, didn't they? I'm glad they incorporated the streamers. Those were my idea."

It's at that moment she figures out exactly what I'm doing.

Game on, lady.

"So, Wes tells me you're the nanny."

"I am," I say. "Though I'm more than that. I've been helping out in any way he needs."

She gives me another once over. "I'm sure you have been. Wes does have a thing for bigger girls."

Oh hell no. She didn't just say that. Do I have curves? Yes. Do I embrace them? Hell yeah I do. I was told as a size eight in high school that I was too big to be on the pageant circuit. I politely told them to fuck off as I went on to win or come in runner-up in every pageant I was in.

I see Emerson looking on in the background. I give her a little head tilt to go in the other room with Hank and Magnolia, which she picks up on. She doesn't need to hear this.

I know I'm supposed to go high when someone goes low. But that doesn't apply in the war of Southern women's words. We're passive. We're petty. But no one will leave not knowing where we stand.

And we'll do it with a fucking smile and perfect lipstick.

"He does. Probably part of the reason he had no problem signing the papers. You look great, by the way. That bone broth diet is really paying off. I hear skinny bitch is back in style these days. Oh, and I meant to ask you! I saw the fake Hermes bag you were carrying on Instagram the other day. Where did you get it? I do love a good dupe."

The redness in her face clearly says that I got her. So I do what anyone would do right now—I slap on a smile.

"Bye, kids! See you tomorrow!"

All three of them run back into the room to give me a hug goodbye. I don't look up to see Cara's face, but I know she has to be fuming right now.

"Okay. I'll be back to get y'all in the morning. Or your dad. Or maybe both of us."

I've never seen a look of such hatred as I'm seeing right now. She clearly was never on the pageant circuit.

"Emerson?" Cara stops her as the kids head back toward the other part of the suite. "What are you wearing?"

Emerson looks down, which she also uses as a time to take in a breath, before looking up at her mom. "It's a T-shirt and jeans. I like it."

That's my girl. Confident. Standing her ground.

"Why are you dressing like that? You look sloppy and like a boy."

And with that one remark, I see Emerson's confidence deflate. It's also at this exact moment I learn what the term "Don't fuck with mama bear" is all about.

"Because she wants to," I say. I don't bother telling Emerson to leave because this girl needs to know that people in her life have her back. I also just had a flashback to the first time I tried to wear something my mother didn't approve of. I didn't have a Betsy to stick up for me back then. Like hell I'm going to let this woman put Emerson into more therapy than she's already causing.

"This is none of your concern. You're the nanny."

"It is my concern, because I'm here and you're not," I begin, my anger starting to boil over. "Last week when Hank fell off his bike, I was the one to clean him up. When Magnolia needs a bedtime story and Wes is at a game, I'm the one who reads to her. And when this girl here—this amazing, talented, smart as hell girl—asks me for help because she wants to feel more comfortable in her clothes and body, I'm going to bend over backward to make sure she knows she's loved and to support her. Have you been doing that and I've missed it? Oh wait, you haven't. So, Cara, it is my concern. Don't be pissed at the situation you created."

And because no tell-off is complete without a dramatic exit, I turn on my heel and leave the hotel room. I'm halfway down the hall when I hear Emerson calling after me. When I turn around, she's barreling into me, hugging me harder than she ever has before.

"Thank you."

I hug her back, the adrenaline starting to crash around me. "Anytime, Em. And I'm sorry, you shouldn't have had to see that."

She looks up to me. "It's okay. I knew she wasn't going to like you."

I laugh. "You could have warned me."

"I figured you knew and that's why Whitley brought you your makeup."

"Girl." I give her one more squeeze. "You are too smart for your own good."

We let go of the embrace, but neither of us move.

"You should probably go back."

"Yeah," she shrugs.

"Call me if you need anything?"

She nods. "I will."

"Or if Magnolia forgot something because I didn't check her bag."

"I already did. I switched out the toys for pajamas and clothes."

"That's my girl." I give her one more squeeze.

"Betsy?"

"Yeah?"

"Can I ask for one more thing?"

"Anything."

She looks up at me, her expression a little more devilish than normal. "When you come get us tomorrow, can you wear your Nirvana T-shirt?"

I laugh. Emerson just hit a level of petty I didn't reach until high school. I don't think I've ever been more proud.

"Gladly."

Chapter 21
Betsy

It's after midnight, but I still can't make myself fall asleep. Not after today.

It started that I didn't want to go to sleep in case the kids needed anything. After seeing the way Cara spoke to Emerson, I had no faith in them having a nice night. Emerson promised to text me before they all went to bed, and she did. Apparently, she was better after I left. Who knows if that was because it was only the kids around, or if she realized she was being a horrible human. Either way, I'm glad that, at least for tonight, things went off as best as they could.

I decided to pour myself a glass of wine and come sit out on the porch. Phone in hand, I begin scrolling through *ForU*. And when I say begin, I mean start again since this is what I've been doing all night. I tuck the fleece blanket under my legs, blocking any cold coming in. It might be less than a week until Christmas, but it's not so cold that you can't sit outside. Or camp in the backyard after your buddy gets a divorce.

Yup, I can hear Wes, Oliver, Simon, and Shane all the way from the Taylors' property to my front porch. When Oliver told me what they had planned, I wondered why they were choosing to do it there instead of one of their houses. I mean, Wes has a huge house with plenty of rooms, as well as a pool, hot tub, and more land than he needs. Oliver said something about tradition and the Taylors' backyard is where this needed to be.

I didn't ask any more questions. But it does sound like they're having fun judging by the intermittent laughter I hear from the distance.

My cell phone dings, which surprises me at this time of night.

Whitley: You okay?

Betsy: How did you know I was still awake?

Whitley: Because you just sent me a ForU video, and since you started working for Wes you've been going to bed before ten.

Oh yeah. I forgot. In my defense, I've been scrolling through the app for probably two hours now and don't know what I've liked, shared, or commented on. I've also watched a movie in ninety-two different parts.

Betsy: Yes, I'm fine. Just been a long day.

Whitley: Amelia said the divorce was finalized. How's Wes doing?

Betsy: I don't know. I only saw him for a few minutes after he got back. The guys wanted to take him to celebrate, let him get drunk, do whatever he needed to do. And Cara wanted a visit with the kids before she left. I took the kids to see her and Wes is currently drinking in his parents' backyard like a teenager.

The One I Want

I smile. This is what friendship is. No questions asked but will be an accomplice in a crime without hesitation.

I set my phone down, only to realize that I don't hear the guys anymore. Did they pass out? I mean, they were already going when I got back from Nashville at seven. Though I don't hear the guys, I do hear a rustling in the grass. I look over to my left, only to see Wes, beer can in hand, stumbling toward my house.

"Wes?"

I slap my hand over my mouth to hold in the laughter as

Wes nearly jumps out of his skin. Though that effort is wasted as he can't find his footing and falls to the ground.

"Betsy! You scared me!"

I laugh as I take the blanket off my legs and set my wine glass down. "How you feeling, big guy?"

He starts slowly getting up, though it takes more than a few seconds for that to happen. "I'm divorced."

Oh God is he drunk. "Yes, you are."

"So I'm feeling good. Broke. But good."

"I'm sure your pro football contract won't keep you broke for long."

He stumbles over to me, but somehow finds the step and ungracefully sits on it. I join him, bringing the blanket with me.

"Where are the guys?"

He looks back to where he came from then back to me. I don't know if it's because he's not sure or if he needed to check on something. "Passed out. I'm the only one who can hang."

"Yes, you are," I say as a cold shiver hits my body.

"Are you cold? It's cold out here. When did it get cold out here?"

I laugh. "Well, it's December. And I'm not drunk. Or by a fire. Or wearing a sweatsuit."

He nods. "Very true. You're smart, Betsy. Smart *and* beautiful."

I shake my head, reminding myself to not latch on to any words said by a drunk man. Though a sober man's thoughts are a drunken man's words...

We both fall silent. Neither of us move until I see Wes reaching for the blanket. I hold up the corner, allowing him to come under it with me, both of our legs now covered.

"I'm divorced."

His words are so quiet it's barely above a whisper.

"You are."

"She left us," he says.

"She did."

I know I'm not saying much, but what do I say? That I'm sorry? That he's better off without her? He *is* better off without her. So are the kids. But I don't think those opinions are what he needs right now.

"Have you let it out yet?" I ask.

He tilts his head to the side, and I don't think that's because of the booze. "Huh?"

"Have you let it out? Have you screamed? Have you cried? Have you punched the wall? You're allowed to be angry, Wes. You're allowed to be sad. And you're definitely allowed to be mad. But have you done any of those things? Truly. I'm sure there have been pockets where you've let a little out, but is it still inside you? Are all of those feelings about to erupt?"

He looks up at the sky, clearly thinking. "I did a few times. With the guys. When she first left."

"But you haven't tonight?" I ask.

He shakes his head. "No. I didn't want to talk about her."

"That's understandable," I say. "But Wes, you can't keep it in. I know you put on a tough front for the kids. And because you don't want anyone to see you down. But don't hold it in. Let it out. Right here, right now. Get it out."

He looks over to his parents' house, back to the field, then back to me. "I'll wake everyone up."

I shrug. "Who cares? Go ahead. Get it out."

Wes just sits there, not talking or moving. Maybe I'm wrong. Maybe he is good. Maybe he has let it out in private. But then, just when I think he's not going to say anything, he says what I have to know has been sitting on his chest for two months.

"Fuck her!"

I nod. "There it is."

He stands up, throwing the blanket off his lap. "She didn't fucking love me, Betsy. She loved my fucking money. She blamed me for the life we had. Do you know how fucking angry that makes me?"

"I can only imagine."

"Everyone says they saw it. The guys just told me that she was a bitch to them at our wedding, and the years after, but they never said anything. Hell, for years my dad has been trying to tell me she's not who I think she is. She played me for a fucking fool, Betsy. A fucking fool! I'm angry at her. I'm angry at myself. I'm just...fucking...*angry*."

I don't say anything because I can read a room. And I'm going to let him say whatever he needs to.

"I loved her at first sight. I loved her so fucking much. We had a family. She made me a dad. And all that time she was fucking playing me."

I really want to say something about today, but I don't.

"I hate her, Betsy. I didn't before, but I do now. I don't know when she became this person, but I can say for certain that if this is who she was the whole time, I *never* would have married her. You should have seen her face today when she was told she wasn't getting as much money as she thought she was."

"I bet it was as good as when I told her she was a skinny bitch," I mutter.

He looks over at me. "What?"

Shit. I shouldn't have said that. "Never mind. Carry on."

"I just want to scream, you know?" he says, now in a full-on pace back and forth across my yard. "I'm angry for me. I'm heartbroken for the kids. I'm glad she's out of our lives. I just...I want to fucking yell."

"Then fucking yell, Wes," I say as I stand up. "Yell to no one. Yell to everyone. Get it out. Here, I'll yell with you."

He stops and stares. "You will?"

"Sure," I say. "I believe that everyone needs a good yell and a good cry once a month—to cleanse the system."

He looks again to his parents' house. "My mom is going to be so pissed."

"I'll smooth it over," I say. "Plus, she should have known better when she told Oliver that you guys could drink in her backyard."

"Okay," he says.

"On the count of three."

"One," we say together. "Two....Three!"

"AHHHHHHHHHHHHHHHHHHHHHHHHHHHHH-HHHHHHHHHH!"

We yell together as loud as we can. I hear every ounce of pain and anger being let out of his system. Hell, I'm right there with him. I spent twenty minutes with the woman and I need to yell it out.

We both stop, gasping for breath, when I hear a door open behind me.

"What on Earth was that?"

I turn to see Wes's mom standing on her front porch, robe wrapped around her.

"We were yelling out our feelings, Mrs. Taylor. Sorry!"

"It's okay, my dear," Peggy says. "You two have a good night!"

And just like that, she shuts the door and goes back inside.

I love that woman.

When I turn back to look at Wes, his gaze nearly knocks me on my ass. I thought the night we almost kissed my body was going to catch on fire from his stare, but that night has nothing on this. I can say for certain a man has never looked at me with this much desire in his eyes. A girl would remember that for as long as she lives.

And I'll tell you this: I will never forget how Wes Taylor is looking at me right now.

"Betsy."

His voice is gravelly as he takes my hand and pulls me to him. We are mere inches apart. He smells of beer, cologne, and bonfire. Everything clenches in me as he wets his lips, looking down at me like I'm everything he has ever wanted.

"I thought you said we shouldn't do this?"

He doesn't budge. He doesn't hesitate. There is not one ounce of indecision coming from him right now.

"I know what I said. I also know I'd be a damn fool if I thought anything could stop me from kissing you right now."

He takes his other hand and grabs the back of my neck, bringing me in for a kiss that I immediately feel from my head to my toes.

I can't help but respond. I open my mouth slightly, which he takes within seconds. His hand lets go of mine, only to wrap around my waist so he can bring me in even closer. There isn't a breath between us. I can feel every inch of him.

Every...single...inch...

His body is hard, and not just his growing cock. His arms are muscular and defined. His scruff feels exactly how I thought it would—rough at first, but leaving you wanting to feel it all over your body. His touch is demanding. Just like his kiss. This is a man who knows what he wants and isn't afraid to take it.

Good, because I want him. All of him.

But not tonight. Not like this.

As that thought hits me, I pull away, breathless from the best kiss of my entire life.

"You okay?"

I nod as I give myself some space. Old Betsy wouldn't even

think twice about taking this man inside, continuing what we were doing, and hopefully going a few steps farther.

But I can't.

"I am, but I think we should slow down."

"Yeah, you're probably right."

I put my arms around his neck again. "That was an amazing kiss. One of what I hope are many. But it's late. You're drunk. And it's been a hell of a day. I just don't want us to have any regrets."

He lets out a long breath. "You're right. I'm sorry for—"

"No. Do not apologize. I'm glad we kissed. That kiss was great. Amazing. Ten out of ten, would recommend. I just think, for tonight, that's where this needs to stop."

He lets out a small smile. "Ten out of ten, huh?"

I laugh, sliding my fingers down his arms and taking his hands in mine. "Come in. Sleep here. No need to freeze your ass off. And, if you don't hog the covers, maybe when we wake up you can kiss me good morning."

He surprises me by sweeping under my legs, picking me up without breaking a sweat.

"I like the sound of that."

Damn me for being good now...

Chapter 22
Wes

THE MORNING SUN HITS MY EYES AS I SLOWLY START TO wake up. I'm clearly not at my house. For one, there would be blackout curtains on every window, preventing the sunshine from attacking me. And two, the pillows wouldn't smell like Betsy.

Betsy...

I roll over to see that she's not next to me. But there is a note on her pillow.

Aspirin on the table. Drink some water. I'll go get the kids. And I promise not to throat-punch your ex-wife. See you tonight. <3 Betsy

I laugh at the thought of Betsy hitting Cara as I slowly roll over and sit up in bed. I'm grateful for the aspirin because my head is pounding. I'm also glad Coach McAvoy told me that I could take a few days this week because of the divorce. Our playoff position is locked, and he wanted to give the guys some rest anyway before we head into the playoffs.

I don't get up for a second, instead letting the events of yesterday roll through my head. Of course, my mind goes immediately to Betsy and the kiss I can still feel on my lips.

Yes, I was drunk, but I knew exactly what I was doing at that moment. And I'd do it again. I want to do it again. I want to kiss her right now. I want to reach over for her, roll her under me and kiss her until we each can't breathe.

And that scares the living hell out of me.

My phone starts vibrating on the nightstand. I grab it to see the guy's only group text already alive and well this morning. Yes, we have one without Amelia. There are some things she doesn't need, or want, to hear.

Oliver: Where the fuck is everyone?

Simon: I went home. It was cold.

Oliver: What the fuck! We were all supposed to camp outside.

Shane: Sorry, man. I tried. I snuck into the Taylors' house around three in the morning. Which is where I thought Wes wandered off to...

Oliver: Wes? If you're not at your parents' house, then where are you?

Simon: And who are you with...

I've never once lied to my friends. I'm really considering it right now. Because I know once I say what I'm about to say, I'm opening a box that I'm never going to be able to close.

Wes: I'm at Betsy's.

For a few seconds, no one types anything. No dot bubbles pop up. Nothing.

Then the flood hits.

Oliver: OMGGGGGGGGGG

Simon: Fuck yeah!

Shane: Do you need me to distract your mom
as you do the walk of shame from her
tenant's house?

Wes: I fucking hate you all.

Shane: No you don't.

Simon: Funny you think that, though.

Oliver: That's it. Mona's Diner in an hour. Not
optional.

❧

I WALK into Mona's Diner, the go-to spot for a greasy spoon breakfast or a patty melt for lunch in Rolling Hills, only to find my three best friends already waiting for me.

"And here I thought being five minutes early would be enough," I say.

"Sorry, my friend. Not today," Oliver says as he flags down the waitress. I order coffee and water, and we all order enough pancakes and bacon to feed a football team.

"So, Betsy huh?" Simon says. "Worried I was going to make my move?"

I shoot a look at him. "I will fucking kill you."

This only makes him smile. "There it is, my friends. The reaction I've been trying to get out of him for a month now. Glad to see I still have my touch."

"You're an asshole."

He holds up his cup of coffee to me. "You know it."

I feel my phone vibrate in my pocket, which I quickly take out.

Betsy: Kids secured. We're going to McDonald's. If anyone needs a Happy Meal right now, it's these three.

I smile at her gesture, but know that I'm going to have to find out, either from Betsy or Emerson, how the visit with Cara went. Because that sounds...less than great.

Wes: Sounds good. See you at home later?

Betsy: You know it. <3

I feel myself smiling as I put my phone away. I don't know why those little hearts get me, but they do. When I look back up, all three are staring at me, each wearing their own shit-eating grin.

I sigh. "Fine, what do you want to know?"

"Everything," Oliver says. "Every detail. Otherwise I'm never going to forgive you for leaving me outside by myself where I could have been eaten by a bear."

Shane gives him a look. "You were sleeping in the bed of your truck. You were fine."

"Ignore these two," Simon says. "Go on."

I take a sip of coffee as I try to figure out where to start. Because I haven't processed anything about last night. All I know is that the second I get her alone, I'm going to kiss her again.

"You guys were passing out and I got bored and stumbled up to her house," I say. "She was outside on her porch, so we started talking."

"Talking with your dick, you mean," Simon says.

"No, you idiot. Actually talking. I know you guys let me

vent last night, but I really didn't get everything out. For some reason, with Betsy, I did. The beer helped. I let it all out. The anger. The sadness. The confusion. The relief. Everything."

I might have been drunk, but I remember every minute of last night with her. Even if we hadn't kissed, last night would have been one of the most memorable nights of my life.

"So what else?" Oliver asks. "It can't end there."

"Then—" I start laughing, trying to imagine how ridiculous we had to have looked. "We yelled."

"Yelled?" Shane asks.

"Yup. Yelled. Screamed. I just got it all out of my system."

"Wait! That was you?" Oliver says. "I thought it was a coyote."

"Nope. All me. And her."

The waitress comes over and sets down our food, but no one touches it. No one even reaches for the syrup. All eyes are glued to me. Even Shane, who usually couldn't care less about something like this.

"Then I kissed her."

It's a good thing no one had a fork picked up. They probably would have dropped them.

"You kissed her?"

I nod at Oliver. "I kissed her."

"Back up," Shane says. "Wasn't it just a few weeks ago where you two almost kissed and you said it wasn't a good idea?"

Simon slaps me on the arm. "You two almost kissed before this and didn't tell me? What the fuck, man?"

"You were out of town. And in my defense, I only told Oliver."

Oliver's eyes go wide. "And I told Shane because I needed to tell someone and I knew he wouldn't tell anyone else."

"Next time, put it in the group text," Simon says, reaching for the syrup. "Where important things should go."

"Noted," I say. "But yes, we kissed. Then we went inside and we fell asleep. Fast forward to this morning and you are now all caught up."

"Not all caught up," Simon says, passing me the syrup. "The question now is, what are you going to do?"

"And the words 'take it back because it was a mistake' better not leave your fucking mouth, or I will beat your ass."

I look at Shane, shocked he's so invested in this. "Noted."

He nods. "Good."

"I don't know what I'm going to do," I say. "I didn't see her this morning. She left to go pick up the kids in Nashville before I woke up. I'm going to see her later when I get home. I guess I'll talk to her and see what she thinks."

"But what do you think?" Oliver asks. "What do you want to happen? Remember, as of yesterday, you are a single man."

I take a second to think about my answer, because while some things have changed, some have stayed the same.

"Yes, I am," I begin. "But there are some things that haven't changed. She's still my nanny. I give her a paycheck. My kids love her. If we tried this, and it didn't go well and she left, my kids would be devastated. They might take that harder than the divorce."

"And?"

I look over to Shane. "And what?"

"And you're scared."

"I'm what?"

"Scared," he says. "Listen, most guys take time after a divorce. Especially one that uprooted your life as much as it did. If you didn't date for two years, I don't think anyone would bat an eye. But here you are, fresh out of one relationship and thinking about jumping into another one. Which is scary.

You're allowed to be scared. The question is if she's worth jumping into something this soon. Is she the real deal, where the timing just happens to be shit? Or do you think it's just a matter of convenience?"

Shane doesn't say a lot, but when he does, the man is spot...fucking...on.

I am scared. I hate to admit it, but I am. I was just left by the woman I thought I'd spend my entire life with. Thinking about another relationship is scary. The fear of being left again. The fear of not knowing what I'm doing because it's been more than a decade since I've been with another woman. Those things, and a slew of others I can't even think of right now, are fucking terrifying.

What if Shane is right? What if she's here, in front of me, and I'm having feelings for her because I'm going through a hard time and she's being nice to me and my kids? That's a real possibility.

Then I think about the kiss. It set off fireworks inside me. I haven't felt like that from a kiss in my entire life. She felt so good in my arms I never wanted to let her go. When we went to bed, she wrapped her arm and leg around me, using my shoulder as a pillow, like we've slept next to each other a million times.

And that's what it felt like. It didn't feel weird. It didn't feel awkward. It felt like she was home. Where she was supposed to be.

I have thought for weeks that she felt like part of our family. Last night proved that she's meant to be there.

"No," I say.

"No what?"

"No, she's not convenient. No, I don't have feelings for her because she's at the right place at the right time. I would be miserable if I didn't at least try. I would hit Simon in the fucking jaw if he hit on her again. I want her. All of her. I can only hope she feels the same way."

"Hell yeah," Shane says.

"This is beautiful," Oliver says. "I can't wait until you propose."

"Easy there, Romeo," I say. "I'm not you."

I look over to Simon, who hasn't said anything. Usually he would have some smart ass remark about now.

"Nothing?"

He holds up his coffee mug, and we all follow.

"To Wes and Betsy," he says. "At least we all like this one."

Chapter 23
Wes

"Hey! I'm home!"

I don't hear anything, which is odd. Betsy's Jeep is parked in the driveway. I know the kids were picked up hours ago. If I didn't already know from Betsy, I would have from Cara, who texted to tell me thank you for allowing her to see the kids. As well as adding a dig about Betsy.

I continue walking into the house, but still, silence. Which in this house, usually means trouble.

"Hello? Anyone?"

I walk through the kitchen and into the living room. No one there. I check in the playroom, where usually I can at least find Magnolia, but again, nothing.

It isn't until I start walking up the stairs that I start hearing giggles coming from the spare bedroom. I walk toward it, now able to hear conversation.

"Do you think Dad will like it?" Magnolia asks.

"Of course he will," Betsy says. "One, it's awesome. And two, it's from you guys. Which makes it extra special."

"I don't know if Mom liked our presents," Hank said, sounding worried.

"Why would you say that?"

"I don't know. She just didn't seem excited."

"I'm sure she was," Betsy says. "Everyone just shows excitement differently. Now, come on, let's finish wrapping these presents before your dad gets back."

I have to bite my fist to prevent myself from not screaming or hitting a wall. I really want to do both. Since this started, I told myself I'd never deny Cara the chance to see the kids. Even though our custody agreement only has summers and certain holidays, if she called and said she wanted to see them, I'd let her. But after hearing that? Oh, we are going to have a talk. A *long* one.

I take a few deep breaths, doing my best to reel in my anger. I can't let them see me like this. I also don't want them knowing that I overheard everything. I turn to walk away, but before I can get anywhere, the door swings open.

"Daddy!" Magnolia screams, holding up her arms for me to pick her up. I do as she asks, because I will never not hold my daughter when she asks me to. She's six, and soon these moments are going to stop. But I never want them to. When Emerson started doing things for herself, yes, I was sad, but I had Hank behind her. Then soon Magnolia. But now there's no one left. When these moments end, that's it.

So yeah, I'm going to hold my daughter. And I'm not letting go until I have to.

"What's going on in there?" I whisper.

Her baby blue eyes get big as she looks back to the door then snaps her head back to me. "Nothing. Nothing for you to see. Can I have a snack?"

The teenage years will be easy if she continues to be this bad of a liar. "No snack, we're going to have lunch soon."

"Oh, well, then let's go make lunch." She wiggles down from my hold and grabs my hand, pulling me down the hallway. "I think you should make me lunch."

I have to hold in my laugh. "Shouldn't we get your brother and sister?"

"They can do it themselves."

We only get a few more steps when I hear commotion behind me.

"Dad!" Hank yells, running toward me. Emerson follows out of the door with Betsy, who shuts the door behind her.

"What are you guys up to?" I ask as I give Hank a hug.

"Top secret," Betsy says. "No Dads allowed."

"Well, far be it from me to interrupt," I say. "Hey kids, why don't you go downstairs and get out what you want for lunch. Betsy and I will be down in a second."

"Just don't go in the room." Magnolia turns to Betsy and points her finger at her, putting on her most determined face. "Don't let him in there."

Betsy crosses her heart. "I wouldn't dare."

The kids run off, though Emerson does give us an assessing look before she makes her way down the stairs.

"Hey, I don't know how—"

I don't let her finish the sentence. Actually, the next sound out of her mouth is a gasp as I pull her into my bedroom and slam the door shut. That gasp is quickly muffled as I take her lips with mine.

We immediately sink into the kiss. My arms wrap her around her waist, bringing her in as close as I can. God, she feels good. I thought she did last night. But part of me was worried it was all made up in my head. That somehow it was the byproduct of yesterday's events and last night's booze.

But it's not. She feels even better. Her lips are sweeter. Her curves are softer. Her purrs as we move our bodies against each other are the most perfect sound I've ever heard.

If I had any remaining concerns of this being a bad idea, that's gone now. A man can't experience this and choose to not want it again.

I slowly pull away, leaving her searching for breath as she leans against the door.

"Hi."

She smiles at me, which I think knocks me more on my ass than that kiss. "Hey."

"Thanks for getting the kids."

"It's no problem," she says, walking toward my bed and sitting down. "I figured you needed your rest."

I raise an eyebrow. "No problem? Nothing happened with Cara?"

Betsy shakes her head. "Nope. Not a thing. Smooth transition. She was gracious and nice."

Okay, now I know she's lying.

"You're a worse liar than Magnolia, but we'll go back to that later," I say, taking her hand in mine. "I thought we should talk without the kids."

She nods. "You're right. Because we've kissed now." She lowers her voice to a whisper. "Multiple times."

I laugh, but then all of a sudden forget what I was going to say. We're now just staring at each other, and every time I open my mouth, nothing comes out. On the drive back to the house I knew exactly what I wanted to say. But now that I'm in front of her, with the taste of her lip gloss still on my tongue, I can't think of a single word.

"Can I ask you something?"

I let out a breath of relief. "Anything."

"I just need to know—was last night, and what happened two minutes ago—you wanting comfort after everything that's happened? I can understand if you do, and I wouldn't fault you for it. Last night was emotional. The whole day was. I get needing the comfort of another person. And I'm glad I could be there for you. But one minute you're telling me that we shouldn't do this and then you're giving me the best kiss of my life. I just need to know which way is up."

Wow, she just went right for it. And I'm not going to forget that whole *best kiss* thing.

"Is a little bit of everything an option?"

"Depends on the explanation."

She turns to face me as I bring her hand into mine. "Yesterday was a lot. I don't know if I've ever felt that many different feelings all in one day."

"Understandable."

"I wasn't prepared for the roller coaster of it all. I thought I was, but I wasn't. I was off balance all day."

"That all checks out."

I give her hand a squeeze. "Do you want to know the only time I felt balanced?"

She smiles. "Guessing by what I heard last night, sometime after the Shania Twain karaoke?"

This gets a laugh. "No. It was when I kissed you. When I kissed you, and finally felt you in my arms, it was like all of a sudden my world wasn't spinning. For the first time in months, I felt centered. And that wasn't because of a kiss. It's because *we* kissed."

"Wow," she whispers. "Okay then."

I kiss her hand. "Now, I need to ask you a question."

"All right, but don't expect an answer like that. That was good."

"Why thank you." I take a breath, wanting to make sure I get every word right. "I know this is probably the worst time for me to start something new. I have three kids. I pay you to help me raise my three kids. I'm a few months from ending my career and have no clue what comes next. And it's been fifteen years since I've done any of this."

She laughs. "Is there a question in there?"

I shake my head. "I want to try this. With you. If you want to. I can understand if you don't. You probably shouldn't. I was never a friends-with-benefits kind of guy, and I don't think I'm one now. But the idea of never kissing you again is a thought I don't want to entertain."

Betsy doesn't say anything. Instead she crawls toward me and throws her leg over my lap, so she's now straddling me.

"You broke the pinkie promise."

I'm confused for a second, but then it hits me. "I assumed, didn't I?"

She nods. "When are you going to learn not to assume? It just so happens that recently divorced dads with gray eyes and scruff are my type."

"I didn't know that."

"Because you *assumed*." She puts her arms around my neck, her fingers lightly stroking at the nape. "Wes, this is new for me too. No, I haven't been married, or know what it's like to date a single dad. But I do know that we can't go back. I don't want to go back. I don't know what the future holds, and we can figure it out as we go along. As long as we're in it together."

I'm glad she sat on my lap. It makes it much easier to kiss her.

I didn't realize kisses could feel different. Last night, I might have been drunk, but I remember every moment. I remember the anticipation of finally feeling her lips against mine. Earlier, it was more of a reminder that I wasn't making last night up in my head.

But now, this kiss feels free. Unrushed. Unhurried. There's no desperation. There's no questioning of whether it will be the last time. No, this is the first kiss of many more to come. It's why I'm not sad when we break away. There's going to be more where that came from.

"We probably shouldn't tell the kids right away," she says. "Maybe wait until after the holidays?"

I nod. "Agree."

"Oh, and I should probably tell you," she says, biting her lower lip before continuing. "I kind of, sort of, told off your ex-wife."

I smile. "Oh really?"

"Yes. But! In my defense, she was being a bitch. She called me fat and was knocking Emerson's clothes to her face. I was livid. She's lucky I didn't take off my earrings. Anyway, I was just defending us. And I'd do it again. So if you had hopes of peaceful co-parenting, I probably threw that out the window."

I bring her in and kiss her harder than I did before.

"Oh," she says when we break apart. "So that was okay?"

I laugh. "If I was Oliver, I'd propose to you right now."

She leans in, giving me one more small kiss. "And like his prospective brides-to-be, I would have said no. But I appreciate the sentiment."

Chapter 24
Betsy

I feel the light from the morning hitting my face, but I don't want to wake up, or get out from under this warm comforter.

It's Christmas morning, and for the first time in my adult life, I'm not waking up with immediate dread, knowing I have to spend the day with my parents. Nope. Since Thanksgiving, I've gone no contact. I don't know if they realize that. They've texted a few times, but I haven't responded.

Today is all about things I want to do. Later I'm going to Peggy's for Christmas dinner, but this morning I told Wes it needed to be just him and the kids. So, my day is consisting of, in no particular order: drinking coffee, watching the parade on television, eating every single cookie Peggy brought over, and binging as many cheesy Christmas movies as I can find, especially if they feature Rolling Hills' very own Hollie Berry.

I reach for my phone and see a text message from Wes, which immediately puts a smile on my face. It's only been a few days, but I've already come to love seeing his text messages, which he sends first thing every morning.

Wes: Do you sleep naked?

I have to blink a few times to make sure I read that text right. He normally sends "Good morning, beautiful" or something like that. Has he already dipped into the egg nog?

Betsy: Wow, didn't realize we graduated to dirty texting.

Wes: We didn't. Though that could be fun…

Betsy: Oh, it is. Just you wait. And Merry Christmas.

Wes: Merry Christmas, beautiful.

Now that's better.

Wes: No, the reason I asked is because the kids wanted to come over to surprise you, as in full Mission Impossible, break into your house to surprise you. Which I was all for. Then I realized that you might sleep naked, and I'm not ready to have that conversation with Hank yet.

I laugh. They are too sweet.

Betsy: I am fully dressed and will even pretend to be asleep for the surprise.

Wes: Good. Because we're in your driveway.

I laugh and set my phone back down. I hurry and bury myself under the covers, hoping I can pull this off.

I hear their little whispers and footsteps coming down the hall, and it takes all I have not to smile. God I love these kids. Whatever happens with us and Wes, these kids have become more important to me than I ever thought imaginable. And now I'm even more secure in my decision to cut off my family. This is the family I want in my life. For as long as they'll have me.

I hear the door creak open, and I let the smile fall from my face. I try not to move as I feel them approaching.

"What should I say?" Magnolia whispers.

"Probably Merry Christmas."

"Well, duh, Hank. But what else? How do we wake her up?"

"Here, let me do it," Emerson says. "You two be ready."

I deserve another one of Peggy's cookie trays for not reacting to Magnolia's salty response to Hank.

I feel a little nudge on my shoulder. I slowly blink open my eyes and do my best to make a shocked face.

"What in the..."

"Surprise! Merry Christmas!"

I sit up, rubbing my eyes like I'm just waking up for the first time. Magnolia and Hank jump into bed with me as Emerson takes a seat.

"Wow, you guys! What a surprise!"

Wes gives me a wink as he sits at the foot of the bed. It's then I notice that all of them are wearing matching white, red, and green pajamas—Wes included.

Fuck me, that's adorable.

"We wanted to come see you and give you your presents!"

I hug Magnolia, kissing her on the head. "What a great Christmas surprise. Did Santa come and see you guys?"

At the mention of Santa, all three of them start talking a mile a minute. Yup, even Emerson, who in no uncertain terms this week told me she knew the truth about Santa. She also told me she knew it was her job to continue to go along with it for Hank and Magnolia.

I really want to be Emerson when I grow up.

I look over to Wes, who's sitting on my bed staring at me. His smile is the most relaxed I've seen since we met. He looks free. He looks *happy*. He's wearing matching freaking pajamas with his kids.

He's the whole damn package.

"So," he says, handing me a wrapped box. "It's Taylor tradition to spend all day in pajamas. It's the way Santa wanted it. So, Betsy Sullivan, your Christmas morning can't begin until you open this."

I smile as I begin ripping the paper off of the box. I feel Magnolia bouncing on the bed. I think she's more excited than I am. I finally get to the box to open it and see white, red, and green plaid pajamas tied with a bow.

"Did you guys get me pajamas to match you?" The three of them nod so fast they look like bobbleheads.

"Thank you, guys," I say, wiping a tear away. "This is the best present ever."

"Just wait," Hank says as he jumps off the bed. "We have lots more for you. Put on your pajamas and let's go!"

The three kids run out of the room as Wes stays behind. As soon as they are out of earshot, he leans in for a kiss.

"Merry Christmas."

I give him one more, because he deserves that and so much more. "Merry Christmas."

"Are you ready for your first Taylor Christmas?"

"Am I ready for a few presents and some Christmas cookies for breakfast? Absolutely."

He shakes his head. "Oh no, beautiful. You're in for the whole day. I'll get the coffee ready. You'll need it."

~

I DON'T KNOW what I was expecting when I came into my living room, but it definitely wasn't this.

My Christmas tree is lit. Carols are playing in the background. Cookies are on the coffee table, surrounded by steaming mugs of what I'm guessing to be coffee and hot chocolate.

And under the tree are a *pile* of presents.

"What's all this?" I say to no one as Wes comes out of the kitchen.

"Santa came," he whispers as he hands the last mug to Emerson. I come into the room and sit by the fireplace, and Magnolia immediately comes to my side.

"I thought we weren't doing our Christmas until tomorrow?"

"We didn't want you spending Christmas by yourself," Hank says.

"Plus," Emerson says as she hands me a present, "we were up at five this morning. And we don't have to go to Gram's until this afternoon. We had time to kill."

"Very pragmatic," I say, taking the present from her. "Wes? My presents for the kids are in the back room."

"Already here," he says, motioning to the other side of the tree. "Now quit stalling. Open."

I smile as I unwrap the first present, which is from Hank. I want to take my time, but he looks so excited I think if I go any slower the poor kid may blow. I open the box to find an authentic green and white Slytherin scarf.

"I didn't like picking it out," he says with a shake of his head. "But you can't go against the Sorting Hat. Plus, I'd like to think Draco and Harry became friends as adults."

I hold out my arms, which he comes into for a hug. "I think so, too."

For years, Christmas for me was never things I wanted. I

never got the dolls I wanted, or the games. I got "appropriate" clothing or "sensible" items. I had to pretend to ask for my first iPad under the ruse of school. Little did my mom know that night I was creating my first social media account.

But these presents? They are all from the heart, and with each one I have to fight back the tears. Along with my scarf from Hank, he also got me my own glow in the dark ball. So "I could practice when I wasn't at the house," he said. Magnolia picked out a makeup set. She said it was for me, but I'm pretty sure she had some personal motivations behind it. I don't blame her. It's a great set.

"And this must be from Emerson," I say, picking up the heavy gift bag. She looks nervously at me as I open it to find a stack of books. I look at the covers, and my jaw drops.

"Are these what I think they are?"

She nods. "Yeah. They are the special edition covers to the series we read together. They even have bonus scenes so there's new stuff in them."

I wipe away the tear that escaped, because yup, that one broke me. "Well, it seems to be we both had books on the brain this Christmas."

I reach over and grab her present and hand it to her. And yes, I wrapped each one individually and bound them together with a book belt. It's all about the details.

She opens the first one, her jaw dropping when she sees it. She doesn't say a word though. She speeds things up, ripping off the wrapping paper for the second and third books.

"What are they?" Magnolia asks me since Emerson is still speechless.

"These are some of the most timeless books in history, and some of my favorites," I say. "I found all the original covers for them. We have *The Outsiders, The Secret Garden,* and my personal favorite, *Pippi Longstocking.*"

Emerson drops the books and leaps into my arms. I don't think Emerson has ever hugged me this hard before. She didn't even hug me like this after I told off her mother. "I'm glad you like them."

"I love them," she whispers. "Thank you. For everything."

And now I'm full-on crying. I hurry and wipe them away and catch Wes, sitting on my couch. Shit, is he crying too? I can't handle it if he is. I know men say they can't stand to see a woman cry, but a man secure enough to cry in front of people is just hot as hell.

"Hank! Magnolia! Grab your presents!"

I use the time to gather myself, and I think Wes does too. We lock eyes and have an entire silent conversation. At least, I hope he understands what I'm trying to say. I want to thank him, not just for today, but for hiring me. For letting me be a part of this. For taking a chance on us. When I came to Rolling Hills, I was looking for something different. I never thought it would come in the package that is Wes Taylor and family.

"There's one more present," Hank announces. "Daddy? Who's this for?"

He nods over to me. "It's from me to Betsy."

I give him a look. "I thought we weren't exchanging presents?"

"Did we say that? I must have forgotten."

I shoot him a look that clearly says I'm going to get him back for this. I honestly have no clue what it is. We talked about the kids' gifts, because we wanted to make sure we got everything on their lists, but that was it.

I drop the box as soon as I see what's inside of it. My hand goes over my mouth, and the tears I thought I got rid of moments earlier are now back with a vengeance.

Because Wes Taylor got me a Bratz doll.

"How?"

He shrugs. "You asked Santa for it. I happen to have a line with the big guy. We made things happen."

I stare at the box for I don't know how long. I can't believe he did this. I can't believe he remembered.

"Do you like your presents?" Magnolia asks.

I put down the box and hug her so tight I don't think she can breathe. "Oh, sweetie. This is the best Christmas ever."

Before I know it, all the kids are gathered around me in a group hug. I look up to Wes, who has his phone out, making sure to get a photo of this moment.

"Thank you," I whisper.

He puts the phone down and comes down on the floor with the rest of us. He wraps us all in a hug that starts off sweet, but quickly escalates to some sort of tickle war.

I sit back and watch the four of them. This. This is what family is about. If I had any guilt about not going to Birmingham today, it is gone like a puff of smoke.

Because I wouldn't trade this day for all the presents in the world.

Chapter 25
Wes

GROWING UP, MY BROTHERS AND I WERE ALWAYS ALLOWED to stay up to watch the ball drop on New Year's Eve. It was our favorite night of the year. We used to get pizza, junk food, soda, and everything else we could think of for an epic night. We'd play cards, board games, and Dick Clark would be on in the background. As we got older, we started inviting friends over until it became a tradition to do New Year's at my parents' house.

And tonight, that tradition picks back up.

I always wanted to do this with my kids. But she-who-will-now-not-be-named always put her foot down. I forget what her reason was. I stopped asking for it after the fifth year she said no.

Well, that was then. This is now. And this New Year's Eve, I'm all about leaving the past exactly where it belongs. All I care about is the future.

"Uno!" Oliver yells, smacking down a red five on the table. "Your move, little man."

Hank looks over his cards, his nose wrinkled as he deeply thinks about how he wants to play this.

"Red six. Uno."

I know I shouldn't do this, but you play to win.

"Uno reverse. Which leaves me also with Uno."

We get a chorus of "oohs" from the table as I lay down my card.

Betsy leans in and whispers to me, "You're really going to Uno Reverse your own kid?"

I let my hand fall under the table, giving her leg a squeeze. "I never said I play nice."

She shakes her head, but the smile on her face tells me she is remembering exactly what I am. We've come such a long way in such a short amount of time. And we're just getting started.

"Oh man! Dad! Why'd you have to do that?" Hank says, slowly looking over his single card, his head shaking like he doesn't know what to do. That's until he looks up. "Then again, if you wouldn't have done that, I couldn't do...this!"

With all of the flare and dramatics he can muster, Hank lays down a Red Draw Four. "Pick up four, Uncle Ollie. And I believe I have just won."

The room erupts in laughter as Oliver is left wondering what just happened. That only makes Hank laugh harder.

This. This is what I wanted tonight. Good times. Good company. Nothing but good to lead us into the New Year.

"I'm going to go get a refill," Betsy says as all the kids scatter from the table now that this round is over. "Anyone want anything?"

"I'll come with you." That comes from my brother Luke's surprise guest tonight, Olivia. "That taco dip is addicting."

The two women head back toward the kitchen as Oliver, my dad, me, and Luke stay at the table.

"Well, this is nice," Oliver says, breaking the awkward

silence. "Thanks, Mr. Taylor. Always great to be back at your house."

"Cut the crap, Oliver," he says. "I need to talk to my sons."

"Okay then," Oliver says as he stands up. "I'll just be—"

My dad signals for him to sit back down. "No. Stay. I need you to make sure that this one over here"—he points to me—"isn't trying to blow smoke up my ass."

Oliver slowly sits back down as Luke and I look at each other, wondering what we did. If he's finally going to yell at us for breaking the patio window, then he's about fifteen years too late.

"I'd like to think that we're close," he says. "Wes, we've always had that kind of relationship. And Luke? I'm passing my construction company to you. Those are special bonds."

We look at each other again, both clearly confused as to what's about to happen.

"So, I'm just wondering why Luke has a girlfriend and we're just learning about her tonight. Oh, and not to mention that we just finished the remodel of her house a few weeks ago."

"I—"

"Shush," Dad says, holding up his finger. "Then there is my oldest. The one fresh off a divorce but is apparently already dating *his nanny*? Am I right on these things?"

Neither one of us say anything. We can't lie. We might be grown men, but we both remember the wrath of Henry Taylor.

"Anyone?"

"Yes, I'm dating Olivia," Luke says. "But I promise you, it didn't start until after the remodel. I know the rule about not dating clients."

Dad looks over to me. "Wes? Anything?"

"I, well, see..."

"Oliver? Is he blowing smoke?"

Oliver's face is pale white. "Yes, sir. He is." He sends me an apologetic look. "Sorry, Wes. You know I'm not good under pressure."

I let out a sigh, rubbing my hand over my face. "Fine. Yes, Betsy and I are trying this out. It's new. Very new. And we didn't tell you because we haven't told the kids yet. We wanted to get through the holidays."

"Well you're doing a shit job," Dad says. "Listen, I don't care who you two date. All I've ever wanted is for my sons to be happy. But you can't hide or spring this stuff on us. Because what you two don't realize is that when you leave, I have to hear about it from your mother. And I love the woman, but when she's the last to find something out, she's damn hard to live with. So please, just remember that for next time."

We nod. "Yes, sir."

"Good," Dad says as he stands. "I need more taco dip. Luke, I like her. She seems good for you. And Wes?"

I look up at him. "Yeah?"

"This is what I've always wanted for you. That's how you look at the woman you're supposed to be with."

Neither of us says anything as Dad walks away.

"Fuck," Luke lets out as he exhales. "I thought we seriously did something."

"I did too," I say. "So Olivia? Were you not going to tell me that you were dating a Fury cheerleader?"

He shrugs. "Like I said, it's new."

"Is this the same woman I called you out for last month when you were helping me move?"

"Possibly," he says. "But enough about me. Betsy? Seriously?"

"Quiet!" I whisper yell. "The kids don't know. I don't want them finding out about it this way."

"Emerson knows," Oliver says.

"Why do you think that?"

"Because the girl has a shitty poker face, and she saw you two sneak a hand hold tonight. It was the best smile I've seen from her in ages."

While that makes me feel good, I don't want her to think we're hiding. Tomorrow. We have to tell them tomorrow.

"Daddy!" Magnolia comes running into the room. "It's about to be midnight!"

We stand up and make our way to the living room. My three kids are in front of the television, noise makers in hand. My mom, Olivia, and Betsy come out of the kitchen, each holding flutes of champagne that they pass around to us. Luke takes his from Olivia and brings her into his side, giving her a kiss on the temple. Betsy hands one flute to Oliver, then the other to me, as she stands between us.

"My dad knows," I whisper to her. "I just got an earful."

"I think your mom does too. I kept getting veiled comments," Betsy says. "The only thing that saved me was Olivia. We need to take her and Luke out sometime. I owe her at least dinner."

"Noted," I say.

We're standing in the back of the room, which is what I planned. If I can't kiss Betsy the way I want to at midnight, I need to at least have a moment with her. I reach down for her hand, which she immediately grabs on to and laces our fingers as the countdown begins.

"Ten! Nine! Eight!"

This year is about to be over. The worst year of my life is officially in the past...

"Seven! Six! Five!"

On to new beginnings. Back in the town that I love. With the people I love.

"Four! Three!"

And to new beginnings. The planned ones, as well as the unplanned ones...

"Two! One! Happy New Year!"

The kids start jumping up and down as the adults turn to their loved ones for the traditional kiss. I turn to Betsy, wanting nothing more than to kiss her until neither of us can breathe.

"Happy New Year." she says.

"Happy New Year, beautiful."

We lean down and give each other a quick kiss. What it lacks in longevity it more than makes up for in sensation. It's not nearly as deep or as intense as the others we've shared. But somehow this means more. Maybe it's the night. Maybe it's doing it in front of people. I don't know. But I do know this: Betsy Sullivan is a part of my future. That is a damn fact.

"Happy New Year, Dad! Happy New Year, Betsy!"

We both reach down and hug each of the kids and give them kisses on the cheek. The girls even attack Oliver, who is here by himself. If anyone shouldn't be alone tonight, it's him. When he finds a woman who loves him the way he can love, it's gonna be game over.

"Hey," Betsy whispers. "Follow me."

She tilts her head toward the hallway and leads me into one of the spare bedrooms.

"What are you doing?"

She gently shuts the door, but as soon as it's closed, she takes a handful of my shirt and pulls me in, crashing our lips together.

My body immediately responds. I don't know if it's because of the sly glances, or the soft touches all night, or the tease of the kiss just minutes ago, but I want her. All of her.

I pick her up under her ass and she immediately wraps her legs round me. I take a few steps over and sit her on the dresser.

The kiss deepens, our tongues finding each other's in a

perfect frantic harmony. Her hands are in my hair, which is driving me crazy. It's taking every ounce of control to not rip her clothes off. But I know I can't. Hell, we shouldn't even be doing this. I know I need to stop. But I can't seem to do it.

"Betsy," I moan. Just as the word is out of my mouth, I hear the door open. The sound is an immediate ice bath to us as I jump back from the dresser and Betsy does her best to smooth out her hair, and close her legs.

"Oh, my! I didn't know people were in here," Mom says.

I know guilt is written all over my face. I'm not quite sure what to say. I never got caught making out with a girl in high school. This is foreign territory.

"We were..."

I trail off, but judging by the look on my mom's face, she wasn't going to buy whatever excuse I came up with.

"You were what? I didn't see anything."

She gives us a knowing smile as Betsy pushes herself down from the dresser. "Peggy, I'm so..."

"Don't you say another word my dear. Like I said. I didn't see anything."

I look back and hold out my hand for Betsy's. She smiles as she walks up to me, joining hers with mine, while also wrapping her free hand around my arm.

"Thanks, Mom."

"What are you thanking me for? Again, I didn't see anything. Or know anything. I'm sure you have your reasons why you are or are not saying certain things, or telling me certain life events, and I'm just going to go along with that."

We laugh. "We're telling the kids tomorrow. It will be all in the open after that."

She nods. "Good. And speaking of the kids, it's late. Way past their normal bedtimes. I actually think as soon as the ball dropped, Magnolia crashed on the couch. Why don't they stay here for the night? No sense in dragging them home. We'll make pancakes in the morning. And you two...well, you can have the rest of the night to yourselves."

We look at each other, our eyes both wide, before we look back to my mother. I knew for years she was the best woman on the planet, but this solidifies her status.

"Thank you, Mom," I say, dropping Betsy's hand to wrap my mom in a hug. "For everything."

"Oh, I've done nothing," she says. "Now, you two go off and enjoy the night. And sleep in. I'm guessing you'll need it."

I ALL BUT flip my SUV as I speed out of my parents' driveway. Yes, my house is only two miles away, but right now, it feels like it's twenty.

"You know, we could have gone to my house," she says as she puts on her seatbelt.

I look over to her and put my hand on her thigh, giving it a squeeze. "I want you all to myself tonight. I'll wait another ten minutes for that."

She smiles as she wraps her arms around mine, leaning her head against my bicep. I look down at her just for a second and notice her red-painted fingernails slowly stroking up and down on my forearm. They aren't digging into me. No, they are leaving the perfect touch, which sends shivers down my spine.

All of a sudden, pictures in my head are flashing a mile a minute. Those nails running through my hair, pulling it slightly as she begs for more. How they'll feel when they dig into my back as I drive into her. What they would look like wrapped around my cock.

And just as suddenly as those thoughts pop into my head, I feel a sweat start to break out on the back of my neck. I have to actively slow down my breathing, because right now I feel like I'm being suffocated. I try and take a few deep breaths as I pull into the driveway.

Have I thought about being with Betsy? I'd be a liar if I didn't. Since that first kiss, that's all I've been able to think about—and a few other times before then. I want her. I want her more than anything. But for some reason, right here, in the span of two miles, it just hit me that I've only been with one woman for more than a decade. And those last few years haven't been anything to brag to your buddies about.

I look over at Betsy. God she's so damn beautiful. Young. Vibrant. Exciting. Just being in her orbit makes me feel alive.

Shit...what the fuck am I doing? Do I even know what I'm doing? I really should have consulted Simon on this one.

"Hey," she says as she laces our fingers together. "You okay?"

I look over to her and somehow, I immediately feel a sense of calm. I don't know how she does it, but it's been happening since the moment we met. She just always knows what I need. Or knows what to say. She can read me like a book. And right now, with her beautiful brown eyes looking at me with such care and concern, she's done it again.

I lean in and give her a soft kiss. I let it linger for a bit, but I don't want it to get too deep. I'm saving that for later.

"I'm fine, beautiful," I say. "Let's go inside."

Chapter 26
Betsy

Shit, he's scared.

I know he'd never say it out loud, and I know he said he was fine, but how can he be? I mean, the first night with anyone is a nerve-racking experience, especially if you care about them. It's one thing if you know it's a quick fuck and flee, but the first time you're with someone you truly care about? It's everything. You build it up so much you think there's no way the real thing could live up to the fantasy. Add on the fact the Wicked Witch of the Exes is the only woman he's been with in a long time, and I can't imagine what's going through his head right now.

I don't want to bring it up. That would only put more pressure on him. I don't even care if we spend the whole night clothed, six feet apart, and talking about the weather. I just want to be with him.

Okay that's a lie. I'd like to kiss him. Because I really like kissing him.

I drop my purse on the counter and kick off my shoes as we walk through the garage into the kitchen, when all I see in front of me is the light shining from the back patio.

"I have an idea," I say.

He shuts the door behind us before he wraps his arms around my stomach, leaning down to nibble my ear. "I bet you do."

I turn around and give him a look. Oh, this is going to be even better. Mr. Assumption is already at it again.

"What's that supposed to mean?"

"I'm just saying that we're here, alone, no kids, and you attacked me earlier with your mouth. Based on those facts, I'd place a very safe bet on what's on your mind."

I shake my head. "There you go, assuming again."

"You're telling me that I'm wrong?"

"Oh, Wes," I say, raising up on my tiptoes to give him a small kiss before I step away, taking his hand as I bring him along. "One of these days you'll learn to stop assuming things about me."

I lead him back to the sliding glass doors that open to the patio. Waiting for us is a pool, which is way too cold to swim in right now. But I'm not looking for that. No, it's the hot tub next to it that's calling my name.

"Really?"

"Yes really," I say, sliding the door and stepping out. "I've had my eye on this thing since day one. What better way to break it in than right now?"

I let go of his hand, taking off my shirt as I walk toward the hot tub and tossing it aside.

"Betsy..."

I turn around to look at him, and he's frozen in place. I don't know if he's blinked in the last ten seconds. I think he needs rebooted.

"You okay back there?"

If he picks up on my playful tone, he doesn't show it. No, there's nothing playful right now about the way he's looking at me. Knowing I have his full attention, I make a show out of shimmying off my jeans, stepping out of them delicately so I'm left standing in a satin and lace set I was hoping would get this kind of reaction.

Some girls might feel unnerved by the way he's staring. Not me. I love this. That there could be a hurricane coming through, and I don't think he'd notice? Now that's fucking powerful.

And, when the time comes, I'll show him how appreciative I am.

I start to say something, but just at that moment, he starts slowly walking toward me, his eyes never leaving mine. It's cold tonight, probably somewhere in the thirties, but my body is heating up with every step he takes. He walks past me, taking off the cover of the hot tub and pushing it to the concrete. He hits a few buttons, bringing it to life with bubbles and soft rainbow lights from inside the tub. It puts me into a trance for just a second, which is how I miss Wes turning back to me and scooping me into his arms.

"You're shivering, beautiful. Get in. I'm going to need you to be nice and relaxed for later."

"Is that so?"

"It is. Oh, and Betsy?"

"Yeah?"

"Don't forget to use those sweet Southern manners and ask nicely for what you want, beautiful."

I don't say another word as he lowers me into the water. I can't. I've never seen this side of Wes before. It's intense. Passionate. Like he could consume all of you with just a look.

This is Wes Taylor, the man. I've only known Wes Taylor, the father. Wes Taylor, the best friend. Or Wes Taylor, football legend.

And just like that, the roles are reversed as I'm staring

slack-jawed at the sight in front of me. If my body was hot before, it's now on fire. And it has nothing to do with the water. No, this has everything to do with Wes Taylor slowly unbuttoning his white dress shirt, torturing me on purpose as he methodically works through each button. Then the bastard doesn't take it off. No, he leaves it open as he works his belt off, ripping it from the loops before unbuttoning his jeans and pushing them down. He steps out of them and makes his way over to the hot tub in nothing but his boxer briefs and an unbuttoned white shirt.

Fuck me.

Literally. Fuck... me...

Wes Taylor in just a pair of boxer briefs is enough to make me come on sight.

"Come here."

I glide back to the edge of the hot tub where Wes is standing. I find one of the bench seats and sit on my knees, making it all that much easier for him to kiss me. Because if this man doesn't kiss me in two seconds I can't be held accountable for my actions.

"Kiss me."

He leans in close, but just far enough away I can't reach his lips. "Is that how we ask nicely?"

I never took Wes Taylor for a tease. It appears I've met my match. "Do you really want me to ask nicely?"

He leans in just a touch closer. "Say please."

Every feminist cell in my body wants to keep toying with him. I love this cat and mouse. And we do it so well.

But right now if a please is going to get me what I want, I will say it literally forty-two times and throw in a pretty-please-with-a-cherry-on-top.

"Please."

My breathy word is barely out before his lips are on mine.

His hands are holding my face as I grip onto his shirt. It's the only thing holding me steady right now.

God, this man can kiss. No matter whether it's a quick peck, or the kind of passion and want he's pouring into a kiss like this, you feel it in every part of your body. My toes have curled before, but not in a kiss. A kiss has never made me lose my mind and forget my name. But that's what happens when Wes Taylor kisses you. It leaves you breathless and wanting more.

So much more.

I allow my hands to travel up his chiseled chest, appreciating every rippling muscle as I slowly make my way up to his shoulders. I let my hands go inside his shirt, pushing it off him. My nails slowly brush his arms, landing on his defined biceps.

"Betsy," he groans, his mouth now paying special attention to the curve of my neck as he kisses his way across to my shoulder. "I'm going to need you to stop doing that."

"Is that how we ask nicely?"

I hear a growl into my skin, which I wasn't expecting to feel in my pinky toe. "Oh beautiful, you don't know what you just did."

He gives me a bite on my shoulder, just enough to distract me for the second he needs to move his hands under my arms, guiding me to stand up. I don't know how this happens, probably because I'm still feeling his kiss, but somehow I end up in Wes's arms as he carries me away from the hot tub.

"Where are we going? Don't you need to turn it off?"

His steps are long and determined, making it back into the house in seconds. "It can wait. I have more important things I need to do right now."

Water drips from me as we head through the first floor and toward the stairs. He doesn't turn on or off any lights as he makes his way to his bedroom. I've only been in here a handful of times, and all of them being when we snuck away for a kiss. One of these times I'm actually going to look and see what color his bedspread is.

Right now, I couldn't care less.

He sets me down, my legs a bit wobbly from the hot tub and his kiss. I link my hands behind his neck, hoping it helps me keep my balance.

"Hey," I say, suddenly feeling like the mood has shifted from just a few minutes ago.

He holds me at the small of my back, bringing me flush against him. "Hey, beautiful."

He leans down to kiss me, instantly warming me up after leaving the hot tub. This one isn't as intense or deep as the one outside, but it's hitting me just the same. Toe curling. Name forgetting. All consuming.

He slowly starts kissing away from my mouth, leaving small kisses as he goes across my cheek, down my neck, and across my shoulder before going lower. His hand slowly begins to pull down my bra strap, his lips never leaving my skin. His other hand does the same, letting down the strap ever so slowly before reaching around to unhook the clasp.

"You taste so good..."

The gravel in his voice is enough to make me come undone on the spot, and that's before his mouth takes one of my breasts, kissing and sucking it like he's been waiting his whole life for this moment. His other hand is gripping the other, kneading it as his tongue does wicked, wicked things to my nipple.

My legs feel like they are going to give out if he continues this. And I don't want him to stop. I never want him to stop.

"Wes...."

He guides me back to his bed and lays me down. I want him to follow, but he doesn't. Instead, he hooks his fingers into my panties, gently bringing them down my legs, while his eyes never leave mine.

"You have way too many clothes on," I say.

He looks down then back up at me. "How many times do I have to ask you to say please?"

I sit up on my elbows, biting my lower lip, hoping it looks as sexy as I think it does. "Pretty please, Wes. Get naked. And put your mouth back on me."

He does as asked, sliding his briefs down his thick legs, leaving him very naked, and very hard, before me. I unintentionally lick my lips, because *holy fuck*...he is impressive *everywhere*.

"Cat got your tongue?" He makes his way back over to me and spreads my legs apart. "Now, where was I?"

I fall back flat on the bed as he leans over and begins to feast on my chest. Does he know this gets me wetter than anything else? That if he keeps doing that thing with his tongue on my nipple that I might orgasm right here, right now?

My hands reach to his back, pulling him closer to me. I let my nails slowly scratch from the bottom to the top. I have a feeling he likes it, considering his mouth just left what it was doing, only to grab onto each breast like his life depends on it. He buries his head between them, groaning into my skin.

"Betsy," he says heavily, almost as if he's in pain.

"I want you, Wes," I say, my body begging for more of his touch.

He slides back so he's now completely covering me. "You have no idea how much I want you. How much I want this."

My hands comb through his hair as I give him a slow, gentle kiss. "I'm yours."

Those words light a fire in his eyes as he leans over to his nightstand and pulls a condom out of the drawer. I don't know if he expected this, or if they were there just in case. Hell, I don't care if his mother bought them for him. But I am so glad they are here.

He quickly rolls it on, his body covering mine in just seconds. He doesn't enter me right away. No, we just stare at each other. My hands run through his hair. His thumb brushes my cheek.

This. This is the moment I'm going to remember. No matter what happens after this, I will never forget how Wes is looking at me.

"Once we do this, there's no going back."

I wrap my legs around him wanting to feel his length against my center. "I couldn't even if I wanted to."

He lifts himself on one forearm, grabbing his cock and slowly pushing into me, each of us needing a second to catch our breaths and adjust to the sensation of finally being connected. Holy shit, does he feel good. I'm stretched in the best way possible, my body allowing me to take every inch of him as he slowly works in and out of me. He's biting the bottom of his lip so hard I think he might draw blood, which, I can't lie, is fucking hot as hell.

"You're amazing," he says, wrapping me in closer as he continues to work in and out of me, the tingles already starting. My hips meet his, loving the slow pace as we just let ourselves feel each other. He buries his face into my neck, flicking his tongue and sucking at the skin as his hips begin to pick up pace.

I let him set the tone, not wanting to push him too far too fast. Don't get me wrong—I love this. Wes inside me, feeling him kiss and suck every piece of skin he can find, I have never felt more worshiped in my life. And while this is a big moment for both of us, this is bigger for him, and only he knows what he needs. So if slow is what he wants, then slow he'll get.

Or if he suddenly wants to flip me over, spank me, and call me a good girl, I wouldn't say no to that either.

Just as I'm settling into his rhythm, he reaches under my ass, bringing me up slightly. I think for a second he's just trying to hit a new angle, but he pulls out and surprises me, flipping me over onto my stomach.

Well, then. Good girl it is.

I grasp onto the pillows for dear life as Wes's hands grip my hips and he slams back into me and I cry out. His thrusts speed up as he brings my body back to meet him at a furious pace. I lift my ass higher, wanting more from him, the pace and the spot he's hitting are just too perfect.

"Wes, I'm close," I breathe out as I start to feel the orgasm coming in fast and strong.

"Give it to me. Give me all of it."

As if I could deny him anything right now. I collapse with a loud moan as Wes drives into me one final time before I come apart in the most glorious way.

"Betsy!"

He cries out my name as he slams into me one final, glorious time, shuddering as he comes.

Wes collapses on top of me, but I don't mind the weight. It's actually perfect.

Our breathing is heavy. Our bodies are sweaty.

Simply? It's perfection.

Happy New Year, indeed.

Chapter 27
Wes

I slowly open my eyes and check the clock. Ten in the morning. Shit, I don't remember the last time I slept past seven. Then I feel Betsy roll over, her arm and leg immediately flinging over me as she makes herself comfortable on my chest. I wrap her in my arms, not wanting to let her go.

I never want to let her go.

Last night was...I don't know if I can even think of words right now. It was a spectrum of emotions I didn't even know existed. But like always, Betsy knew exactly what I needed.

I just hope I was enough for her.

"Turn off your brain," she groans, gripping me tighter. "You're thinking so loud it's waking me up."

I brush the hair off her forehead and lean down to kiss her. "It's ten."

"Still early. Need sleep."

I laugh as she grips me tighter. "What about breakfast?"

"Overrated," she says, her eyes still closed.

I take her hand that's on my chest and bring it to my lips,

giving a soft kiss to each knuckle. "It's actually my favorite meal of the day."

"Let's order it then," she says. "Take it out of my paycheck."

"Actually," I say, putting her hand to the side. "I'm a fan of breakfast in bed."

Before she can say anything else, I grab her leg and lift it off me, which lets me easily roll her to her back. Her eyes go wide as they lock with mine before I start kissing my way down her perfect body. It's so soft and smooth. Curves in places that curves should be. I had a feeling the moment I met her in that tight, red devil costume that her body was made for sin. I was right. And I will worship it every chance I get.

I snake my arms under her legs, bringing my hands up to rest on her stomach as I kiss across her pelvic bone, down her leg, before going back up to the place I want the most. I can't help but lick my lips before my tongue gently slides from bottom to top, earning me a quiet whimper from Betsy. With just one taste I am instantly hard, but I ignore that. After what she did for me last night? This morning is all about her.

After a few slow drags of my tongue, I speed up, letting myself fully taste her. I want to hear her scream out my name. I want her to wake the neighbors. Her hands are immediately pulling at my hair, and just knowing it's those damn red nails doing it only makes me double down in my efforts.

I keep one hand on her stomach but free up the other, sliding two fingers inside her as I kiss and suck on her pussy. My tongue is going rapid fire, flicking her clit as I work my fingers in and out of her. I have to tighten my hold as her hips are trying to move in every way they can.

"Oh God, Wes...fucking yes. Yes!"

I allow myself to watch her as she chases her orgasm and I almost bust right then and there as I watch her playing with her tits. She's rolling her nipple on one side and massaging the other. Holy shit, I could watch her do this all day. I have to physically stop myself from reaching down and stroking myself, the image of this goddess in front of me too much to handle.

I curve my finger, and like I flicked a switch, she stills before she comes undone on my hand.

"Ah!"

Yes. That was the scream I wanted. She grabs onto my arm, her back arching as the orgasm flows through her.

That was the hottest thing I've ever seen.

And I think she needs another.

I reach over to the night stand, thankful for the box of condoms. I grab one, quickly sheathing myself before rolling back to Betsy, who is still coming down from her orgasm.

"Are you awake yet?"

She turns her head to me, and I have to swallow the lump in my throat from the sight of her. Her hair's a mess. Her face is fully flushed red. Her lips are swollen from last night, and her cheeks are slightly scratched from my beard. I call her beautiful because she is, inside and out, but now? I've never seen her look more beautiful in my entire life.

"I don't know if I'm alive."

I can't resist and lean down and give her tit one quick kiss and suck, letting the nipple pop out of my mouth. "I think you are. And I think I know exactly what you need to start your day."

"What's that?"

I don't answer her with words. Instead, I roll her on to me. "Now, what was it you were doing before? I feel like I didn't get to see the entire show."

It doesn't hit her for a second, but when it does, I instantly see the fire burn in her eyes. "Well, we can't have you missing that."

She sits up before lowering herself onto me. I have to hold

myself back as I watch. Her hands grip my thighs as she arches back, pushing her breasts toward me, allowing herself to stretch to my size. She takes one hand and starts to roll her nipple like she was before. It's fucking hot. The way she moves her hips, the way she lets her head hang back as she's embracing every sensation. It makes me want to make every one of her fantasies come true.

She does this for a second before picking up her speed, her hands coming to rest on my chest. Her tits are slowly swaying in front of me, begging me to take one in my mouth. And I do. I suck on it like it's the only thing keeping me alive. I begin to massage the other, which makes Betsy ride me harder. With every squeeze, her pussy tightens around me. So I keep going. And going. I switch my mouth and hand, loving the weight of each as I continue to drive her wild—which is driving *me* wild.

Fuck, this woman is going to be the death of me.

I never considered myself a dirty guy, or kinky, for that matter. I've heard some of the things Simon has done in his life, and by that standard, I am definitely vanilla. But one night with Betsy has unlocked a safe of desires I didn't even know I was guarding. I want her in every room. On every surface. I want her anywhere I can have her and in every way.

"Wes," she pants out, her hands now exactly where I wanted them. She's rubbing herself like she can't help it. It's fucking sexy. "I need you."

I grip her hips and flip her over. "Ask and you shall receive."

I fling her legs on my shoulders and hammer into her, knowing that she needs this fast and hard. So do I.

"Fuck! Wes!"

Hearing my name yelled like that sends me into the stratosphere. I think I black out as I fall to the bed. I roll over, but only because I don't know if I can breathe if I stay face down.

I shut my eyes for a second, only to be jostled awake by a banging on the front door. I turn to look at the time and it says two o'clock.

Shit.

"Betsy," I whisper, shaking her awake.

She rubs her nose in my chest, slowly blinking open. "Hmm?"

I kiss her forehead. "Someone's at the door."

She doesn't react for a second, which isn't good considering I can't get up if she's laying on me. Then it hits her. And when it does, she nearly kicks me as she makes her dismount.

"Oh, shit! It's your mother. It has to be. Oh God. This is bad. She can't catch me violating her son two days in a row!"

I laugh, giving her one more kiss as I sit up. "Considering she volunteered to watch the kids, I'm pretty sure she knew what you were about to do to me."

"Doesn't make it better."

I swing my legs out of bed. "You get dressed. I'll go answer it and keep the kids out."

Her eyes grow wide. "The kids! They kids can't see me! What do we tell them when they ask why I'm here?"

I smile leaning back in for another kiss. "We tell them exactly why. Because today's the day. We're coming clean."

Chapter 28
Betsy

I have done the walk of shame plenty of times in my life. Hell, one year I did it after Halloween, leaving me to walk home as the slutty cop. It wasn't my finest moment.

Then again, I've never done *the walk* in front of children and my boyfriend's mother.

Oh my God. Wes Taylor is my boyfriend! When did that happen?

I lean down into the sink and splash one more handful of cold water onto my face. I dry it, doing my best not to get the shirt I borrowed from Wes wet. I couldn't wear my clothes from the night before because they are still on the patio. I wasn't about to put back on my panties. So here I am, in a Fury t-shirt, Fury sweatpants, my hair thrown up on the top of my head with a hair tie I think is Emerson's, about to go downstairs and face his mother and children with sex written all over me.

Maybe the slutty cop wasn't so bad.

"You got this," I say. "Now don't fuck it up."

With one more breath I exit the bathroom and slowly walk out of Wes's room. As I approach the stairs, I hear the voices getting louder. I take a few steps down and see the three of them are sitting on the couch, all talking a mile a minute. Well, everyone except for Peggy. She's sitting opposite of Wes in one of the chairs, smiling as she watches her son and grandkids.

Just as I get to the bottom of the staircase, Magnolia sees me and jumps off the couch to give me a hug.

"Betsy's here!"

I lean down and open my arms to her. "Happy New Year, Miss Mags!"

We walk over to the couch as she begins talking nonstop about her morning. I am usually very good about listening to her, but right now all I can do is look at Peggy. She knows, right? She has to. She knew last night. Like Wes said, she did volunteer to keep the kids after walking in on us after I attacked him. Does she hate me now? Does she think I'm not the best person to watch the kids? Oh God, what if she likes Cara more than me?

"Betsy," Peggy says when Magnolia takes a breath. "Can you help me with something in the kitchen before I head back?"

I look to Wes, who is wearing quite the smirk. It's giving me "haha, you're in trouble and I'm not" vibes.

He's going to pay for that at some point.

"Sure."

I slowly follow her into the kitchen, bracing myself for what's about to come. Then she does the last thing I expect. She hugs me. Hard. Like I can't breathe or move my arms.

"Happy New Year?"

Peggy gives me another squeeze before pulling away. It's only then I notice that there's a tear rolling down her cheek.

"Peggy! Why are you crying?"

I grab the box of tissues on the kitchen island, which she waves away. "I'm sorry, dear. I'm just so happy it's leaking out."

"Happy? You're not mad at me? Or disappointed? It's okay if you are. That's kind of my thing when it comes to parents."

She shakes her head. "Do you know how long it's been since I've seen my son smile?"

All I can think of are sarcastic quips that probably aren't the right time and place right now. So I just shake my head no. Seems like a safe move.

"The answer is: I don't remember. Maybe when Magnolia was born? But that was a different kind of smile. No, sweetie, when I walked into this house today, I knew my son was truly happy for the first time in a long time. And that's because of you, and I'll never be able to thank you for that."

Well, shit, now I'm going to cry.

We come together in another hug, each sobbing, and then laughing because we're both crying.

"I thought you were going to give me an earful."

"Why would I do that, dear?"

I step away, and signal at my outfit. "Because I snuck away with your son last night to kiss him and you caught us and then kept the kids so we could do what you know we did, but I don't want to say it out loud because this is new and I really like Wes and I really appreciate and like you and I don't want to ruin this because you think I'm a whorish Jezebel."

Peggy blinks a few times, clearly confused. "Whorish Jezebel?"

I shrug. "It felt right."

She laughs. "Oh, dear. I'd never think that of you. I don't even think of Cara like that."

"You don't?"

"Oh no," she says, guiding me away from the kitchen back to the living room. "I think she's a fucking cunt."

I dead stop as those words come out of sweet Peggy Taylor's mouth. My jaw is dropped, my eyes are bugging out, and I'm pretty sure I don't know words at this point.

"What?" she asks, picking up my jaw for me. Literally. "We call a spade a spade in this family."

I continue walking out of the kitchen, still stunned from Peggy's choice of words, when Magnolia comes walking up to me.

"Betsy? Why are you wearing one of daddy's clothes?"

What is it with Taylor family members throwing me for loops today?

"I think I'll be going now," Peggy says, giving me a kiss on the cheek before she goes to grab her jacket. "Good luck, you two."

She kisses the kids goodbye, leaving me still standing, unsure how to answer this question. Then I happen to catch Emerson's glance. Her smile says it all: She knows. And not only does she know, she's happy about it. The nod of approval is all I need to calm myself and give me the courage for this conversation.

Damn, she really is my life coach.

"Well," I say as I sit on the couch, patting the seat next to me for Magnolia. "I spent the night."

"Why?"

I take a breath. Because I don't know how I'm about to answer this. "So remember when we met and I started off as your friend, and then became your nanny?"

She nods. "And you started doing my hair."

"I did." I look over to Wes for some guidance, who is sitting on the other side of Magnolia. "Well, just like we got to be closer, so did me and your dad."

"And you know," Wes chimes in, "that your mom and I aren't married anymore."

"That's why she lives in California, and we live here," Emerson adds, looking directly at her siblings. I love how without talking down to them, she explains something that they might not put together. This kid is so damn smart.

"That's right, Emerson." Wes takes a breath and reaches across the couch, signaling for my hand. I give him a clear "are you sure?" look, which he just answers with a nod. When I do, Hank's eyes double in size.

"Guys, you know how Uncle Oliver has girlfriends? How he goes on dates with them and they hold hands and maybe sometimes kiss?"

The two youngest nod as Emerson continues to just smile away.

"Well, what would you guys say if Betsy was my girlfriend?"

No one says anything for a second, which puts my panic level at fifteen out of ten.

"Will she still be our nanny? I like our get ready routine," Magnolia says.

I stifle a laugh at my sweet girl's question. "Yes, nothing will change when it comes to you guys. I'll still be here every morning, ready to go for hair, food, and clothing duties."

Wes looks over to Emerson. "What do you think?"

She shrugs, though I can tell she's trying to hide her smile. "I like it. I think you two are good for each other."

"Really?" I ask. "How so?"

Emerson comes over to the couch with us. "You bring out the fun side of him. I mean, he was always fun, but not all the time, because Mom wouldn't let him. And he keeps you focused. When we met you, you were a bit of a mess."

"Hey!" I say, playfully hitting her with a pillow. "I was figuring things out."

"Sure..." she says. "But in all seriousness, I'm good with this. I like how everything is going, and if you two make each other happy, then we're happy, too."

I push back the tears as Wes opens his arms for Emerson. Out of all of the kids, he needed to hear that from her more than anything. She knows enough to know that things weren't easy for him during all of this. She knows Cara's true colors. She had to grow up more in these past three months than any eleven-year-old should have to.

"Dad?"

Wes looks down to Hank. "Yeah, buddy?"

"I have a question, if Betsy is now your girlfriend."

"Ask away."

"Are you going to ask Betsy to marry you?"

Wes and I look at each other, an equal look of terror and "way too soon" going through our eyes.

"Well, that maybe could happen," he says. "But that's a long time away, buddy. Why do you ask?"

Hank shrugs. "Because you said it was like Uncle Oliver having girlfriends, and I know he asks them that. But they say no and they leave. I just don't want Betsy to say no, so if you're going to ask her, I want to make sure you're doing it right."

We all bust up laughing. I snort. Wes has actual tears. Magnolia falls off the couch from laughter, but she's just laughing because she doesn't know why everyone else is laughing and she doesn't want to be left out. Emerson is laughing so hard she runs to the bathroom. I've never seen her laugh like that.

I can't believe I was worried about how this would go. From the second I met this family, I immediately felt a connection. Like I had finally found where I was supposed to be.

Who knew I'd also find someone who I'd want to be with.

"So," I say as the laughter dies down. "What do we want to do today?"

"We?"

"Yes Miss Mags. You're stuck with me now on all days of the week. And, it's a holiday. Your dad doesn't have practice today. So, I think we should do something fun."

"Like what?" Emerson says as she comes back into the room.

"How about a family date?"

The kids look at each other, clearly confused.

"What's that?" Hank asks.

I look over to Wes, who gives me the nod to go ahead. "It's a night where all of us go out. We go to dinner. Maybe a movie. Anything we want. And best of all? You guys get to pick. But it has to be something all three of you agree on."

Hank's eyes go wide. "Anything?"

"Anything," I say. "Just keep it legal. No need to get Uncle Shane involved."

The three gather in a little huddle, and I wish I had my phone. This is freaking adorable. Wes and I each hold in a laugh as their whispers become not exactly whispers. Emerson keeps looking up at us, like she's making sure we're not bluffing.

"Ready, break!"

The three of them clap their hands as they leave the huddle. Tell me your dad is a football player without telling me your dad is a football player...

"What did you guys decide?"

Hank and Magnolia look to Emerson and give her a nod.

"We've decided that we want dinner at The Joint. We want Uncle Porter to make us wings and onion rings, and we will need quarters to play the pinball machine."

Wes nods. "If we go early enough that will be just fine. I bet we can even get Uncle Porter to give you the quarters. Just have Magnolia turn on *the face*."

Magnolia gives a thumbs up. "Got it Dad."

"Good," Emerson continues. "There's more."

I laugh as Wes pretends to be taken aback. "More?"

"Yes. We want to go bowling."

Chapter 29
Wes

"Uncle Simon! You're not supposed to put it in the gutter!"

Simon snaps his head around to Magnolia, who has a confused look on her face. I don't know if it's because she's wondering why she has a higher score than Simon, or why all of a sudden the eleven adults in attendance are suddenly silent. If any of us would have said that to him, he would tell us to go do things to ourselves that aren't anatomically possible. But in the presence of my kids? The only people in the world who bring out the side of him that isn't an asshole? This ought to be interesting...

"Wait! I'm not?" He dramatically looks to the lane before turning back to Magnolia. "Well, someone told me the wrong directions."

We all hold in our laughs as he continues his antics. "It's okay," she says. "You can use my bumpers next time."

That sends us all into laughter as my kindergartener unintentionally roasts her godfather. Yup, Simon Banks, the man who loves money more than most people, is the godfather to my youngest daughter.

And he takes his responsibility very seriously. It's also why we had to get cell phones for our other kids because Uncle Simon got one for Magnolia when she turned five. Cara was pissed. I laughed.

"Who's next?" Hank asks.

I look at the board. "Amelia. Show 'em how it's done!"

Amelia rubs her hands together as she makes her way to the lane. I take a second to look around, my heart swelling

Yes, this was supposed to be family date night. Then we ran into Amelia, Jake, Whitley, and Amelia's kids, Luke and Mariah, at dinner. Next thing I know Hank's inviting them to come with us. Anyone who thinks it's hard saying no to Magnolia has never seen Hank in full action.

Before I know it, Emerson's asking me if I can call the uncles. She used the logic that it's a family date night and that they were family. Even Luke and Olivia joined us.

And yes, Amelia gave her son the same name as my brother. She insists it wasn't on purpose, and that it was the only name she and her ex-husband could agree on. I'll blame him since he's a piece of shit.

I hear laughter to the right of me as Amelia taunts Simon after she rolls a strike. To the left of me is Mariah, who is helping Magnolia with her ball on the lanes we have set up with a bumper.

I don't know what constitutes a perfect night, but this has to be damn close. My friends. My family. My girl. All in one place. Just having a good time with no worries or drama.

"Can I ask a question?" Betsy asks.

"Of course."

She nods over to our right. "How did all of you become friends? What's the origin story?"

I laugh, my head falling back as I recall how the five of us all wound up together.

"Guys," I say. "Betsy wants to know how we became friends."

Oliver laughs, Simon groans, and like normal, Shane doesn't say anything. Then there's Amelia, who comes over and parks right next to me and Betsy.

"Do you want to tell it or me?" Amelia asks.

"I can do it."

"You can," she says. "But sometimes you like to leave certain parts out."

"I promise I won't," I say.

"I've actually never heard this before," Jakes says, him and Whitley taking a seat next to me and Betsy. "I just remember one day I was Amelia's only brother and the next she had four more."

Oliver pours himself another beer before passing the pitcher. "And there's more to the story before that."

I put my arm around Betsy, settling in for arguably the greatest story ever told. "It begins in kindergarten, when two kids have their desks put next to each other."

"That was me and Shane," Oliver says. "The teacher thought it would be good since we were so different."

"The fucker wouldn't leave me alone until I shared my crayons with him," Shane chimes in. "I did it once to shut him up. Look where that got me."

"You love me and you know it," Oliver says. "I'm sorry, Wes, please continue."

I tip my beer to Oliver. "I was in the other kindergarten class, so I didn't meet them until that next summer when our parents all signed us up for tiny mite football."

"Tiny mite?" Betsy asks.

"Yes. Tiny mite, and we were adorable."

She leans in and kisses me on the cheek. "I'm sure you were."

A napkin hits my head, which I realize was just thrown by Simon. "Hurry up and get on with it."

"Fine," I say, throwing it back at him. "For the next few years, it was the three of us. And we were doing just fine."

"And then!" Simon yells. "I move to town! This is the good part."

Shane gives him a look. "I think you need to rethink your definition of the word 'good.'"

Simon shakes his head. "Nope. I know it. I'm comfortable with it. And it's not just good, it's fucking great."

"Uncle Simon!" Magnolia yells from a lane over. "Swear jar!"

Simon groans but takes out his wallet and holds up a five. "How about you just take the money and go to the concession stand?"

"Okay!" Magnolia runs over, but instead of grabbing the bill, she takes his whole wallet. "Thanks, Uncle Simon."

We all start laughing as Magnolia recruits all the kids for snacks on Uncle Simon's dime.

"Can we get back to the story so I can forget that my goddaughter just robbed me?"

"Fine," I continue. "Now comes fourth grade, and there are three classes. Oliver and I are in one, Shane is in another. One day at recess, we noticed a new kid. No one seemed to know his name. So we went about our business."

"Translation," he says, looking directly at Betsy. "They were threatened by my good looks from day one. It's not too late, you know."

She laughs, but snuggles in closer to me. "Thanks, but I'm pretty confident with my choice."

I look down at her. "*Pretty* confident?"

"Don't get hung up on the words," she says, giving my legs a squeeze. "Keep going."

"Fine, but we will be revisiting that later," I say. "So, a few days later, the three of us notice Amelia crying."

She holds up her beer. "Yes, the first time I cried over a boy was in the fourth grade."

"Randy fucking Dalton," Shane growls.

"Yes, Randy Dalton," I say. "One of those kids who was an asshole when we were young and an asshole when we were older."

"In my defense," Amelia chimes in, "he had a CD burner and made me a mix. I was a goner after that."

"Don't need to tell me, sister," Betsy says. "My third-grade boyfriend had an iPod Shuffle. I was also a goner."

"Anyway," I continue. "We go over to check on Amelia, and she tells us what happened."

"He called me ugly because I had just gotten my braces and broke up with me."

"How rude!" Whitley exclaims. "Did you guys beat him up?"

Amelia looks over to Shane. "This one tried to."

The two lock eyes like they have so many times over the years when we tell this story. This might have been the first time Shane came to Amelia's defense, but it wasn't the last.

"Before we could stop him, Shane was marching over to Randy," I say. "When he gets there, he demands Randy apologize to Amelia. Of course Randy said no, so Shane pushed him. Randy pushed back, but Shane being Shane..."

"I hit the fucker."

"Yes, you did," Oliver says. "The problem was, Wes and I were across the playground still with Amelia. We couldn't get to him in time before Randy's little crew came out of nowhere and jumped Shane."

"So the three of us started running over," I say. "But before we could get there, we realized that Shane wasn't alone."

Simon puffs out his chest. "I was there to save the day."

"I could have taken them," Shane says.

"You've been trying to sell me that bullshit for twenty years. It's not working, my guy."

"Why did you help?" Betsy asks. "It wasn't your fight."

Simon shrugs like it's no big deal. "I was in the same class as Randy and Amelia. The guy was an asshole. Copied her homework. Said mean stuff behind her back. And he broke up with her on the playground right before they were supposed to get married. You don't do that. It's just not the manly thing to do."

We all laugh. "And that is how our group was officially formed."

We each hold up our glasses, toasting to the memory. And not just that memory, but all of the ones since then. The days on the football field. Days playing ball in the field behind my parents' house. As we got older, things didn't change. We went as a group to all of the school dances. We were there the day Shane told us he was going to enlist in the Army. We were there when Amelia found out she was pregnant with Luke right after graduation. They were there for me when each of the kids were born. They threw me my divorce party."

These people have been a part of nearly my entire life. I don't know what it would have been without them, and I don't want to.

"So that's us," Oliver says, pointing to Whitley and Betsy. "Now, what I really want to know is how the two of you found each other."

They look at each other and start giggling. "We met at the Little Miss Camelia pageant when we were ten years old."

"Oh, this is going to be good," Simon says.

"Wait," I say. "I thought you two didn't meet until you were teenagers?"

Whitley shakes her head. "No, that's when we became friends. But we actually met when we were ten."

"I beat her for Ultimate Grand Supreme," Betsy says with a flip of her hair.

"The only time she beat me," Whitley adds in.

"We don't need to bring that up."

"So wait," Oliver says. "Aren't beauty pageants cutthroat? If you beat her, why did you become friends with her?"

"Because," Whitley begins, reaching for Betsy's hand. "Much like your story, ours involves a bully."

"Her name was Cyndi Mae Thornton, and she was a bitch."

"She was," Whitley continues. "We were competing for Miss Teen Alabama. That's a major competition, so everyone's nerves were high. We were rehearsing, and I dropped my baton."

"Wait!" Jake yells. "All of these years we've been together and I'm just now finding out you were a baton twirler?"

"Focus, Jake," Whitley says. "Anyway, I was practicing, and I dropped it more than I usually did. I was flustered, and it didn't help that Cyndi was in the wings making snide remarks. I was just going to ignore her. Every pageant has a Cyndi."

"But, like Simon, here I come to save the day," Betsy says. Simon tips his glass to her as Betsy bows in her seat.

"What did you do?" Oliver asks.

"What no one else had the courage to do," Betsy says.

Shane's eyes go wide, clearly engrossed in this story. "Kick her ass?"

Betsy shakes her head. "And break a nail before pageant day? No. See, we Southern women don't get violent. We get personal. So I did what any other teenager would do in the late

2000s—I went and friended her boyfriend on social media, liked a bunch of his photos, and also replaced her hair gel with Vaseline and hid all of her left shoes. She dropped out the next day."

Everyone stands up, giving Betsy a well-deserved standing ovation. She just laughs as Whitley gives her a side hug.

"What's so funny?" Hank asks as all the kids come back, their arms loaded with sodas, candy, pizza, and nachos.

"Betsy was telling a funny story."

"Was it about how you aren't going to be like Uncle Oliver and ask Betsy to marry you?"

The group gets quiet exactly when Hank says this. Oliver is shocked. Shane and Amelia are trying not to laugh. Simon spits out his drink.

"What?" Hank asks. "I'm just speaking the truth."

Hank heads back to the kids' lane as everyone starts to laugh. That is everyone except Oliver, who is left dumbfounded.

Shane walks over and slaps Oliver on the back. "You heard the little man. This is how bad you've gotten. Now *Hank* is roasting you."

Yup. Tonight is exactly what I needed.

Chapter 30
Betsy

I woke up this morning and thought it was going to be a great day.

Then I opened my eyes.

Wes had to go into Nashville early. The playoffs have started, so that means longer hours at the facility for training and practice. Which is no problem. I've done plenty of mornings by myself. This one shouldn't have been any different.

Until Emerson lost a notebook, so we spent most of the morning looking for that. That meant I didn't have my usual time with Magnolia, so she started crying because she felt rushed and didn't like her hair. I get it. You can't mess with a morning routine.

Unfortunately, I had to load her and the other two into the car with only a few minutes to spare before school started. That meant Pop Tarts and juice boxes during the commute. I should have known that was going to end in disaster, which it did when Hank's leaked and got juice all over his pants. I told him to hang out in the office until I could run home and grab him a new pair of pants. And a new outfit for Magnolia, because she decided to run through a mud puddle on her way inside.

When I got back to the school, new outfits in hand, Hank informed me that he forgot a permission slip for a field trip—which of course was due today. And had to be signed by Wes. For a field trip Wes *organized* to go to the Fury stadium. I asked the secretary if I could sign it, and she said no. When I asked again if she felt like it was redundant for a father to sign a permission slip for his son to go to his place of employment on a field trip he organized, she just gave me a look like I had answered my own question.

So I went home and got it. And signed his name. I'm not even sorry about it.

At this point I was hangry, so I stopped at Mona's for lunch. I tried to call and have Whitley meet me, but she had "important work" to do and couldn't get away. What good is owning your own business if you can't play hooky whenever you want?

Now I'm sitting in the pickup line, which is ten cars deep because I think people camp out here two hours early. And don't get me started on the white SUV that pulls up at the bell and drives straight to the front of the line. Every. Day.

Maybe some retail therapy will work? Yeah. Wes won't be home until late. There's a good mall between here and Nashville that would have something to make me feel better, as well as a toy store for Magnolia and Hank and a bookstore for Emerson. And, of course, we'll stop for dinner because after the day I've had, I'm pretty sure the kitchen would catch on fire.

The line starts moving, and I pull up to where I normally can see the kids. Except they aren't there.

"Oliver!" I yell out the window. "Where are the kids?"

He looks around, seemingly confused. "Honestly, I haven't seen them. How about you pull around and go to the end of the line so they have time to come out?"

I look back to the line, which has to have at least fifty cars in it now. "Are you kidding me? Can't I just stay here? They have to be coming soon."

"Sorry, Betsy," he says as he directs a kid to the car behind me. "Have to keep the line moving."

I say a few choice words under my breath and pull around. This day just keeps getting worse.

It takes me twenty minutes to get back to the front of the line. I know this because I listened to a song that's ten minutes long—twice. There's no one behind me and still, there is no sign of the kids.

Now I'm worried.

"Oliver!" I yell as I jump out of the car. "Where are they? This isn't normal. I'm calling Wes."

He puts his hands over my phone to stop me. "That won't be necessary."

"Won't be necessary? Oliver, the kids aren't here. Where are they?"

He tilts his head to the door. "They're right there."

I look to the exit of the school to see the three of them walking out, and I immediately start crying.

Emerson is rolling my overnight bag. Hank is carrying a bouquet of flowers. And Magnolia has a card tied to a balloon.

"What's all of this?"

"Here," Magnolia says, handing me the card. "You're supposed to read this."

I carefully remove the balloon and tie the string to Magnolia's wrist so it doesn't fly away. Then I rip the letter open, because I don't know what Wes did, but I have a feeling it's going to make me cry even more.

Betsy,
Take your suitcase from Emerson. Don't worry,

Whitley packed it all. Oliver is going to stay with the kids tonight. Here's the address to our hotel for the night in Nashville. It's time I finally take you on a proper date.

See you soon, beautiful.

Wes

P.S. I don't know what the kids actually did this morning, but I know I probably need to apologize for it. Once I told them I needed to cause chaos, their imaginations went wild.

I look up and see each of them with the most mischievous smiles on their faces. I've never wanted to cry and laugh all at the same time before.

"So this morning...?"

"We were good, weren't we?" Hanks says proudly.

"You were." I look over to Emerson. "The notebook?"

"When have you ever known me to lose anything?"

"Very true. And what about you, Miss Mags?"

She shrugs. "Daddy always says I'm extra. He told me to be *extra* extra."

I laugh as I kneel down, holding my arms out, which they all come running into. "Thank you all."

I give them all a kiss on the cheek and stand back up.

"Thank you," I say to Oliver. "Sorry I went a little crazy there."

He shakes his head. "Nothing to apologize for. Shows how much you love these kids. Now, get on. You have a man waiting on you in Nashville, and I have a night of board games to win."

～

"This is stunning," I whisper, looking around at the gorgeous, and romantic, ambiance of the restaurant Wes picked for the evening.

"Not as beautiful as you," he says, reaching across the table for my hands.

I take them, but give him a side eye. "You know you're already getting laid tonight, right?"

He laughs. "I was hoping so, but it never hurts to bank a few points."

The waiter brings over the desserts we ordered. We arrange them in the center, each wanting to try the other's selection.

"Now this is how you do dessert," I say, enjoying every bit of the tiramisu. "Why limit yourself to one?"

"Agree," Wes says, digging into my bananas foster. "I forgot how much I loved dessert."

"How do you forget that you love dessert?"

He gives me a look that clearly states "Do you want me to answer that?" Which is code for Cara.

"Noted," I say. "Thank you again for tonight."

Wes takes back my hand, rubbing my knuckle with his thumb. "You've thanked me six times. And I haven't even got to the good part yet."

"There's a good part?"

He lifts up my hand and places a kiss on it. "Just wait until we get back to the room."

This whole night has been perfect; I can't imagine what he has in store for when we get back. When I arrived at the hotel, I was ushered to the suite he rented for the night. He was still at practice but left me a note that instructed me to take a hot bath and to pour myself a glass of champagne, knowing I had a rough day. When he finally arrived in the room, I was in the midst of getting ready. I knew we had to be going somewhere expensive, judging by the tight black dress Whitley packed for me. It's one of my favorites and considering I had to make sure Wes didn't rip it off me before we left, it's now one of his favorites, too.

"Can I ask you a question?"

I swallow my bite of the bananas foster. "I mean, it is our first date. I feel like questions go with the territory."

He laughs. "You're right. When I first offered you the job to watch the kids, you made a joke about having multiple jobs and none of them working. Then I once heard you making that same joke with my mom. How many jobs have you had?"

I set down my fork and dab my mouth with my napkin. "Do you really want to know? How about asking me about men I've dated? That's an easier conversation."

"Sorry. This is the question. Inquiring minds want to know."

I do a quick mental count in my head. "Counting this job, and the one I had with Whitley, I've had roughly thirty-three jobs since I graduated from college."

Wes's wide eyes, that haven't blinked in a few seconds, is all the reaction I need from him. "Thirty-three?"

"Well," I say, doing the mental math. "Let's call it thirty-two. I only worked for my dad's firm for a day. I don't even know if they processed my paperwork."

Wes takes a big gulp of his water, clearly trying to figure out how to react that isn't wide-eyed horror.

"Say whatever it is you want. I've heard it all," I say.

"I'm just...I don't know whether to be impressed or not?"

"That's a fair reaction."

"None of them worked out?"

I shake my head. "Not really. There was one I liked, but unfortunately it didn't work."

"What was that?"

I let out a breath. "Promise not to laugh?"

He crosses his heart. "I would never laugh."

"Okay, well, you know how Jake is a star on that app, *ForU?*"

"I've heard that but I've never watched his videos," Wes says. "I just can't make myself watch Amelia's little brother dancing half-naked in front of a camera."

The thought of that makes me laugh. "Yes, that would be weird. But anyway, I thought about making some sort of video content. I really liked the idea of doing something creative that I could have fun with."

"Then why didn't you do it?"

Here comes the embarrassing part. "Because I didn't know what to do."

"What does that mean?"

"On an app like that, you have to find your niche. Some people dance. Some are funny. Some give tutorials. I tried a few different things, but nothing felt right. So I gave up."

I hate saying that out loud. I honestly thought I could do it. I knew it was going to be hard work, but at least it was going to be hard work I controlled.

"Anyway," I say, wanting to change the conversation. "That's my sad job history."

"I'm sorry. For what it's worth, I think you'd be great at something like that."

"You're just saying that because now you have to."

He laughs. "I don't have to say it. You're charismatic. You're beautiful. You're funny and smart. You'd be a hit if you just found that thing you think you're missing."

I reach over for his hand. "You really are getting laid tonight."

He brings up my hands and gives them a kiss. "Don't feel bad. If it makes you feel any better, I have no clue what I'm about to do when football is over."

"You're not just going to cruise into a life of retirement with golf every day and becoming one of the old men sitting around and gossiping outside of Mona's?"

"No. Shane, Oliver, Simon and I are saving that for after the age of sixty-five."

"Sounds about right."

"But no, I don't have an answer to what I'm going to do. I was an education major in college. I never thought I would get drafted, so I figured I'd probably end up being a high school football coach and a teacher. But could I do that now? I don't think I could. Things have changed so much. So what am I going to do when this season is over? I haven't figured that out yet."

I give his hand a squeeze. "Maybe you can stumble into a nanny job. I hear they not only come with pretty good paychecks, but if you play your cards right, you can start dating the boss."

"I'll consider it."

We both laugh as the waiter comes to take the check from Wes. I might have just made a joke about becoming a nanny, but the more I think about it, I think the joke is about to be on me. When I first signed on for this, I told Wes I'd be here through the season. It's completely possible that if the Fury lose, his season is over in three days. What would I do? Go back to work for Whitley? Find another job in Rolling Hills? Do I stay in Rolling Hills? Does he want me there?

I must have a panicked look on my face because Wes is suddenly moving his chair next to mine and taking both of my hands in his.

"Hey? Are you okay?"

I look up at him, his gray eyes so sincere and concerned. And fuck, the man looks so damn handsome tonight it's almost too hard to look at him. His black dress shirt and black slacks, combined with the cologne that I've never smelled on him before, is enough to scramble my brain.

"That's a loaded question," I say.

"Well, unload it for me."

I take a breath, giving his hands a squeeze. "What's going to happen with us when the season is over?"

He looks confused, which I don't know why because I feel like this is a serious question. "Why would you ask that?"

"Because..." I pause for a second, making sure I'm choosing the right words. "When you first brought me on, you said it was for the season, which is rapidly coming to a close. Do you need me after that? And now that I think about it, we never talked about the weirdness of my boyfriend signing my paychecks. I just...I don't need you to make me a promise I don't think either of us are ready to make right now when it comes to our relationship, but I need to know if I need to start making plans."

He doesn't say anything. Instead, he frees his hands, only to cup them around my face and bring me in for possibly the softest, most emotional, kiss we've shared. I grip onto his shirt, hoping he can tell how much I need this.

"Oh, beautiful," he begins as he slowly pulls away. "You're not going anywhere. I don't care if I'm playing football, teaching, or selling Tupperware, I need you in my life. The kids need you in their lives. As for the paycheck thing, just stop talking about that because you can call it a salary, or me providing, but either way your bank account is going to be filled. Now, if you found a job that you really wanted, I would never stop you. I want you to be as happy as you make me, and that includes you continuing to be the bad ass, strong, feminist woman you are. But you need to know, when it comes to me and the kids, Betsy Sullivan, you're stuck with us."

I feel a tear sneak out of the corner of my eye, which Wes tenderly brushes away.

"Thank you," I say, feeling much better already. "But can I make a suggestion?"

He smiles. "Sure."

"Don't sell Tupperware. I tried it. Doesn't pay well."

We both laugh as we come together, sharing another kiss that is probably a little too deep for being in public.

But I don't care. Because for the first time in my life, I am truly happy. The future might be unknown, but if I'm with Wes, it doesn't seem as scary.

Chapter 31
Wes

I take a step outside to my patio as I shut the sliding glass door behind me. The music and excitement from inside is instantly muffled, which is exactly what I needed. I don't blame anyone for being loud and having fun. I'm glad they are. Hell, this is one of the best nights of my life. I just need a minute to myself.

I'm going to the fucking championship game.

I laugh to myself as I sit back on one of the chaise loungers, still not completely processing everything. After you play professional football for as long as I have, there are things you want, but you start to believe they aren't in the cards for you. For some guys it's all-star nods or record-breaking seasons. For me, it was a league championship.

There were some seasons with the Fury that I think we were eliminated from contention before we played a game. That's how bad we were. Then Coach McAvoy came in and started turning the ship around. Once he got comfortable, and our franchise quarterback figured his life out, we started clicking. We've come close the last few seasons. Last year we fell a game short of making it to the big one. It's what motivated us all year. It's why I knew that if it didn't happen this season, it wasn't in the cards for me.

And even better? My whole family was there to watch, blood and extended. And then everyone made the trek back to my house to continue the celebration.

The best part was that the kids were there to see me in my final home game. I take out my phone, looking at the picture Betsy snapped of the kids celebrating with me on the field. We aren't posed. I'm kneeling as all three ran into my arms. I'm getting emotional just looking at it. I know I was gone for a lot of their childhood. Yes, football, in comparison to other sports, is a shorter season, but it's still a significant amount of time. I missed school plays and ball games. I missed lost teeth and bad dreams.

I just hope that one day they realize that I did it all for them.

"Whatcha looking at?"

I smile as Betsy comes over to the chair, sitting on the end of it. "The pictures you sent me from today."

"They are good, aren't they?"

I reach for her hand, bringing her in so her back is against my chest. "This one is my favorite."

I show her the picture of the five of us. I need to thank Whitley, because she was the one insisting we take it. Everyone is decked out in Wes Taylor jerseys, and each of the girls have the Fury logo on their cheeks. Emerson and Hank are in front of me and Betsy as I hold Magnolia. Betsy's hand is on my chest, and her smile could light up the stadium.

It's perfect.

"Everything okay in there?" I ask.

She nods. "I just put Magnolia to bed. She passed out on the couch holding a piece of pizza."

I laugh. "Thanks. I just needed to get away for a second."

"Do you want me to go?"

I squeeze her tighter. "Don't you fucking dare."

I feel her relax against me as we just lie there, taking in the crisp, clear night. I gently stroke my fingertips up and down her arms, just loving the feel of her against me.

"So, what's it feel like?" she asks.

"Surreal," I say. "I don't know if it's actually hit me yet."

"Going to the championship, or playing in Nashville for the last time?"

Huh...I never thought of it like that. "I guess both. The championship will hit me when we land in Arizona next week. As for it being the last game, probably not until next year when I don't report back for camp."

"That makes sense," she says. "But until then, just enjoy the moment."

I look over to the house, where I see Emerson and Hank dancing on the kitchen island, Oliver and Simon each there dancing on the floor, making sure neither of them fall. Shane and Amelia are talking at the table. My mom is cleaning up, because that's what she does, and I'm pretty sure Dad is lounging in the living room, watching replays of the game. My brother was here with Olivia, though now I don't see them. I'm guessing they pulled an Irish goodbye.

I look down at Betsy. Her eyes are closed as she rests her head against my chest. God, she's beautiful. She's now changed into one of my Fury hoodies. I've made sure to stock up on her Fury clothing options, but she still prefers to steal my stuff. I don't care. I'd give her my whole closet if she wanted.

I've already given her my whole heart.

It's scary to think about how fast this woman has weaved her way into my soul. I've always wondered about fate and destiny. To me it seemed like a bunch of shit. But knowing that

Betsy came into my life exactly at the moment I needed her to, well, put a point in the destiny column.

I feel her shiver beneath me as she tries to tuck herself more into my hold.

"Let's go in," I say.

She shakes her head. "I'm not that cold. Plus, inside is loud."

I laugh, stroking her arms again, causing goosebumps to break out. The sensation only makes her cuddle against me more, and I don't think she's trying to turn me on, but fuck if she isn't. I can't help it. Betsy is what a woman should be—sexy and confident. Smart. Funny. Compassionate. Caring. And her body? Which is right now trying to wrap around me like a vine? I'd fucking start a war over it.

"Betsy…"

"Hmm?"

"I know you're just trying to get comfortable, but if you keep that up I can't be held accountable for my actions."

She doesn't open her eyes; instead the vixen plays innocent despite her chest beginning to rub against me.

"Betsy…"

She continues her torture as her hand slowly slides down me, beginning to stroke me through my pants. "I don't know what you're talking about. I'm just lying here."

I suck in a breath, doing my best to control myself. That all goes out the window when her hand slides back down, goes underneath my pants, and begins working every inch of me.

"Dammit, Betsy…"

Two can play at this game. I check the house again, making sure no one is looking at us. No one is. I can see in, but we are tucked away, out of direct viewing. Plus, I'm not taking off any of her clothing. Nope, if this is the game she wants to play, then I'm all for it.

I let my hand travel down her pants, letting my fingers crawl to the spot I'm searching for. I swallow a groan. Fuck... she's already wet. My fingers easily slide into her center, finding the spot I know will set her off.

"What are you doing?" she asks, her hips grinding into my touch.

"I never said I play nice."

I curve my finger, which usually makes her scream. Tonight, she holds it in, choosing to bite onto my shirt.

"Wes, I can't stay quiet."

"Well, then, we should probably go somewhere where you can scream."

I yank out my hand so I can quickly pick her up as we run toward the pool house. It's not the best place for this, but it's private, and she has a wall to hold onto.

She's going to need it.

I set her down and shut the door. It's dark in here, so when I turn around I'm confused as I don't see the outline of her body. It's only when I feel her pulling down my pants I realize what she's doing.

"Betsy."

The cold air hits me as my sweats fall to the floor, but I'm immediately warmed by her touch.

"I never actually told you congratulations. So this is how I'm going to show you."

I hit my head against the wall of the pool house, but it's easy to ignore the pain as the feeling of Betsy's mouth overwhelms my senses. She takes me all in, her tongue rolling around as I hit the back of her throat.

"Shit..."

That only spurs her on. She picks up her pace, her hand working in tandem with her mouth as she takes me in and out. I grab her hair, needing the balance as she takes me at the perfect pace.

My eyes begin to adjust to the dark, so I look down at this magnificent woman. I don't know when she did it, but at some point she took off her shirt, her heavy tits bouncing in her bra as her red lips swallow me. And there they are—the red nails. Working me. Stroking me in tandem with her mouth. I dreamt of this. Fantasized. Stroked myself to the image of those nails around my cock.

This is better. So much fucking better.

"Bra off," I say through clenched teeth.

She doesn't hesitate. And she doesn't take her eyes off me as she stops what she's doing, releasing the front clasp of the black lace bra.

"Fucking perfect," I say.

I lift her up, bringing her lips to mine in a hard kiss when I realize I'm a damn idiot.

"What?" she asks as I suddenly pull away. "Is everything okay?"

"I don't have a fucking condom."

"Oh babe," she says, bringing me in and stroking her fingers down my cheek. "I'm on the pill. And I'm clean. And you're it for me."

I let out a sigh of relief as I bring her into me. "And you're it for me."

I kiss her again, just as hard as before. "Now turn around," I direct, spinning her around so she's facing the wall. "Hold on, beautiful."

Making sure she's placed her hands on the wall, I pull down her leggings and line up my cock to her center, sliding right into her. Holy fuck. Feeling Betsy for the first time without a condom is...heaven. That's what this is. She's fucking heaven.

"This is going to be quick," I grunt, slamming into her as I hold onto her hips.

"Yes, please," she says, leaning over a little more.

I thrust into her over and over, her ass jiggling with every pump. Fuck, I could stare at this all day. She throws her head back, and I allow myself to take each of her tits in my hands. I squeeze them, holding on for dear life as I begin to feel my balls tighten.

"I'm close," I grunt.

"I'm ready," she moans, digging her fingers into my fore-arms. "Make me scream."

I reach down and rub her clit, making sure she gets just as much pleasure out of this as me.

And that does it. With a few more pushes, I feel our orgasms hit at the same time. I grab onto her, holding her tight. It's the only way we both don't fall to the ground.

Holy fuck...

I don't let her go as we do our best to slow down our breathing.

"That was..."

Her words trail off, but I know exactly what she was going to say. Or at least I'd know how I'd describe it.

Intense. Passionate. Consuming.

Everything.

Chapter 32
Betsy

The kids have been in bed for two hours. I've done the dishes. All the laundry is put away. I have lunches made for the morning and I've already started packing our bags for when we fly out for the game in two days.

And now I'm bored.

I would have called Whitley, but she and Jake already flew to Arizona. They decided to go for a pre-wedding vacation before the game on Sunday. I even called Oliver to see what he was doing, but grading tests didn't sound like my cup of tea.

So here I am, aimlessly scrolling through one of the streaming services, trying to find a true crime documentary I haven't watched, knowing full well that I'm just going to find my favorite one and watch it for the hundredth time.

I miss Wes. Which is ridiculous. He left two days ago. I'm going to see him in another two. I got spoiled with him having home games since we officially got together, meaning his time away wasn't as bad as when he's on the road.

For just a fraction of a second, I feel bad for Cara. I've only had to do this for a few games; she had twelve years of being the only parent for chunks at a time. Then again, if Wes were to tell me after Sunday that he changed his mind and wanted to stay in the league another year, I'd pull up my girlfriend pants, get a rhinestone jean jacket with his name on it, and be the best football partner I could be.

Hmmm...Do I have time to make a rhinestone jean jacket before we leave?

I launch the app to my favorite online store, where I know I can get a jean jacket delivered in one business day, when my FaceTime signals that Wes is calling.

"To what do I owe this surprise? I figured since we talked before the kids went to bed I wouldn't hear from you again."

He's laying on his hotel bed, one hand behind his head, giving me a spectacular view of his bicep.

"I missed you."

"You said that earlier."

He laughs. "I did. And I still miss you. We're done with our media obligations, so I turned in for the night."

"Well, thank you," I say. "I was actually just laying here feeling very alone. So you have impeccable timing. Now, tell me about your day. And don't give me the edited kids' stuff. I need to know all of the gossip."

Wes starts talking about the media event and how it was relatively low key. Over the past few years, there has been plenty of drama and headlines within the Fury. Some of it is public, like the quarterback's battle with mental health. Some of it I only know because of Whitley, like the time the star wide receiver started dating a crazy ex-girlfriend of one of the offensive linemen. The same offensive lineman who is now married to the quarterback's twin sister.

But Wes isn't giving me any of that. Instead, he's going on about the questions the reporters asked him, and other things like that. Normally, I listen to every word he says. But tonight I'm distracted.

His freaking arm keeps flexing, and I don't know if he's doing it on purpose or not, but it's hot as fuck. And considering it's been more than a few days since we last saw each other...

"Hello? Earth to Betsy?"

Hearing my name snaps me out of my daze. "Yeah. Totally. Yup."

"You didn't hear a damn word I said, did you?"

Thank goodness he's laughing, or I would have felt bad. "Sorry."

"What were you thinking about? I'm guessing something good because you had that spaced-out, post orgasm look on your face."

"My what!" I squawk then slap my hand over my mouth. I forgot the kids are asleep across the hall. "I do not have that face."

Wes starts to laugh, which somehow makes his bicep flex more.

Fuck me...

"Yes, you do. And just like the rest of you, it's beautiful. Then again, I put it there, so I do take a bit of pride in it."

In the past, if this were any other guy, I'd call him out on his cockiness. But I can't with Wes. The man speaks no lies.

"But seriously," he says. "What were you thinking about?"

I look over to the door to double-check that it's closed. "You really want to know?"

He sits up a little more against the headboard. "Considering you just did the double-check to make sure none of my children were around, hell yes."

"If you must know"—I pause for dramatic effect—"the way you're sitting, your arm keeps flexing. And, well, it got me thinking..."

I watch his eyes go from curious to blazing. I'm used to getting turned on from just one of Wes's looks, but this is a whole new level.

"What were you thinking, Betsy?"

His gravelly voice hits me straight at my core. "That the little toy I left in your drawer might get some use tonight."

"Get it out. Now. And lock the bedroom door, no interruptions."

I don't ask questions. I don't hesitate. Because I have many favorite sides of Wes Taylor, but Boss in the Bedroom Wes Taylor might be my favorite.

I hurry to the door and turn the lock. On my way back to the bed I reach into the bedside drawer, grabbing my bullet I brought over a few weeks ago. He didn't believe that I had a waterproof vibrator. So of course, I had to show him.

Turns out he showed me.

I rearrange a few of the pillows on the bed, situating myself at the perfect angle.

"Why are you still wearing clothes?"

I put the phone back in front of my face to see a shirtless Wes. Damn he works fast.

"Because I was locking the door and getting the toy. I can only do so much at a time."

"Well, then." He puts his arm back up where it was, only this time he knows exactly what he's doing. "Go on."

I look around, wondering how I'm going to prop the phone up. I decide to set it against the lamp on the nightstand. If this is going to be a show, I might as well do it right.

I take a few steps back, making sure he's getting all of me.

"What do you want first?"

He lowers his hand, sliding it out of range for the camera. Naughty boy.

"Leggings."

I do as he asks, slowly shimmying them down my legs.

"Next?"

"Panties."

I repeat the motion, lowering them before kicking them to the side.

"What else?"

"Nothing. Get back into bed."

"Really?" I ask as I grab my phone and get situated again. "You, Wes Taylor, *don't* want to see my tits?"

"Don't worry, I have the photo you sent me," he says. "Plus, I like knowing that I'm going to make you come while you're wearing my shirt."

Well, when he puts it like that....

"Do you have it?"

I reach to my side and grab the bullet, bringing it to life. "I do."

"Put it on your clit."

I do as he says. No, he can't see it, I'm keeping the camera at my face, but he'd also know if I was faking. The man can read me like a book.

My body slightly jerks when I feel the first vibrations. I close my eyes, allowing myself to settle in to the purr of the tiny toy.

"That's it," he says. "What are you thinking of?"

"You," I say, opening my eyes so I can look at him.

I see his arm moving, which only drives me wilder, knowing he's stroking himself as well.

"What am I doing to you? Tell me everything."

"You're doing that thing where you suck on my tit while fingering me. I fucking love that."

"Mmmm," he groans. His arm is picking up speed. "What do you love about it?"

I continue working the toy, making sure I hit every nerve

and hot spot. "I love how you make me feel. I love how you make me come. I love how much you love my body."

"I do fucking love your body," he says. "I love it when you ride me so I can watch your fantastic tits bounce in my face."

I smile, loving how the tables have turned. "What else?"

"I love the feel of your skin when I kiss you everywhere."

Shit...that one is hotter than the tits thing. "I love it when you touch me. How you make me feel desired."

"I wish I was touching you now."

"I do too," I say, though this vibrator is doing quite the trick. "You know exactly what I like. What I need."

"What do you need, Betsy? Tell me."

I take a couple breaths as my orgasm begins to creep up. "Tell me to come, Wes. I need it. I need you to get me there."

His arm starts working faster. Just thinking about his dick is enough to send me over the edge. But then he moves the camera down and I see how hard he is stroking his cock.

That's it. I'm done for.

"Do it, Betsy...come for me, beautiful."

"Yes...Yes!"

Holy shit, I think I'm seeing stars. And judging by the groan Wes just let out, so is he.

I look down and see the shirt I'm wearing has risen up so my breasts are now exposed. I lazily brush my thumb along my nipple, prolonging the orgasmic tingles a little longer. A smirk creeps over Wes' face knowing I was still imagining it was him touching me.

"That was—" I say, breaking the silence.

"Fucking amazing," he finishes.

We finally look at each other, both of us smiling ear to ear. I slowly slide back down to the pillows, covering my breasts back under Wes's shirt, my body feeling completely relaxed.

"Get some sleep," he says.

I let out a yawn. "Who knew FaceTime sex would take me out?"

This makes him laugh. "See you in two days."

I smile and blow him a kiss. "I'm counting down the hours."

"So am I, beautiful. So am I."

Chapter 33
Wes

"All right guys, this is it," Bryce Donald, our quarterback, says as he enters our huddle. "For all the fucking marbles."

The huddle erupts in claps and chants of "Let's go!" as we get the play call from our league MVP quarterback.

I put my toe on my mark, my fingers dangling as I look down the line while Bryce yells out the cadence. Our receiver, Dexter, goes into motion as the play begins to run.

This is it. Our last chance. We're down by four, so a field goal does us no good. There's less than thirty seconds left. It's now or never.

"Ninety-two red...ninety-two red...set...go...hike!"

I run my route exactly as planned. I'm not the first option for Bryce, but as I'm going, I see an empty pocket in the end zone. My defender is a few steps behind me, guessing the wrong way I was going to run. If I turn on the jets I think I can make it to the end zone. I only hope Bryce sees me.

I say a prayer to the football gods that I still have the speed I need to make this work. As soon as I turn up a gear, Bryce has locked eyes with me. He fires back a pass, just past the tips of the first line of defense. I have to jump slightly for the ball, holding it for dear life as I come down into the end zone.

"TOUCHDOWN FURY!"

I hear the whistle blow, and before I know it, my teammates are mobbing me in celebration. I've never been a showy guy, but I just made a fucking touchdown in the fucking championship game. So I stand up, toss the ball to the referee, and start doing the dance I saw on one of Hank's video games. I must be doing something right because my teammates are jumping and hyping me up.

I hear the crowd roaring as we jog off the field as the extra point team comes on. I celebrate with Coach McAvoy and Davis before Bryce and I give each other one more pat on the back.

"Hey," Bryce says. "Turn around. This moment is yours."

I'm confused, but do as he says. And I'm so glad I did.

The crowd is standing in applause as they chant my name. I'm overwhelmed. I'm glad I don't have to say anything right now because I don't know if I could get any words out. I raise my hand and wave, showing my appreciation to the fans who have stuck by me, and this team, for the past twelve years.

I try my best to bask in the moment. Because this is it. This is how I want to go out. With that play. With this memory.

As I'm waving to the crowd, I somehow pick out my family in the crowd. Probably because they are cheering the loudest of all of the seventy-thousand people in the stadium.

My mom and dad are hugging as they wave to me. My brothers are next to them, giving me the slow clap they always do when I score a touchdown. The kids are celebrating like they caught that pass themselves, which makes me laugh as I also hold back the tears. Hank is giving me a thumbs-up, obviously for my amazing dance moves. Emerson is crying, which only makes me cry harder. Magnolia is dancing to the music, living her life to the fullest.

And then there's Betsy. I can see the tears on her cheeks as she holds her hands over her heart. We make eye contact, and like we've done so many times, we have a conversation with just a look.

I love her. I love this woman so much.

I wasn't planning on her. Hell, she just showed up one day and somehow never left. There were days after Cara left that I was so hurt and angry I never wanted to lay eyes on another woman again.

But Betsy made me forget all that. She healed me without even knowing it. She healed my family. When I thought of raising the kids by myself, I always wondered if they would think there was a piece of our puzzle missing. Turns out the piece was a sassy stranger who gave my kids candy and me a reason to smile again.

I see out of the corner of my eye that some of my teammates are grabbing the Gatorade dispenser from the training table. I turn to look at the clock, and there's now just three seconds left in the game.

Holy shit we did it...

Coach McAvoy gets doused with the liquid as we all run and yell our way onto the field. I'm bombarded by teammates and staff as we start jumping around in celebration. Someone hands me a hat that calls us the champions as I make my way through the mob on the field.

I quickly shake hands with a few of the players from the opposing team that I've become friendly with over the years, when a reporter taps me on the shoulder, asking me for an interview.

"Wes, first of all, congratulations. Tell me what was going through your mind on the last play."

Normally in interviews I'm very guarded. I never want anything I say to be taken out of context. Over the years I've become the king of canned answers. But this is my last one, and we just won the whole damn thing.

"All I was thinking about was getting open. I knew it was my last game, and our last chance to win it. I wanted to give Bryce another option and I saw my opening. Somehow my old knees beat out my defender. I'm just glad it worked."

This makes her laugh. "As you said, this is your last game in a Fury uniform. What are the emotions right now, knowing this is the final game of your career?"

"Overwhelming," I answer honestly. "I've had a great career with a great franchise. Players don't often get to spend their entire careers in one place, and I'm so grateful it was with the Fury. I never thought I'd catch the game winner to win the first title in the franchise's history. That's...well... that's once in a lifetime."

"Daddy!" I stop talking to scan the crowd and see Magnolia sprinting toward me, her arms in the air. I lean down and scoop her up, kissing her cheek as she giggles and claps.

"And who is this little one?"

"I'm Magnolia. I'm six. My daddy scored and the Fury won! Wooo!!!!!"

I laugh, realizing my child is for sure about to go viral. "Yes, this is my youngest. I'm just so glad she's here, as are the rest of my kids and family."

I signal behind me where Betsy has Emerson and Hank. "They are the reason I played all this time. They are the reason I'm choosing to end my career. They are the reason for everything."

"Congrats again, Wes."

I nod to the reporter as the camera turns away from me. As

soon as they do, the three of them come rushing over to me, finding any part of me they can find to hug.

"Dad!" Hank yells. "That was so awesome. And you did the dance!"

"Yeah I did, buddy," I say as I lean down to kiss the top of his head before looking over at Emerson. "How'd I do?"

She shrugs, trying to play the role of cool pre-teen. "Eight out of ten."

"I'll take it."

She gives me another hug, as does each of the kids before they realize they can play in the confetti. Before I know it, they are running off, finding some of the other kids they know and begin making confetti angels on the field.

I look over to Betsy, who has her phone up, taking photos of everything she can. "Get it all?"

She nods as she puts it down. "I just videoed everything. I'll take screenshots later. Best of both worlds."

I reach for her hand and bring her in, laying a kiss on her that I know we'll both remember for hours after the game.

"Congrats, champ," she says, smiling up at me like she's never been prouder of anyone in her life. "How are you going to celebrate?"

"I have a few ideas." I lean in for another kiss, only this time I pick her up, swinging her around.

Have I ever been this happy? I'm sure in pockets of time, yes. But here? Now? With my family here, my kids in their glory, I just won a title, and the woman I love in my arms? It doesn't get better than this.

"Hey," I say as I put her down. "Remember the other night when we were saying all the things we loved about each other?"

"Wes!" she looks around, scared as if someone might overhear.

"Get your head out of the gutter," I say. "No, what I was about to say was that I realized that I forgot to tell you one."

"Are you sure my head shouldn't be in the gutter?"

I cup her face, making sure she's looking nowhere but at me. "What I should have said, what I wanted to say, is that I love you, Betsy Sullivan. I love every damn thing about you. You brought me back to life. You found the sunshine in the rain. And there is no one I want to go into this next chapter of my life with other than you."

"Oh Wes..." she says through tears as she grabs my face to kiss me. "I love you. I've never said those words before, and that's how I know I love you. Because I'm not scared of them. You said I was your sunshine? Well you're my anchor. You've helped give me purpose. You've showed me love. You've supported me and believed in me more than anyone else ever has. Wes Taylor, I love the hell out of you."

I pick her back up, kissing her in between laughter and tears.

I always said to myself that I wanted my last moments of football to be memorable. That I wanted to look back and know that no matter when it ended, I gave it my all. That I left no regrets on the field.

And I didn't. Not one damn regret.

Chapter 34
Betsy

"Do you have the presents wrapped?"

I look over to the pile near the window where I stacked Emerson's birthday gifts earlier. I told Wes it was too much. He told me to hush.

"Yes. All accounted for. Except the big one that's just got the bow on it."

"And that's in the garage, ready to be rolled in," Wes says. "Did you get the cake?"

"Picked it up this morning. What about the food?"

Wes dangles his keys. "Porter should be finishing it up now. What twelve-year-old requests bar food for her birthday?"

"The one who has life figured out."

I take a few steps toward him, lifting my chin for a quick kiss, which of course he gives me. "Can you also pick up a few extra bags of ice while you're out?"

"Why do people always stock up on ice?" he asks. "We have an ice maker for a reason."

"You can never have too much," I say. "Can you just get it?"

He leans against the counter, trying to distract me with his sexiness. I won't tell him that it's working. "So this is what it's going to be like, huh?"

"This is nothing," I say, giving him a pat on the chest. "Just wait until our first Halloween party."

Wes gives me a kiss on the cheek. "Just make sure you wear that costume from last year. I'm a big fan."

"I'll keep that in mind," I say. "Now go. Be back within an hour."

Wes waves and shuts the door behind him, leaving me to get the kids ready for Emerson's family birthday party. Yesterday was her friend party and her actual birthday. She chose an escape room, an arcade, and then a sleepover. Wes insisted he could handle it by himself, and that I should stay home with Magnolia and Hank.

I got a call an hour into the day that he needed reinforcements.

He fell asleep before the girls did last night. They were five seconds away from drawing on his face with a Sharpie. I have no idea where they would have gotten the idea...

Because of the late night, the kids all took a nap today before the family, or as Emerson is calling it, the adult party. She chose food from The Joint, a vanilla cake for today because she had a chocolate one yesterday, and a day full of board games.

Sounds like the perfect birthday weekend to me.

I look around the kitchen, making sure everything is set up before I head upstairs to get changed. No, I'm not living here. I just have my cosmetics, my toiletries, most of my clothes, and half of my shoes here. Though now that I think about it, I don't think the Taylors cashed my rent check last month. I'll have to ask Peggy about that. Though I have a feeling I know what her answer is going to be.

I laugh to myself as I walk down the hallway to Wes's

bedroom. It's only then I hear sobs coming from one of the bedrooms. I peek into Magnolia's room, but she's out like a light. Hank's door is open across the hall, and he's so far gone half of his legs are dangling off the side of the bed.

I take a few more steps and put my ear against Emerson's door. And then, clear as day, all I hear is the unmistakable sound of an ugly cry.

I should know; I've had many in my life.

I tap on the door, but she doesn't answer. I tap again and open it a little farther, because the cries are only getting louder.

"Em?" I ask, taking a step in. "Sweetheart, what's the matter?"

She doesn't answer, but does roll over, now burying her head in a pillow.

"Whatever it is, we can work through it," I say, taking a seat at the foot of her bed.

She shakes her head, but turns it enough so I can hear her. "She didn't call."

"Who didn't call?

She slams her pillow down, her face red and blotched. "Yesterday was my birthday, and she didn't call."

I'm gripping on to Emerson's bedspread because she hasn't said who, but I know. And I'm about to lose my shit on this woman. I wonder how long it would take me to fly to California, find that bitch, key her car, rip out her hair extensions, and overall ruin her life. Could I be back before the party starts?

"I am so sorry, Em," I say as I inch closer to her, which just makes her fling herself over to not face me. "I wish I had a better answer."

She doesn't say anything else, just continues to cry as I stroke her hair. There's nothing I can say. I'm not about to make an excuse for that so-called mother of hers. I'm not going to apologize for her. But I am going to comfort my girl, and if she needs to cry it out then I'll go buy every box of Kleenex in Rolling Hills.

"Sissy? Are you okay?"

I look to the door to see both Hank and Magnolia standing in the open frame, looking equally confused. At the sound of Magnolia's voice, Emerson pops up and quickly wipes away her tears.

"Yeah, I'm okay," she says. "Nothing to worry about."

Normally I'm all for Emerson being her little independent self, but not now. Nope. She needs to be pissed and angry at her mother. And if I had to make a wager, so do Hank and Magnolia, even if they don't know it.

"That's it!" I say, jumping up from the bed. "Everyone get their shoes and something warm on. Meet me out back in five minutes."

Everyone gives me a confused look.

"You heard me. Socks! Coats! Shoes! Sweatshirts! Let's go!"

Hank and Magnolia think it's a game, and they bolt for their bedrooms. Emerson just looks at me like I'm mental.

"What are you doing?"

I give her a pat on the leg. "We're going to yell it out. And I think you, my dear, are going to need to yell the loudest."

I walk across the room and grab my boots and a sweatshirt. Do I know if this is the right thing to do? Nope. Should Wes be here? Probably. But then again, I think Emerson hasn't let it out because she doesn't want him to see this.

I've never seen these kids cry about their mom leaving until today. Only occasionally at the beginning would they ask about her. They have to have questions, or be mad about something. Or hurt or angry or sad.

And today, we're going to get it all out.

Five minutes later, I have the three musketeers all outside.

"Emerson," I say, asking her to come next to me. I put my

arm around her, wanting her to know that I'm here. "I know you want to be strong for your brother and sister. That's what makes you the best big sister in literally the entire world."

"She is," Hank says. "She did my math homework for me last week."

I look over to her, but she's now conveniently looking everywhere but at me. "We'll talk about that later," I say. "Anyway, when you both came into Emerson's room today, she was sad, and that's okay. Emerson, do you want to tell them what you were sad about?"

She looks up to me, a touch of fear in her eyes. I give her a nod and a squeeze, encouraging her to go on.

"I was crying about Mom," she begins. "She didn't call me to wish me a happy birthday."

I feel my own tears building as both Hank and Magnolia run over to her, hugging her as hard as they can.

"I'm sorry, Sissy," Magnolia says. "That wasn't nice of her."

"No, it wasn't," Emerson says. "I'm sorry you two had to see me cry."

"Don't say sorry," Hank says. "I cry sometimes too. I miss her."

Oh fuck, I'm going to lose it...

"Hey buddy," I say as I take a seat on one of the chairs, bringing Hank beside me. "That's okay too. It's okay for you to feel sad. It's okay for Emerson to feel sad and maybe angry. Magnolia, do you miss your mom?"

She tilts her head, clearly thinking hard about it. "I get mad sometimes."

"Why, sweetie?"

"Because she says she's going to call and she doesn't. That makes me mad. And sad. I'm sad mad."

"Sad mad is a very big feeling," I say, bringing her to my

lap. Emerson takes a seat opposite of us. "Guys, what your mom did was terrible. I don't like talking bad about people—"

"Because it's not nice."

"That's right, Miss Mags, it's not nice. But as long as I'm around, I'm never going to lie to you. And I'm never going to make you feel like your feelings don't matter. My mom did that to me, and I remember how bad it made me feel."

"Your mom made you feel bad?" Hank asks.

"Yup. She didn't leave like your mom did. But I remember she always made me feel like I was wrong if I was upset about something. Or made me feel bad if I was happy. Feelings are important. Sometimes we need to be angry or sad or mad."

"Or sad mad."

I nod and boop Magnolia's nose. "Or sad mad. But there's a way that we can let all of those bad feelings out so new, happy feelings have room in our bodies."

Emerson gives me a questioning look. "There is?"

"Yup," I say, picking Magnolia up off my lap and signaling for everyone to stand. "We just yell it out. You can just scream. Or maybe get something off your chest you've been holding in. Anything you want. I guarantee when we're done, everyone will feel a million times lighter, just in time for what looks like an epic vanilla cake."

The three of them look at each other, clearly not knowing if I'm serious or not.

So I start it.

"AHHHHHHHHHHHHHHHH!!!!!!"

Now they're looking at me like I'm certifiable.

"What did you have to get off your chest?" Emerson asks.

"Remember that day at the hotel before Christmas?" I ask, and she nods. "Let's just say I've been holding that in since then."

This makes Emerson smile. I watch her as she takes the biggest breath I've ever seen. And then, she just let's go.

"Why didn't you call? I will never forgive you for that!"

"Good," I say. I look over to Hank. "You want to go?"

He nods. "Why didn't you say goodbye? Ahhhhhh!!!!!"

We all look to Magnolia, who is in the process of climbing on to one of the patio tables. "I didn't like the dolls you got me for Christmas! I never play with them!"

Emerson and I each hold in chuckles.

"Very good, guys," I say. "Now, how about all together, we just let out one big one. Get all the big feelings out.

The three of them nod.

"One...two...three..."

We yell so loud my smartwatch goes off for being in a loud environment. When we finally stop to catch our breath, all of us at the same time realize we aren't alone.

"What's going on?" Wes says. "Is this a good ol' fashioned yell-it-out?"

Magnolia's eyes nearly bug out of her head. "You yell it out?"

"I do," he says, kissing me on the cheek. "A very smart woman had me do it once. I felt a lot better after."

"Kids, want to do one more with Dad?"

They all start cheering, leaving Wes literally no choice.

"Why are we yelling?" he whispers to me.

"I'll tell you after the party because you don't want to know now." I turn back to the kids, who are ready for one more round. "Ready kids? All of us together! Three...two...one!"

The yells begin, but quickly turn into laughs as the three of them all of a sudden catch a case of the giggles.

Good. I like giggles. Giggles don't make me want to cut a bitch.

Chapter 35
Wes

Sometimes I just like to sit back and watch Betsy with the kids. The way she connects with them blows my mind. She's a friend. A nurturer. A confidant. It overwhelms me that I found someone who loves my kids with her whole heart.

One of my favorite things to do is sneak peeks of Magnolia and Betsy getting ready each morning. Their little chats about school, life, and the questions Magnolia asks while Betsy does her hair is one of those things I'm so glad they get to share, but that I also get to witness.

And now, so does the world.

Yup, my daughter, with the help of my girlfriend, are becoming social media stars.

"What's the hairstyle today, Miss Mags?"

She wrinkles her nose, thinking about it. "What am I wearing again?"

"Black leggings. Pink sweater and polka dot boots from Tiny Divas."

"Space buns. Definitely space buns."

Betsy nods and gets to work while Magnolia goes on and on

about what's coming up at school today. They're learning about plants because the weather is starting to warm up in Nashville, which means flowers are about to grow. She also talks about a boy named Liam and how he gave her a flower yesterday.

Note to self: figure out who Liam is when I do pickup later today.

I hold in my laugh as Betsy makes exaggerated faces toward her phone, which is recording this whole thing. I wondered what retirement would be like. But I never thought that part of it would include my family slowly but surely becoming one of those influencer families.

Because I nailed it... My kid went viral.

After the championship game, Dean, my agent, asked me to call him. I was a little shocked to hear from him, considering I told him that I wouldn't be needing his services on a full-time basis anymore. He responded that he wasn't calling for me, but for my kid.

A clothing company for young girls called him wanting to hire Magnolia to be a spokesperson. I didn't know that was a thing. Sometimes even I don't know what she's talking about. How's she going to talk about a product?

Then Betsy explained to me how it works. How she just had to make videos wearing the clothes, giving them a certain amount of name drops, and she'd get paid. I didn't like the idea of my child going to work before her kindergarten graduation, but Betsy made the suggestion that we put it away for when she's older. Maybe for her first car. Or college. That I could get on board with.

The deal was sealed when Betsy said she'd do the videos with her. She said she'd do all the filming, editing, posting, and even coordinate the efforts with the brand. All I had to do is sit back, watch, and make the occasional cameo.

I now live in a house with ring lights.

But I'll take it because Magnolia is loving it. She loves the clothes. She loves her mornings with Betsy that have become the niche that Betsy once told me about. And they're having fun.

That's all I can ask for.

"Now for the clothes!"

I hold in my laugh until I know Betsy has stopped recording. I've now seen enough videos to know that's where this part of the video stops before she goes to get dressed.

"Looking good as always," I say, leaning down and giving Magnolia a kiss on the top of her head.

"Thanks, Daddy. Excuse me, I need to go do an outfit change."

I stare at her as she walks into her bedroom, shutting the door behind her.

"Have we created a monster?"

Betsy laughs as she puts away the hair products. "Nah. She's just a girl who knows to feel good, you gotta look good."

"Well, you always make me feel good," I say as I pull her into my arms and kiss her.

"Come on, you two," Emerson groans as she walks past the open door of the bathroom. "There are minors present."

We laugh as Emerson walks away, mumbling something about how we're "cringe."

"I love that she's finally at the age where I'm embarrassing to her just by existing."

"Speak for yourself," Betsy says. "I'm supposed to be the cool one. I'm not supposed to be cringe."

"Sorry, beautiful. You're stuck with me."

She playfully rolls her eyes. "Fine. But that's going to require you being in a video this week."

"You play dirty."

She gives me a devilish smile. "You've known that all along. Yet you still picked me."

I pull her in for one more kiss, but another groan from Hank as he walks down the hallway breaks us up.

"Okay. Enough of that," Betsy says. "What's your day today?"

"I have to run up to Nashville to meet with the Fury media staff. They asked me to do some draft stuff in a few months, and they want to finalize it."

"You're still good to pick the kids up today? I promised Whitley I'd go with her to her dress fitting."

"I got them," I say.

"Betsy!" Magnolia yells. "I can't decide what earrings to wear!"

"Go," I say, giving Betsy a smack on the ass. "I love you."

She turns and gives me a quick kiss. "Love you more."

I have figured out the trick to the parent pickup line.

Get here early then nap in your car. Not only are you one of the first ones out of the traffic, but you're also recharged for the rest of the day.

I'm killing this retirement life.

I bring my hat over my eyes, settling in for my twenty-minute power nap, when a knock on my window scares the piss out of me.

I jump so high I nearly hit my head, only to see my old high school football coach laughing his ass off.

"Coach Lockwood!" I say, getting out of my car to give the man a hug. "Not cool, man."

"It gave me flashbacks when you used to sleep in my history class."

I hold my hands up in surrender. "In my defense, it was right after lunch. I was a goner."

"Fair enough," he says. "How's retirement?"

"Great," I say. "Just taking it easy now. Much deserved break, you know? How are you?"

"Oh fine," he says. "Just heading inside to the superintendent's office."

"Are you in trouble or something?" I joke. "Did someone finally report you for scheduling lifting at five in the morning?"

This makes him laugh. "Nope. And don't tell anyone this, but I'm not going to miss those."

"What are you talking about?" If this man ever changes five in the morning lifts, every alumni of Rolling Hills football will come back and riot. At this point, it's a rite of passage.

"I'm retiring, Wes," he says. "Put in my paperwork at the beginning of the year. But I kept it quiet. I didn't want this being my last year taking away from the kids."

"Wow," I say, completely in shock. This is the only man who has ever coached at Rolling Hills. Hell, he coached my dad, me, *and* my brothers. Even though I know he's up there in age, I just assumed he'd one day coach Hank. Because no one coaches Rolling Hills football other than John Lockwood.

"I'm actually glad you're here," he says. "Because the meeting inside isn't for my retirement. It's for my replacement."

"Why would you be glad I'm here? Do I know who's going to take it? Who are your candidates?"

He just smiles. "You."

I open my mouth to say something, but nothing comes out. Is Coach retiring because he's slowly losing his mind?

"Me?"

"Yes Wes. You."

"But I..." I trail off, because I'm still not sure what to say.

"Coach, there has to be guys more qualified. Some of your assistants? Oliver? I've never coached a day in my life."

"That's true," he says. "But when is there going to be a chance for these kids to learn from a guy who has played at the highest level of football? You have more football knowledge in your pinky than I'll ever have. You were never a great football player because of your skills—"

I clutch my chest and stagger back. "Gee, thanks."

He gives me the look he used to give me at practice when I would interrupt. "What I was going to say is that it was your smarts. You saw plays develop before they even started. You always knew how to get open. That's how you made that catch in the championship game. You were selfless. You're a team player who knew that sometimes you needed to be the guy and sometimes you needed to be the guy who helped the guy. Wes, I've been thinking about retiring for years. But want to know why I didn't?"

"Because Mrs. Lockwood has a honey-do list that's three pages long and you wanted to avoid it as long as possible?"

"That's one of the reasons," he says. "The other is because I didn't have someone to hand it off to. Wes, you're the guy. You're who I've been waiting for. You were one of the finest young men I ever coached. It would make me sleep easier at night knowing I left this program in the most capable hands possible. What do you say? Want to put on the whistle?"

I don't know what to say. This is...let's just say I didn't expect my day to go like this.

"Can I think about it?" I ask. "I want to talk to my family first."

He gives me a pat on the shoulder. "I'd be upset if you didn't. I'll go talk to the administration and let them know what we just talked about."

"Thank you," I shake his hand. "I'm honored, sir."

"We'll talk soon."

He pats my hand before walking away, leaving me stunned next to my car. I barely hear the kids running out of the building. I think I hear my crew telling me hi and getting in the car, but I still haven't budged.

"Hey, are you okay?"

I look over to see Oliver, who looks downright concerned for me. "Coach Lockwood wants me to take over the football program."

"Wow," Oliver says. "What are you going to do?"

I don't know. I honestly don't know.

Chapter 36
Betsy

"WHAT DO YOU THINK?"

I push tears away because that's how beautiful Whitley looks in her wedding dress. It's the most Whitley dress I've ever seen. Lace all over. The perfect strapless, mermaid silhouette. Just enough spark to catch your eye.

She looks like an angel.

"You, my best friend, might be the most beautiful bride I've ever seen." I walk over to her and wrap her in a hug. "Thank you again for making me part of your day."

"Are you kidding me?" She pulls away as the seamstress starts making the minor adjustments the gown still needs. "I would be losing my mind if you weren't my maid of honor."

"Thanks, but you don't need to lie," I say. "I know I've been busy, and I'm sorry. But it's a month until the wedding. Anything you need, I'm here."

"I'm not lying," Whitley says. "You've organized the shower and the bachelorette party this weekend. You've helped with invitations."

"That was more Emerson, but I'll take the credit."

"No matter what, I was helped," Whitley says. "I never said you couldn't outsource."

I sit back and watch Whitley turn this way and that as the seamstress makes some final adjustments to her gown. It's weird to think I'm about to take Whitley to her bachelorette party. It was at another bachelorette party we attended where she met Jake in the first place. It might have been four years ago, but it feels like yesterday.

Who knew they'd be anything after their one night together? Who knew she'd move to a small town in Tennessee for him?

Who knew I'd follow?

Thank God for Jake giving Whitley that lap dance.

"I'm going to go change," Whitley says. "After that, let's get lunch?"

I nod. "Tacos and margs?"

She smiles. "You read my mind."

Whitley goes back into the dressing room, and I grab my phone to pass the time. I've been on it more since Magnolia and I started the channel, but if I'm scrolling on that account, all I see are other families doing other fun things. Which is great and all, but sometimes I need *my* feed—full of celebrity gossip, cooking videos, and my favorite, the muscled guy who cuts down the trees.

Yes, I love Wes. But it doesn't hurt to watch. I call it helping another creator pay the bills.

I start scrolling when an email notification pops up with a subject line that nearly makes me drop my phone.

SUBJECT: Content creator interview, Alabama Now Network

I hurry and swipe away from the app, opening the email.

Why in the world would Alabama Now Network, the largest media company in the state, want to interview me?

Betsy,
Good afternoon. My name is Ted Buckly and I'm the
director of content with Alabama Now Network.
This email might be sudden, but we are expanding our
social media content here at ANN. We are looking to
bring different creators together to give our consumers a
complete content experience. I've heard from your father
that you are in this line of work, and after seeing some of
your videos, we think you'd be a perfect fit.
Please call my office to schedule an interview. Look
forward to hearing from you.
Best,
Ted Buckly

It takes all I have not to throw my phone into one of the twenty mirrors surrounding me.

How fucking dare he? I haven't talked to him or my mom since Thanksgiving, and all of a sudden he thinks he can swoop in and get me a job? And how does he know about the videos? I can't even think about that right now, I'm so damn mad.

I jump out of my chair, pacing back and forth as I try to figure out how to handle this.

"Betsy?" Whitley asks as she comes out of the dressing room. "Are you okay?"

I hold up my phone. "My fucking father is once again trying to save the day."

"Oh no," she says as she guides both of us back to the couch. "Tell me everything."

I do, which of course only makes me madder as I repeat what I just read.

"I mean, how dare he!" I yell, thankful that we seem to be one of the few in here for appointments right now. "Why would he do that?"

"Probably because, like he has before, he thinks the only way you're going to be employed is if he helps you."

"Which is bullshit. The only job I ever took that he set up was at his firm, and I didn't make it a whole day. Unless there were more? Shit, there could be more."

I slump down in the chair, wondering how much he's meddled in my life that I didn't know about. "Want to know what the fucking kicker of it all is?"

"What's that?"

"When I told them last year that I wanted to be a content creator, they laughed at me. They fucking *laughed*. Said it wasn't a real job. Then it wasn't good enough. Now that I'm doing well with it—and by the way, making Magnolia a hell of a nest egg for her college fund—all of a sudden it's not only a job that he wants me to have, he's willing to help make it happen."

I take a few deep breaths, trying to suppress my anger. Because half of me wants to get in the car and tell Whitley to start driving to Birmingham so I can properly tell this man to stay out of my life once and for all. Maybe more than half. A solid seventy-five percent.

"I know this is going to sound like a stupid question, but I need you to say it out loud so I know where you stand. You aren't taking this interview, are you?"

"Hell no," I say with no hesitation. "I like what I'm doing. And not to mention, that job would take me back to Birmingham. And I'm not leaving. I love it here." I reach over and grab Whitley's hand. "My best friend is here. A man that I'm head over freaking heels in love with is here. His kids, who I adore, are here. Rolling Hills is where I'm meant to be. And there isn't a job in the world that could take me away from that."

"HAVE THE BEST DAY YOU CAN!"

Magnolia and I wave to the camera after she says what's become the sign off to our videos. She said it once—no clue where it came from—and people went nuts over it. We now end almost every video that way.

What can I say, little Miss Mags was meant to be a star.

"Can we make another, Betsy?"

I fall back on the couch, exhausted from the day. "Girl-friend, I'm whooped. How about we order pizza tonight and have a good ol' fashioned lazy night?"

"Can we get pineapple on the pizza?"

I scrunch my nose. She knows I hate that. "How about we get one for you with pineapple?"

"Yes!" she exclaims as she jumps on the couch.

Oh, to have her energy.

"What are we celebrating?" Wes asks as he comes back inside from playing catch with Hank.

"That I declared it pizza night."

"Pineapple?"

I roll my eyes at the man I love. I knew he had to have one flaw. "You and Magnolia can split that one."

They give each other a high five as he sits down on the couch, bringing Magnolia to his lap.

"Actually, before we order, I have some exciting news," Wes says. "Emerson! Can you come down here for a second?"

Exciting news? I'm racking my brain, trying to figure out what it is. He hasn't told me anything over the last day or so that I'd deem exciting. Now that I think about it, the only thing he's told me is that Oliver found a date for Whitley and Jake's wedding. The only way that would be exciting is if he *wasn't* already in love with her. Which he is.

"What's up?" Emerson says as she takes a seat on the floor in front of me.

"So, something happened today that I wasn't expecting, and I wanted to talk to everyone about it."

No one makes a sound. Emerson looks back at me with the same confused look I'm wearing.

"When I was at pickup today, I ran into my old high school coach."

"Coach Lockwood?"

"That's right, Hank. Coach Lockwood. Well, like me, he's apparently ready to retire."

My senses start firing off. But I don't want to assume. That's Wes's role in the relationship.

"He was talking to me, and he thought that I'd be the perfect guy to take over coaching the high school football team next year. I told him I was flattered, but I had to talk it over with my family first."

"I think it's awesome!" Hank yells. "Can I be the water boy? I want to go to every practice. Can I?"

Wes laughs. "Easy there. I haven't said yes to anything. But if I did, I'm sure that could be a possibility."

"Why do you need to talk to us?" Emerson asks.

"Because, I thought I was going to be retired," he says. "I wasn't going to be jobless forever, but I thought I'd at least take a year and just relax. Hang out with all of you. This is a job that will take a lot of my time. Not as much as when I played, and the travel isn't like it was, but during football season I'll be gone a lot. Are y'all okay with that?"

"Yes!" Hank says.

"Can I be a cheerleader?" Magnolia asks. Oh, this child...

"Sure, sweetheart. I'm sure we can find you a Rolling Hills cheerleading uniform."

He looks over to Emerson, who is clearly thinking about it.

"Do you want to?" she asks.

He nods. "I do. I've been weighing the pros and the cons all day, and I think I could be good at it. This was the plan after college if I wasn't drafted. I guess it could be the plan for right now."

"Then I think you should do it," she says. "Plus, in a few months you'll be bored. And I don't think you're cut out for being a social media influencer."

This makes all of us laugh.

The laughter settles, and our eyes meet. I can't hold back my smile, because I know he hasn't said it out loud, but he wants this. He wants it bad.

And I'm going to be by him every step of the way.

"Betsy? What do you think?"

I stand up and take the few steps so I'm now next to him. "I think Coach Taylor sounds pretty darn good."

Everyone begins to cheer, and the idea of pizza is quickly tossed out the window and replaced with a celebration dinner at The Joint. Somehow, over the noise, I hear my phone notify me of a text, which I quickly check.

Dad: Did you get an email today?

I ignore the message and toss my phone down. In the midst of Wes's news, I almost forgot about that. Almost.

I debated on whether to tell Wes, but I don't see a reason to. What's the point when I don't even plan on responding?

Wes is here. And I'm going to be wherever he is.

If I wasn't sure about my decision before, I'm damn sure now.

I open up my email and find the message from earlier.

And I hit delete.

Chapter 37
Wes

"The car is leaving in five minutes! If you're not down here, ready to go, Hank and I are leaving without you!"

Hank looks at me, confusion all over his face.

"Why do they take so long to get ready?"

"My son, that is a great mystery of the world. One that I don't think will ever be resolved."

Hank and I sit down on the couch as we wait for the girls to finish getting ready. We have plenty of time, but for them, five minutes really means fifteen, which will get us out the door on time to the annual Rolling Hills Spring Fling. Every year, the kindergarten through sixth grade building holds a dance for parents and kids. All the money made goes straight back to the teachers for everything they've done for our kids throughout the year.

"Are you excited?" I ask Hank. "We never got to have anything like this when I was in school."

"I think so," he says. "Except I really don't know how to dance."

"That's okay, neither do I," I say. "I mean, you saw my touchdown dance."

He shakes his head. "It was cool then, Dad. Please don't do that tonight."

"Because you're my favorite today for being ready on time, it's a deal."

We shake hands as Emerson comes down the stairs.

"Where are the other two?"

"Filming a quick video. They said they'd be down in a second."

I look at Emerson, and it hits me straight in the heart how much she has grown up this year. I don't even know if I realized it until now.

She's wearing a baby blue dress that makes her look seventeen instead of twelve. Her long brown hair that she gets from my side of the family has soft curls through it. She pushes the hair back behind her ears, revealing small sparkling earrings. Thank goodness she's not wearing heels. I don't know if I'm ready for that.

My little girl is growing up. And while I'd like time to stop, I couldn't be prouder of the young woman she's becoming.

"You look beautiful," I say, bringing her in for a hug.

"You think so?"

"I know so." I place my hands gently on her shoulders. "Also, I never thanked you."

"For what?"

"For everything you've done." I take a breath, wanting to get through this without having her see me get too emotional. "You had to grow up fast this year. You never flinched to be there for not just your brother and sister, but for me. You helped Gram and Grandpa when you guys had to stay with them. You helped Betsy get acclimated."

She shrugs like it's no big deal. "Just doing what I needed to do."

I shake my head. "But you didn't have to. And you did. I love you kiddo, and I don't know if I tell you that enough."

"You do." She takes a step forward, wrapping her arms around my waist. "But I'll always want to hear it. And I love you too."

I hug her back, saying fuck it to the tears welling in my eyes.

We stay that way for a second before letting go.

"Okay, enough mushy stuff," she says. "It took Betsy an *hour* to do this makeup. And I'm not sitting through that again."

I laugh as my other two girls come downstairs.

"So this is why you asked Hank and I to wear baby blue ties."

Betsy and Magnolia each come downstairs in their own baby blue dresses. Magnolia's has a puffed skirt, perfect for a little girl who is going to want to spin in circles all night.

Then there's Betsy. If my kids weren't around, we wouldn't be going to a dance. I'd be ripping this dress off her and promising to buy her a new one. It's tight in all the right places and covered in the others, making it the perfect balance of sexy and modest.

"Yes, it is," she says, coming over and giving me a quick kiss. "I didn't know how you'd feel about color coordination?"

She tries to step away, but I bring her back in. "Did you forget about the matching Christmas pajamas? I'm all about coordination."

"Good to know," she says. "That will make our family's Halloween costumes so much easier."

～

"One, two, three!"

We all smile for the camera, which is being operated by one of the parents, as we enter the heavily decorated gymnasium. I almost didn't recognize it, even though I spent many days here in my childhood.

"This is so cool!" Hank says, looking around with wide eyes. "Oh! There are my friends. Can I go?"

"Sure, buddy. Just don't leave the gym without telling me."

He nods and runs to a group of boys sitting at a table under one of the baskets, phones already out playing some game.

Emerson sees her friends and takes off. Luckily, Magnolia still thinks we're cool.

"Daddy? Can I go dance with my friends?"

Maybe not.

"Of course, sweetie. Just save me a dance for later."

She doesn't answer, just runs off to have the time of her life.

"Don't worry," Betsy says as she wraps her arms around mine. "I'll keep you company."

"Hey, Coach! Congratulations!"

"Thank you," I say with a nod.

"Who was that?" Betsy asks.

"No clue."

I was officially named Coach Lockwood's replacement at last week's school board meeting. The response has been great, if a little overwhelming. I can't go anywhere without someone telling me congratulations or giving me their two cents on how I should run the offense.

"I'm still not used to people calling you Coach," Betsy says.

"Same," I say. "Sometimes I forget to respond."

"Well, you better get used to it." She pulls on my shirt, signaling for me to lean down. "If you want, I can start calling you that when I scream your name."

I swallow nothing as I do my best to not pop a hardon at the Spring Fling.

"Probably not a good idea. I don't want to be thinking of that when I have to address the football boosters."

"Fair," she says. "But just say the word and it's done."

"Everyone on the dance floor!" the DJ—also known as Oliver—announces. "Let's see who has the better moves, the kids or parents!"

Betsy pulls me out onto the dance floor, and to my surprise, all my kids join us. Luckily, it's a line dance with very clear instructions of how many jumps to take, which direction to walk, and when to clap.

I hold Magnolia's hand, making sure she's going the right way. Hank is between Emerson and Betsy, doing his best to keep up. I passed a lot of things onto my son. His love for learning and football. My gray eyes. And apparently my dance moves.

"I hate to ask this," Betsy says as we change direction.

"You need video?"

She nods. "Do you mind? It would be great to have a video with all three kids in it. Unless you want to be in it too and then I can ask someone else."

I shake my head and give her a quick kiss. "I'm meant to be behind the camera. Give me your phone. I got this."

I pass Magnolia to Betsy as I take her phone and open the video camera. I've done this a few times, so I know Betsy is going to ask for multiple videos from multiple angles. I learned after the first time if I don't do it right, she'll just have me do it again.

I'm nothing if not thorough.

I begin walking around them as I hit the record button, videoing Betsy and the kids as they dance around in their coordinating blue outfits. Luckily, I have some room, so I'm able to get each angle a few times, making sure she has plenty of options to pick from.

I exit the video app when a text notification pops up on her phone. It's from her dad and it's staring me right in the face.

> Dad: Did you not take the interview? Call me immediately.

I read the text message again, confused about what the hell he's talking about. First of all, I didn't even know she was in contact with her father. And what interview? She didn't tell me about any interview.

She must see the confusion on my face, because she tells the kids to head back to their friend group before making her way to me.

"What's the matter?"

I turn her phone and hold it up to her. "Want to explain this?"

She reads it and shakes her head. "It's nothing."

"It doesn't feel like nothing."

She looks around as frustration grows on her face. "Not here." She takes my hand and pulls me out of the gym. We turn into a hallway, giving us at least a semblance of privacy.

"Why are you in contact with your dad, and what interview is he talking about?"

"Calm down," she says.

"Don't tell me to calm down."

She stands up a little straighter. "I'm telling you to calm down because this is nothing and I don't want it to be something."

"Then explain."

"I'm trying." She takes a deep breath, which I should probably do too. But I'm too thrown by this to think rationally. "A few weeks ago, I got an email from a media company in

Alabama. They offered me an interview to come work for them as a content creator."

"How could you not tell me!"

"Let me finish," she says with a bite. "I didn't tell you because I didn't even consider it. For one, my dad arranged it, and I don't want anything from him. That's why he texted me about it, I'm sure, because he's probably pissed I didn't respond to one of his golf buddies."

"You didn't respond?"

She shakes her head. "I didn't. Besides the whole dad part of it, the job is in Birmingham. I'm not leaving you or the kids for some job I don't even want."

"But isn't making content what you want to do? Why would you not even consider the job? We should have talked about this."

"I am doing it!" she yells. "I love what I'm doing with Magnolia. I love that it's a thing we can do together. Hell, even Hank and Emerson have started asking questions about it and want to start making videos. Wes, I'm happy. I'm doing something I love with people I love. Isn't that the goal?"

"Yeah," I say defeatedly.

She takes a few steps closer to me, grabbing onto my shirt to bring me down closer to her. "I'm sorry I didn't tell you. But I don't want you to stress over this. It's nothing, and I'll take care of it tomorrow. Okay?"

"Okay," I say, giving her a kiss.

"Good, now let's go back inside."

I go back in, but the rest of the night is a blur. I don't hear a single song that's played. All I hear are evil voices taking over my brain.

Actually, just one voice. My ex-wife's.

"Wes, I have nothing to show for my life."

"I want more."

"Living in Rolling Hills? Not exactly the life I imagined."

Even as I go to bed that night, all I hear are those words that Cara said to me playing over and over in my head.

I held her back. At least in her mind I did. I didn't realize she felt that way until it was too late. Is that what I'm doing to Betsy? Holding her back?

She didn't even consider that job because of me and the kids. Does she want it? Should she take it? I don't want her to not go after what she wants because of me.

She has to want more, right? She's not even thirty yet. She should be having fun at bars and clubs on Friday nights, not at school dances. She went from a stranger to a nanny to the de facto mother of three kids in less than a year.

No way that's what she wants for her life.

Cara resented me at the end of our marriage, but truth be told, now that I look back with a clearer vision, our marriage was over long before she gave me those papers.

But if it was fifteen years from now and Betsy left, hating me because I held her back from the job she was always meant to have? Well, I don't know if I'd survive that.

Scratch that. I know I wouldn't.

Chapter 38
Betsy

I don't know at what point in my life I became a person who cleans to relieve stress, but here I am, four months from my thirtieth birthday, scrubbing a kitchen counter like it personally harmed me.

I barely slept last night. And even though Wes and I didn't talk after we went to bed, I know he was tossing and turning as much as I was.

Never go to bed angry. That's the saying, isn't it? Now I understand what it really means. Because I went to bed slightly angry and woke up with a lot of feelings inside that need to get out, and this poor kitchen is paying the price.

Watch out, refrigerator. You're next.

I knew at some point Wes and I would have our first fight, but I never thought this is what it would be about. I have no idea why he flew off the handle like that. I wanted to ask him about it this morning, hoping that cooler heads would prevail. Instead, I got barely full-sentence answers to any question I asked. Even the kids knew something was off. I'm glad they're going to Peggy's for the day. Wes and I need to talk, and it'll be better for everyone if it's just the two of us.

I don't want our relationship to be like this. Emerson has told me stories about how Wes and Cara would fight. That they'd wait until the kids went to bed, but it didn't matter—they heard the arguments. I refuse to be that. I'm not saying we're always going to be rainbows and sunshine, but I never want the kids to have to relive that part of their past.

Just the thought of Cara sends my anger level back to a ten. I turn my cleaning playlist up full blast, letting the song that used to be my college party song fuel my fire as I make this grease stain my bitch.

There's a little trill from the smart speaker, announcing a notification.

"Call from Dad Cell"

I groan.

"Not only do I not want to talk to him, he interrupted my favorite song." I throw the cloth down and wipe my hands up before I hit accept.

"Dad."

"Are you ignoring me or just that forgetful these days?"

"Do you want the truth?"

I hear him let out a sigh that screams of disappointment. "Why are you like this Betsy? What can't you—"

"Don't finish that sentence," I say as I take a seat at the kitchen island, putting the call to speakerphone. "Whatever you were going to say, I don't want to hear it."

"Oh, you're going to hear it," he says. "Why didn't you return Ted's email? He went out of his way to contact you, the least you could have done is written back."

"Because I didn't want the job," I say. "I'm sorry I ghosted your friend. Now he knows what it feels like to be a single woman these days."

"I don't even know what that means, but I guess if it's coming from your mouth it's probably something sarcastic."

"See, Dad, you *do* know me."

He lets out another sigh. Two in two minutes? That might be my new personal best. "You should have taken the interview, Betsy. It would have been perfect for you."

"How do you know that Dad?"

"Because," he pauses, which is a clue that he doesn't know the answer.

"Exactly," I say before he can continue. "Listen, I'm sorry I didn't take your buddy's interview. I'll email him to say I'm sorry if that will get your panties out of a bunch. But I need you to listen: I'm happy here. There is no job in the world that would make me leave, especially one I knew I only got because my dad made a phone call."

"You're going to regret this Betsy," he says. "You're living in a fantasy world right now. One day you're going to realize you need a real job. That being a nanny and making videos with a kindergartener isn't a way to make a living."

"But at least I'll be happy. Bye, Dad. Don't call again."

I hit the end button and let out a breath, coming down from the adrenaline rush.

"He's right, you know."

I jump so high I nearly fall out of the chair at the sound of Wes's voice.

"When did you get back?"

"A few minutes ago." He walks to the other side of the island.

"How much did you hear?"

"Enough to know that I agree with your Dad."

I have to blink a few times because no way he said those words. "You agree with him? About what, exactly?"

He leans down on the white counter, his hands clasped as

he looks down. "I agree with him that you'd be perfect for it. And I agree that you might one day regret it."

I just stare at him in shock. I didn't know how we were going to get this out in the open today, but here it goes. And apparently we're picking up where we left off last night.

"Why are you assuming I want this? What in the world makes you think that?"

The look he gives me is one he never has before, but I've seen it many, many times. It's how my dad would look at me—like I'm stupid and not understanding what he thinks is obvious.

Coming from Wes it hurts a thousand times worse.

"How could you not want it? It's the perfect job for you."

"And you know what the perfect job for me is?"

"Yes. Because you told me this is what you wanted to do. This was the only line of work you actually liked," Wes says. "Did you not tell me that just a few months ago?"

"Yes," I say, hating that he's right. Also how dare he use my own words against me. "But that was then. Before I started the channel and the *ForU* page with Magnolia. Before I found what I was meant to be doing with the people I love doing it with."

Does he not hear me? Didn't we have this exact argument last night or am I hallucinating?

"This is what you're meant to be doing?"

"Yes!" I scream because I feel like that's the only way he's actually going to hear me. "I love getting to share this with her. I love watching her brain work and come up with ideas. Why can't that be enough for me?"

"You're seriously going to tell me that you enjoy making videos with a six-year-old? That doing hair and twirling around in clothes is your idea of work?"

My eyes double in size. "Watch it. You're treading very

close to the line of stupid shit you say when you're mad that you can't take back."

He stops for a moment, running his hand over his mouth.

"Why are you so angry about this?" It's the question that's been on the tip of my tongue since last night. "Should I have told you about it? In hindsight, yes. And I'll apologize for that. But this? You trying to tell me what I should and shouldn't want? I thought you knew me, but clearly you don't."

"I know you better than anyone."

"Bullshit," I say, needing to stand up. "You're assuming again. It was cute before but now it's just pissing me off."

"Pissing you off?" he yells. "I'm trying to help you."

"Help me? How in the world are you helping me?"

"To make you see what you want!"

"I want *this*, you asshole!"

What is not processing for him? Why is he being so damn insistent on this?

"What has gotten into you?" I ask. "Where is all of this coming from? And I swear if you say because you think it's right for me I'm going to lose my shit."

He looks at me, frustration written on his face. And...is that sadness?

"Because." He pauses before continuing. "I don't know if you're thinking about the future."

"The future? Do I all of a sudden have a crystal ball to see what's going to happen in the future?"

"Yes. The future," he says. "Yes, what you and Magnolia are doing is fun right now. But is that sustainable? What about five years from now? Ten? Twelve? You aren't thinking about the long term, so I'm trying to do it for you."

I open my mouth to say that I clearly don't need him to do anything for me when something he said hits me...

Twelve...

Holy shit.

"So that's it," I say. "You think I'm going to leave."

He shakes his head. "I didn't say that."

"You didn't need to, Wes. I'm not Cara. You think that after we're together for a while I'm going to up and leave you too. Wow. I didn't realize you had that little faith in me."

"I don't think—"

I hold up my hand. "No. Clearly you do. And all of this, the assumption of what I want, the pushing me away, you're trying to get ahead of this. Don't you want me here? I thought you loved me?"

"I do."

"This is how you show someone you love them? By pushing them away?"

"I just want you to be happy."

"I am happy!" I'm now screaming because I can't with him anymore. "Every moment except for this fucking fight I have been happier than I've ever been in my entire life. Why would you think that I'd leave? How could you think that? Don't you know how much I love you? How much I love the kids?"

He looks up at me, his eyes now completely void of emotion. "I thought she loved us too."

"Fuck you, Wes," I say, fighting back angry tears. "If you for one second think that I don't love you, and I'd pull the same shit she did, then maybe I should leave. Hell, maybe I'll take the interview! It's what you want, right?"

He doesn't say anything for a second.

"Right?" I ask. "Isn't that what you want?"

He looks up at me and I almost break, seeing the range of emotions in his eyes. It reminds me of the night the divorce was final. Hurt, sadness, and anger. The only difference now is I know my eyes have the same look.

"Deep down, it's what you want," he says. "You just don't know it yet."

I laugh, but it doesn't have an ounce of humor in it. "Of course it is. Because everyone knows what I want better than me."

I storm toward the door, grabbing my keys and slipping on the shoes lying on the mat.

"Betsy! Wait!"

I turn around and shake my head. "I'm sorry she did what she did to you. She's a horrible person. But to even put me in the same sentence as her...after everything we've been through...that's the worst thing you could have ever said to me."

Before he can respond I march out the door and get in my car and start driving. Angry tears are blurring my vision, but it doesn't stop me. Somehow, I end up at Whitley's. But I don't even make it to her door. As soon as I open the Jeep and step to the ground, my legs give out.

And I just sit in the driveway and cry.

Chapter 39
Wes

"Fuck!"

I rip the tie off and toss it on the counter. I've tied ties probably a thousand times in my life. Hell, I've already taught Hank how to do it. But for some reason today I can't seem to get this damn thing to go on right.

"Dad!" Magnolia comes stomping into my room. "You owe the swear jar like, a gazillion dollars!"

"Sorry, sweetheart," I say. "I'm just trying to get my tie on for the wedding."

"I bet Betsy could fix it."

I look down at Magnolia, who is tilting her head at me, daring me to challenge her.

"Magnolia, we talked about this."

"I know. I still don't like it."

I take a breath, wondering how I'm ever going to make this right with them. Betsy texted me a day after the fight saying that she was going to stay at Whitley's this week—after she "got back from Birmingham." She asked that we not make any more decisions, or speak again, until after the interview and wedding.

I nearly threw my phone across the room when I read that. Even though I know everything she's doing is because of me.

That doesn't make it any easier.

When the kids asked where she was and I told them, they each gave me a look like they knew I was full of shit. Even Magnolia. Later that night Emerson asked me if we were broken up. I told her we weren't, that she was just staying at Whitley's for the week. It's not a lie, but I think she could tell that I wasn't exactly being honest.

"I know you miss her, sweetheart," I say as I lift her up and sit her on the bathroom counter.

"She misses us too," she says. "She said so."

"When?"

Magnolia's eyes double in size as she realizes she said something she wasn't supposed to.

"It's okay, sweetheart. If you talked to Betsy you won't be in trouble."

She lets out a breath. "Good. Because we've talked to her every day."

This is a surprise. "Every day?"

"Yup. She calls Emerson every night before bed so she can tell us goodnight and remind us of stuff for school."

I didn't know this. "Before or after I put you guys to bed?"

"Um...Before? Yes. Before. We don't get out of bed to go talk to Betsy."

I rub my face. I'm not mad, I'm just...surprised? I shouldn't be. That's the most Betsy thing ever. It's also kind of sad that she calls the kids more than their mother does.

The woman you compared her to...

"Betsy showed us her dress for Whitley's wedding today. Daddy, she's going to look like a princess."

"I bet." My jaw is clenched, and I'm gripping onto the counter like I'm about to rip it out of the wall.

I did this. I know I did this. But I stand by what I did. It sucked and it hurt, but she needed to be pushed in the right direction. She needed to try for that interview. She needs to see what else is out there.

I know all of that. That doesn't mean I have to like it.

I also know I need to change this subject before Magnolia somehow gets it out of me that I'm the reason Betsy isn't here anymore.

"Is your bag packed to go stay at Grams?"

She shakes her head.

"How about you go do that then?"

"Fine," she groans as I lift her off the counter. "Daddy, make sure you tell Betsy she looks pretty tonight. Girls like to hear that stuff."

I give her a kiss on her nose. "I love you, sweetheart."

The kiss makes her giggle as I set her down, and she sprints out of my bathroom.

I grab the tie and sloppily put it on. Whatever. I was dreading going to this wedding anyway, knowing Betsy was going to be there. But now? Fuck, I don't know if I can see her.

I walk out of the room after spraying my cologne and grabbing my wallet.

"Kids! Let's go!" I say. I'm taking them to my mom's for the night, which they're probably grateful for. I haven't exactly been a load of fun this past week.

All three kids meet me at the front door, overnight bags in hand.

"You guys ready?"

Emerson opens the door and ushers Magnolia out, who apparently is moving into my mother's judging by the three bags she's carrying.

"Dad?"

I look down to Hank. "Yeah, buddy?"

"Are you going to see Betsy tonight?"

I swallow the lump that suddenly appeared in my throat. "I'm sure I will."

"Can you give this to her?"

I look down at the folded piece of paper. "Absolutely."

He walks out the door, the normal bounce in his step gone.

I make sure he's not looking before I open it. Which was the wrong thing to do.

The drawing is of him and Betsy. I'd guess. It's a boy, wearing a maroon and gold scarf, holding hands with a woman with blonde hair, donning a green and white scarf. They are each holding wands with their other hands, pointing them up to the sky.

I fold it back up, unable to look at it anymore.

The kids were obviously devastated when Cara left. And yes, they cried. They asked questions. They also very much understood it was her decision to leave. Not because I told them it was. But because kids are smart and they see things it sometimes takes adults years to comprehend.

I look out to the car where Emerson is loading them up. She looks back at me, and all I see is disappointment all over her face.

I can't blame this on Cara. This one is reserved for me.

I'm the disappointment. I'm the one who is causing them pain. But this time I don't have anyone to blame but myself for their hurt.

I just hope one day they can forgive me.

~

"Scotch. Neat."

The bartender flinches at my tone. Which I get. I basically just barked at the man. I can't imagine that many other wedding guests are coming up here and aggressively demanding drinks because the idea of being here right now is a personal hell.

A week ago, I couldn't wait for this wedding. Because Whitley is the sister of my former coach, the guest list is flooded with my old teammates and coaches. And because Jake and Whitley are basically town royalty, the entire town is here. Everyone is happy. Dancing. Smiling as they celebrate the couple.

And then there's me.

Pissed.

Bitter.

Alone.

I pushed her away. Apparently that's what I do. I know we aren't technically broken up, but we aren't here together. I did that.

And I can't even be mad at anyone but myself.

I look around, and because whoever is controlling the universe hates me, my eyes land on Betsy. She's on the dance floor, twirling around Whitley's nephew, Cameron, who served as ring bearer. He's Coach McAvoy's son, so I got to see him a few times over the years. Cute kid. And, by the way he's looking at Betsy, the boy might have his first crush.

I get it, kid. I absolutely get it.

She looks stunning. It physically hurts to look at her, that's how beautiful she is in her pale pink dress. Her hair is done and pulled off to the side, leaving her shoulder exposed. My lips are begging me to kiss it. To kiss her.

I just want you to be happy...

I take my scotch and slam it back. I see her begin to look my way, so I quickly turn back to the bar.

"Another."

"Whoa there," Simon says, sliding up next to me as the bartender hands me my drink. "I don't know who you think you are, but I'd like to remind you that Wes Taylor is shit at holding down liquor."

I shoot him a glare. "Fuck you."

"Fuck you too," he says taking my drink out of my hand and slamming it back for himself. "What's the matter with you? You've had a pissed off look all day."

I order another drink because fuck him for doing that. "I don't want to talk about it."

"Well, that's not going to happen." Simon grabs his drink, and the one I just ordered, and heads back to our table. I follow him, not because I want to talk, but because the fucker stole my drink.

"Boys, we have a problem here."

"Did they run out of liquor?" Oliver said, his words more slurred than mine. "Because I need a refill soon."

Shane looks at his empty glass then back to him. "Why are you drinking like prohibition is starting tomorrow?"

"Because Shannon broke up with me. This morning."

We all look at him, waiting for the inevitable next part.

"Did you?" Simon asks.

Oliver hangs his head. "Maybe."

Shane smacks up in the back of the head. "How do you 'maybe' propose?"

"When you propose during sex."

We all stare at him. I think this is a first.

"Don't you all say a fucking thing! Plus," he stops mid-sentence to point over to me. "I'm not the one who broke up with the perfect woman because he's scared or some shit."

I feel my face getting red as all three of them shoot a look my way.

"You two broke up?" Shane asks.

I shake my head, suddenly feeling very ashamed. "We never said the words. But we had a huge fight. She hasn't been at the house all week. How did you know?"

Oliver sits back, taking his empty glass with him. "Emerson came to talk to me this week. She needed a person but didn't want to go to you or Betsy."

"Thanks for doing that," I say.

"How could you not tell us?" Simon asks. "And why did you break up with her?"

"We aren't broken up."

"Okay, then what did you do to make her go stay at Whitley's for the week?"

"Who said it was me who did it?"

"Am I wrong?"

I shake my head. "She got an interview in Birmingham that she didn't take. Because of me and the kids."

"Okay," Shane drawls. "I don't see how that leads to where you are now."

"Because," I say, trying to figure out how to explain it. "She just dismissed it. Didn't even consider it. Said she wasn't interested in it."

"Wow, a woman who loves me so much she'd turn down a job to stay with me. Yup, I can see how that's a very unattractive quality in a partner."

I shoot a glare to Simon. "It's not like that."

"Then tell us what it is, dear friend," he says. "Because what I'm hearing right now is you thinking, like you like to do, that you know what's best for everyone."

"I'm not assuming," I defend. "She wasn't thinking about the future. Her future. I didn't want her to have any regrets."

"Speaking of regrets," Simon says, his eyes trailing somewhere behind me for a second before he continues. "I don't have many. But I do have one, and it's not telling you what a money-hungry bitch Cara was. We all agreed to keep our mouths shut because you seemed happy. Well, guess what? I'm going to speak now. Only this time *you're* being the little bitch."

"What are you saying?"

"I'm saying we didn't do anything to save you from your first wife. But I am going to try and save you from being miserable for the rest of your life. Betsy is it. You're not going to do better than her. If you fuck this up, her future will be fine. It's your future that's going to be alone and miserable."

"But her future is what I'm trying to save!"

"Is she not a part of your future?"

I look over to Shane. "What did you say?"

He leans his elbows on the table. "I said, before this fight, was Betsy not part of *your* future?"

"Of course she was."

"Then why can't you be part of hers?"

I sit for a second and let that resonate with me. "Because..."

"Because nothing," Oliver says. "You love her. She loves you. You two are both part of each other's futures. But because you thought you knew what was best, now that future is in jeopardy."

He stands and changes seats to the one next to me. "She loves you Wes. She loves the kids. She's the kind of woman you hope to fall in love with one day. I don't know what's going on in your head, but don't push that away. Some of us look for this kind of love our entire lives. You have it. And now look at it."

Oliver nods to the dance floor as he stands up and makes his way to the bar. I hear Simon yell something to someone as he walks away. But I can't seem to give two shits what my friends are doing. Because through a sea of people on the dance floor, all I can see is Betsy, dancing with my ex-teammate Dexter.

"Fuck no!" I yell, slamming my hands on the table as I stand up. Before I can get anywhere I feel Shane's hand on my arm, pulling me down.

"No," Shane says. "You did this. You pushed her away. That could be you. So you can't be pissed about this. Want it to be different? Then you need to fix it."

All I can do is glare at the dance floor, watching Betsy and Dexter's every fucking move. That fucker better not let a hand slip or he won't have anything to catch footballs with next year.

Out of all the fucking guys here tonight, she's dancing with Dexter? The manwhore of the Fury? He'll fuck any woman in front of him and not think twice about it.

This is it. This is my worst nightmare. This is the thought I had at the bar all those months ago. Betsy in the arms of another man. Smiling at him. Making him feel like he's the only one in the room. I see her laughing right now at something Dexter said. He's not funny. It has to be fake. But even if it is, she's making him feel like he could conquer the world.

I remember that feeling. I've never felt anything like it in my entire life.

That should be me. I should be holding her. I should be feeling her against me. I should be making her smile. I should be kissing her and making her promises for the night.

Fuck. I fucked up. I fucked up so damn bad.

"Shane?"

"Yeah?"

"I need to fix this."

He takes a sip of his drink before answering. "No shit, Sherlock."

Chapter 40
Betsy

Every part of me is tired.

My feet. My legs. My head. My heart.

I'm just...tired.

I plaster on another smile as someone from Whitley's distant family that I met once a million years ago says goodbye to me as we wrap up the post-wedding brunch. I should be used to this by now, I've been wearing this fake smile for the past two and a half days since we arrived at rehearsal on Friday night. Pretty soon this face is going to become permanent.

"Save me," Whitley whispers as she passes by me, only to be greeted by another extended family member.

I crack my neck, ready to put my maid of honor hat back on.

"Excuse me, Whitley?" I say. "So sorry to interrupt, but the hotel manager needs to speak with you."

She apologizes to Great Aunt Somebody and follows me out of the hotel's dining room and down the hall, where we sneak into one of the bathrooms.

"Thank you," she says as she falls into one of the chairs. "I just didn't have talking to one more person in me."

I take a seat in the chair next to her. "I get it. I'd be peopled out if I were you."

She looks over to me, a sad look in her eye. "How are you?"

"Don't," I say. "I'm fine. This is still your wedding weekend and all talk of my love life is off the table."

"Nope," Whitley says. "I'm married. And if we stay in here long enough, all of the relatives will leave. Which means my wedding weekend is all but over."

"What if I don't want to talk?"

"Too bad. What the bride wants, the bride gets."

"Didn't you *just* say that your wedding was done?"

"Technicality," she says, giving me a stern look. "Now talk."

I let out a sigh. "He didn't speak to me at all last night."

She reaches over and takes my hand. "I'm sorry."

"It's not like I expected him to," I say. "He hasn't tried to reach out to me all week. I don't know why I thought last night might be different."

"I hate that you had to put on a happy face all day while you were hurting so much."

I put my free hand on top of our clasped ones. "The only thing that kept me going was you. Thank you for letting me be part of your day and reminding me that love does exist."

"I just hope you didn't have a horrible time. I did see you dancing with Dexter though. How was that?"

I roll my eyes. "He is...quite the character."

"You can say that again," Whitley says with a laugh. "Did you have fun dancing with him?"

I shake my head. "I tried. He asked me to dance so I said why not. He was telling awful jokes and I pretended to laugh. But it beat sitting at a table alone."

"If it makes you feel better, I walked by Wes's table a few times last night. He looked miserable."

I want to say good. That he deserves it. But thinking of Wes being miserable only makes me more miserable.

Because I love him. Even after all the things he said, and the idiot he was being, I still love him.

"So what now?" Whitley asks. "You know I love you, and whatever you need from me I'll—"

I shake my head. "No. I love you for everything you've done for me over the past week. Hell, the last six months. But I need to figure out what's next. And if I can get out of my lease."

Whitley's eyes go wide. "What do you mean get out of your lease?"

I take a breath, bracing for what I'm about to say. "If Wes and I are done, I think it's best if I leave Rolling Hills."

"What? This doesn't sound like you. The Betsy I know doesn't give up like this."

"What am I supposed to do Whitley?" I hold back the tears of frustration, though they are seconds from spilling over. "If he and I can't work this out, can I stay here? Can I live in a house owned by his parents? Whit. I love you, and I know no matter where you are, or where I am, you're going to be my best friend. But I don't know if I can be near him. It hurts too bad. Hell, I could barely survive last night. I can't imagine just seeing him around town, or just randomly running into him at the grocery store."

"What about the kids?" she asks.

And there go the tears. "I don't want to leave them. They already have abandonment issues, and I don't want to add to that. But can I stay for kids who aren't mine? I don't know Whitley. I'm so confused."

She reaches over for my hands. "Let me ask you this. Hypothetically, if you were to leave, where would you go? Did you get the job in Birmingham?"

I shake my head. "I didn't get it."

"I'm sorry, Betsy."

"Don't be," I say, trying to stop the tears. "I didn't get it because I never went to the interview."

"What? I thought you did?"

"I couldn't go through with it. I emailed them from the parking lot saying that I changed my mind and best of luck to them."

In a moment of rage after Wes and I fought, I emailed back Alabama Now Network asking if they were still interested. They got back to me immediately and told me I could come in the next day.

So that morning, I got in my Jeep and drove to Birmingham. I had on my best interview outfit and was ready to wow them so much they would just have to offer me the job on the spot.

Then I pulled into the parking lot and I just sat there. I couldn't make myself open the door. So I told them no thank you and turned around and drove back to Rolling Hills.

"Wow," Whitley says. "So what would you do? If you decided to leave?"

I shrug. "I don't know yet. I'll figure it out. I always do."

She stands up, pulling me up with her. "Damn right you do."

We hug for at least a minute, each of us crying for the same, yet different reasons.

Could I leave her? This town that I've grown to love? The family I found here?

Whitley brought me to Rolling Hills, promising that it would heal me.

That promise was kept. She healed me. Wes healed me.

The kids healed me. I became the person I always wanted to be.

But all chapters end. Sometimes you see them coming. Sometimes you don't.

Maybe this is where mine ends.

"Okay," I say, wiping the tears from my face. "I need to go."

Whitley nods. "I've hid for long enough. I'm sure Jake is probably wondering where I'm at."

"Either that or he's still fending off your mother's friends."

This gets a laugh out of her. "You'd think now that he's married they'd quit asking for lap dances."

"That's what you get for marrying a thirst trap."

She rolls her eyes. "Don't I know it."

We laugh and link arms as we walk out of the ladies' room and back toward the restaurant. I stop mid step when I see Oliver standing in front of me, looking pretty worse for the wear, holding a sign that just has an arrow, pointing toward the door.

"Oliver?" I ask, very confused. "Are you okay?"

He shakes his head. "You're lucky I like you."

"Okay..."

He nods me out the door, where I'm stopped in front of Shane, holding another sign with another arrow. I look back to Oliver, then back to Shane, now seriously confused.

"What are you guys doing?"

"Just keep going," Shane says.

I do as he says, continuing to walk through the hotel parking lot. I could either go left or stay straight, but Amelia has a sign telling me to go left. She gives me a smile and a nod as I turn, only to see Simon in front of me, a sign pointing for me to go straight. Then he holds up a finger and shows another piece of poster board. I giggle when I read what it says.

Just so you know, we're Team Betsy.

I whisper "thank you" as he steps out of the way, letting me see where my Jeep is parked. Though even if I didn't know exactly where it was, I couldn't miss it right now.

It's covered in balloons. Multi-colored streamers are flying in the wind.

And there's Wes, standing there, somehow still looking so damn handsome even though his eyes look just as heavy as mine, standing with his own sign.

Forgive me?

Chapter 41
Wes

I TAKE IN A BREATH AS SOON AS I SEE HER TALKING TO
Simon. She hasn't looked my way yet, which gives me a few
more seconds to remind myself what I need to say. And also
another few seconds to panic that this isn't going to work.

What's taking him so long? Does he have another sign?
What the fuck did he do? I'm nervous enough as it is standing
here. I knew putting him last was a mistake.

I can feel the sign shaking under my fingers as I do my best
to hold onto it. Then she turns my way and everything goes
still.

God I've missed her. She looked gorgeous last night. But
this morning? Barely any makeup, her hair on the top of her
head and a pair of leggings that make me damn near bite my lip
off? Fuck, I've never seen her look more beautiful.

I can't fuck this up. Not again. I need her in my life. *We*
need her.

I just hope it's not too late.

"What's all this?"

I let out a small laugh as I look back at her Jeep. "My friends seem to have taken a liking to decorating cars."

She smiles. "The streamers are a nice touch."

"Thank Shane for that."

"You mean Oliver?"

"No," I say, shaking my head. "Actually, we couldn't find Oliver this morning until the last minute. The decorating was the rest of the crew, which Amelia was excited she got to be a part of this time."

"Wow," she says. "I don't know what to say."

"Don't say anything," I put down the sign and take a deep breath. "All you need to do is listen."

"Okay."

I want to reach for her hands, but I don't want to push my luck too soon. "I need to start by saying that I'm sorry."

She nods. "Go on."

"I was an asshole."

"Correct."

"And you were right. About everything."

"I know."

"When I saw that text message, it set me off in a way I wasn't expecting."

"And I'll apologize again for that," she says. "If I would have known that you would have that kind of reaction, I would have told you. But that day you had just been offered the coaching job, and you were so excited. I wasn't about to ruin it for something I wasn't even considering."

"I know that. Technically I know that. But that one omission of knowledge set off a spiral in my brain I didn't know was on the brink of overflowing. Suddenly every bad voice I've ever had in my head over the past few years, and in the months after the divorce, came flowing back."

"I'm sorry, Wes."

I shake my head. "Don't you dare say you're sorry for anything. This was all me. Pushing you away, assuming things about your life that I had no right to, that wasn't me talking."

"But it was, Wes," she says, signaling me to follow her to a nearby bench. I'm glad she did because somehow sitting, and being close to her, makes me instantly feel more relaxed.

"Those things you said? They hurt. They hurt me deep," Betsy continues. "So I know they came out harsh and heated in the moment, but they happened because somewhere in your mind, you had already thought them. Maybe not daily. Maybe not actively. But somewhere, they were there."

"Wow," I say. "When did you become a psychologist?"

She shrugs. "It was one of my minors. I have four."

That's a conversation for later. But she's right. I didn't come up with those off the cuff. They came to me when I needed a response for a situation.

"You're right," I say. "They were there."

"Can I ask a question now?"

"Please."

"Do you think I'm going to leave you? Deep down in your gut, do you think that I'm going to up and leave you because one day I might get bored?"

I nod, which I'm already ashamed of doing. "I know you wouldn't. I heard myself saying those things and somehow, I was making myself believe it. In the logical part of my brain, I know you aren't my past. I know you aren't her, and I don't want to even say her name because comparing you to her *was* horrible. I know you're different. I know you wouldn't do that. But somewhere, some voice in my head got really loud and convinced me that you were going to do that. And yes, the voice is quiet now, but I don't know if he's gone. And that scares the shit out of me."

She reaches for my hands and takes them in hers. "You know it's okay to be scared."

I shake my head. "I don't want to be."

"I'm scared too."

I pop my head back up. Is she serious? She's the most confident woman I've ever met. What does she have to be scared about?

"I have been a failure at everything I've ever done," she begins. "I have never held a job. Never had a successful relationship. I am such a screw-up my own parents think of me as a failure. Do you know how scared I was that first time I watched the kids? I was terrified that someone was going to choke, or break a bone, or that I would set your house on fire."

"But none of those things happened."

"They didn't, but that doesn't mean I'm not still scared. I'm scared of how much I love you. And how much I love the kids. I'm scared that the words you said are true and you don't want me anymore. I'm scared I'm not enough. And I want to be enough. I want to be everything you need."

"Betsy..." I wrap my arms around her, bringing her tight into me. She grips my shirt like she needs it to stay upright.

I didn't know she felt like that. Any of it.

Turns out both of us were keeping in some loud voices.

"We're quite the pair, aren't we?"

This makes her laugh in between the tears that have started falling. "A match made in baggage heaven."

We pull away, but I make sure I take her hands back in mine.

"I'm sorry again." I know I've said it, but I need to make sure I say it one more time. And every day for as long as she'll let me. "I'm sorry I let the voices and insecurities get the best of me. I'm sorry I tried to dictate your life. Somehow, I thought I was protecting you and your future, even as you were telling me that's not what you wanted."

"We can't predict the future. I could have taken that job, thinking it was perfect for me, and then in five years the company could go under. At any point in your football career you could have gotten a season-ending injury that would have changed the course of your life. We don't know, Wes. And we don't know what's going to happen with us. I could move in and you could resent me for needing a closet just for my shoes. You could leave beard hairs in the sink that make me the subject of a true crime podcast one day. Or, we could live happily ever after and be that gross couple that the kids will be embarrassed about. We don't know. No one does. We have to trust each other. We have to talk to each other. We can't let little voices in our heads grow so loud that one day we vomit them out. If we let that happen, then we are done. But if we know what we need to do, and make sure we do those things every day, then we can be end game."

I cup her cheeks in my hands, bringing our lips together. As soon as we connect, I feel the world shifting back to normal. Somehow, just feeling her lips on mine, grounds me in a way I've never felt before.

And she's right. All of it. We need to talk to each other. We need to listen to each other. And most importantly, we need to be there for each other.

Because that whole thing about being old and gray and embarrassing the kids? Well, I had that growing up. And I want it now more than anything.

"Wait!" I say as I quickly back away from the kiss. "What about the interview? Didn't you take it? I know I insisted you did, and if you got it then I can't be mad if you go. But I really don't want you to."

She slowly smiles, instantly relieving the tightness in my chest.

"I didn't go."

"What?"

"I didn't go. Well, I went. I drove to Birmingham. And then I couldn't get out of the car."

"Why?"

She gives my hands a squeeze. "Do you want the reason I told myself then or the reason I know now?"

"How about both?"

That makes her smile. "The second I pulled into the parking lot, I knew it didn't feel right. I've been through enough bad jobs to know pretty early when something isn't going to be a good fit."

"Now the other reason?"

"My heart wasn't in it," she says. "Because my heart was still with you."

Chapter 42
Betsy
~One month later~

"Woo hoooooo!"

Wes and I laugh as Hank hoots and hollers as he sprints out of the school toward us as we stand outside the car in the pickup line.

"I'm officially a third-grader now!"

Wes laughs as he ruffles his hair. "Yes, you are."

"Daddy! Betsy!" Magnolia yells as she also runs to us. I get it. Everyone is running. It's the last day of school. I'd be running too.

"How was your last day, Miss Mags?"

"Great! We played outside all day. Liam asked me to marry him. And I got to take home all of my artwork so we can hang it up!"

I stifle a laugh as Wes nearly chokes on his own spit. "Liam asked you what?"

Magnolia rolls her eyes in the most adorable way. "I told him no, Dad. Geez. I don't have time for boys. Isn't that right, Betsy?"

I nod. "Darn right you don't. We have an empire to create."

"Those videos aren't going to make themselves," she says with a nod.

I laugh as I pick her up, giving her a kiss on the cheek.

Usually Wes and I don't tag-team pickup duties, but since it's the last day of school, we decided it would be fun to go together to get the kids and take them for ice cream. Maybe start a new tradition for their first last day of school in Rolling Hills.

"Where's Emerson?" Wes asks.

I look around the sea of kids, trying to pick her out. I look for the yellow T-shirt she had on this morning, but can't seem to spot her. This is unlike her. Usually she's one of the first ones out of the building.

"There she is!" Magnolia says as she points to the flagpole.

I turn to my right to see Emerson and I nearly drop Magnolia in the process.

Because at that moment, I see a boy, who I think is named Jay, lean in and give her a kiss on the cheek.

I hurry and look at Wes, who has started talking to Oliver and thankfully didn't see that. My man is many things, but ready for his oldest daughter to start getting kisses from boys is definitely not on that list.

"How about you two get in your seats," I say as I open the door so they can climb in. "Your Dad and I have a surprise for you guys."

That's all Magnolia and Hank need to hear. When I look back for Emerson, I see her walking toward me, the boy maybe named Jay walking toward the buses.

I meet her halfway, which she doesn't see at first. But when she does, I'm all knowing smiles.

"Hey there, Em. How was your last day of school?"

Her face gets instantly red. "Fine."

"I bet it was," I singsong.

This gets me the loudest groan I've ever gotten from these kids. I'm officially entering cringe territory, and it's all I can do not to cackle.

"Betsy, please don't."

I laugh, bringing her in for a side hug. "Don't worry. Your secret is safe with me, and your dad didn't see anything."

This seems to relieve her. "Thanks."

"No problem," I say. "And you know, if you have any questions, about anything, you know you can talk to me, right? And if you want to know why you should always use extra caution for any man whose name starts with 'J', I can explain that as well."

This gets me a laugh. "Thanks, Betsy."

She stops and gives me a hug, which I return with an extra squeeze.

How did I get so lucky? Yes, I got lucky with Wes. The man is...well...he's not perfect. But neither am I. But we're perfect for each other.

Where I truly got lucky is that I get to be in the life of these three amazing kiddos. A wise woman once told me that I'm the only one who knows my destination. I didn't know it at the beginning, but since these three walked up to my porch, they were my destination. This family saved me in more ways than I think they know. And I count my blessings every day for them.

"Buckle up," I tell the three of them. "I'm going to go tear your dad away from Uncle Oliver then it's surprise time."

They all cheer as I walk over to Wes and catch the tail-end of his sentence.

"You're seriously not going to tell me who you're going with?"

Well, this gets my attention.

"Where are you going? With who? How have you not told us? Did you already propose to her?"

Oliver shoots me a look. "Vegas. Not telling. Because I haven't. And no."

Wes laughs. "I'm sorry, man. It's just that you always tell us everything. You being secretive is throwing me off balance."

"It's no big deal," Oliver said. "I met someone. She has an extra ticket to Vegas. She invited me to go. That's it."

Wes and I look at each other, clearly knowing that's *not* it, but silently agreeing to let it go. It's Oliver's last day of school. No teacher deserves to be grilled on the last day of school.

"Well, I hope you have fun," I say, leaning in to give him a hug. "Bring us back a souvenir."

He smiles. "Will do."

He and Wes do their man-hug thing before we head back to the car.

"He's going to propose again, isn't he?" Wes asks.

I snort. "He's going to Vegas," I say. "That man is going to come back married."

The two of us laugh as we get in the car, all the kids anxiously waiting for us, and their surprise.

"Dad?"

Wes looks back in the rearview at Hank. "Yeah, buddy?"

"Can Markie come over and swim tomorrow?"

I laugh. I was told by Wes, and a few of the moms I've become friendly with, that summer break means a lot of snacks, and a lot of requests for activities. I didn't realize this was going to be starting so soon.

"Probably not, buddy," he says as he exits the parking lot. "We have Dr. Kelly tomorrow, but maybe the next day."

He nods and goes back to whatever he was playing on his tablet. It's a relief that the kids don't moan and groan when the subject of Dr. Kelly comes up. Because that woman has been a life saver.

After Wes and I talked everything out, I immediately moved in. Was it the best move? Who knows? But we both knew it was inevitable. So, for the second time in less than a year, I packed my stuff and changed my address.

Only this time I'm pretty sure it's permanent.

The kids were over the moon when I told them that not only did Wes and I make up, but that I was moving in. We knew that was going to be their reaction. What we didn't know was how they were going to react when we told them that we thought it would be best for all of us to start talking to a family therapist.

Because as Wes and I both realized, not only do we each have some traumas that could be treated, but so do the kids. Cara did a number on them, whether they vocalize it or not. And we don't want that to carry into their teenage and adult years.

Dr. Kelly has been amazing. Somehow she connects with Magnolia as much as she does with Wes and me.

It also helps that we go to The Joint for dinner after. Food is therapy as much as anything else.

"All right, Emerson, question time," Wes says. "What are we most excited about this summer?"

"Disney. Definitely Disney."

"That's right!" I say, reaching back for a high five. Once I made mention to Wes that we should try to take a vacation, the kids immediately asked to go to Disney World. When I said that I'd never been, there was no further discussion on where we were going. Hank just wanted to make sure that we were also going to Universal to see our favorite wizarding world.

As if he had to ask.

"How about you, Hank?"

"Going to see Mom."

I reach over and give Wes's hand a squeeze at the mention of the trip to California.

Per the divorce agreement, Cara gets one month in the summer. Because he had a feeling something might happen, Wes never told the kids this. It was a good thing, because a few weeks ago she called, asking if she could shorten the time from a month to two weeks. Something about getting tickets to a music festival or some shit like that.

It was one thing for the kids to spend the night with her in Nashville at Christmas, but Wes was worried about two weeks away. Easy enough. I suggested that after our Florida trip, we go to California with them. The kids go to Cara's, and we find a place close enough that we can get to them in an emergency—or if she decides she's done parenting—but far enough away that we can have an adult vacation, just the two of us.

He liked the sound of that.

I liked the sound of getting two weeks with Wes. Alone. Preferably naked for much of that time.

"That whole trip is going to be so exciting," I say. "Magnolia? What about you?"

I look back at her as she taps her little finger to her mouth before her eyes get big as she comes up with her answer. "Getting a baby!"

Wes whips around and stares at me. I shake my head so hard it almost rolls off my neck.

"Mags, sweetie, where are you getting a baby?"

"At the mall," she says, her tone communicating just how exhausting it is to deal with idiots like us. "Uncle Simon told me he'd take me shopping if I got good grades. Which I did. So I'm going to have him buy me a new baby doll."

Wes and I let out a collective sigh of relief. Hell, I think Emerson does too.

"What about you?" Wes asks me as we pull into the ice cream shop. "What are you looking most forward to this summer?"

I turn to him as he puts the car in park. "I think you know."

We lean in for a kiss, which of course gets a chorus of "ews" and "gross" from the kids as they pile out of the car. Sometimes I think he does it in front of them just to embarrass them. I also know they secretly love it.

"And how about you?" I ask. "What are you looking forward to this summer?"

He smiles. "That's easy."

"Oh really?"

"It is."

"You can't say two weeks of sex," I say. "That was my technical answer and no copying."

He laughs and pulls me closer. "I wasn't going to say that, but it's high up there."

"Then what is it?"

He leans in, giving me a slow, but promising kiss, as we steal these few minutes alone. We don't get these often, which makes them even more special.

"You."

"Me?"

He nods. "Yeah, you. Every day with you is an adventure. Every day I count my blessings that you're in my life. Every day I learn that I love you more than the day before. So yeah, my answer will always be you."

I kiss him again, because how do you not kiss a man after he says those kinds of things to you?

You don't. You can't. And they usually end up with you being naked.

I love this man. So much. When I came to Rolling Hills, I didn't know what was in store for me. I definitely didn't think

I'd meet the man of my dreams and find a love I didn't think existed.

I was just a lost soul trying to find her way. I ended up finding a home.

And my home is Wes Taylor.

Epilogue
Oliver

"She loves you Wes. She loves the kids. She's the kind of woman you hope to fall in love with one day. I don't know what's going on in your head, but don't push that away. Some of us look for this kind of love our entire lives. You have it. And now look at it."

I nod to the dance floor where Betsy is dancing with one of Wes's former teammates. It's a slower song, a wedding staple if you ask me. Everyone who's here with a date is on the dance floor.

Which means that's my cue for another trip to the bar.

I love weddings. If I do say so myself, I'm the best wedding date there is. I like to dance and have fun. I will lead any conga line. Need a dancing partner for the great grandmother? I'm your guy. Need someone to hype the newlyweds up? I'm your man. And when it comes to catching the garters? No one is better than me. Most guys run away from it. Not me, I'll grab that thing every fucking time and celebrate like I just caught a foul ball at a Tennessee Arrows game.

The old wives' tale is that when you catch it, that means you're next.

Bullshit. It's all bullshit. I've caught seventeen of them. Yet here I am, still alone.

"Jack and Coke."

I don't know why I needed to say it. I've been to the bar so many times tonight this man knows my drink by now. He sets it in front of me and I turn around to watch the couples on the dance floor.

I should be out there. I thought Shannon and I had something going. Yes, it was stupid to say what I said. And I apologized. Apparently she's never said or done anything stupid before like proposing during sex.

Whatever. That just means she wasn't the one. She's out there somewhere. One day I'll find her.

"Jack and Coke. Make it a double."

I look to my left and nearly lose my footing. And not because of the six Jack and Cokes I've had tonight. She's that damn gorgeous. Her red hair is sleek and smooth, running down her back. The gold dress she's wearing is sexy as hell. And a woman who drinks Jack and Coke? Now that's my type.

And because I'm so drunk, I'm seeing two of her. Double the pleasure, double the fun.

"Do you want to dance?"

She turns to look at me and even in my drunkenness I can tell she doesn't know if I was talking to her.

"Excuse me?"

I nod to the dance floor. "I asked if you'd like to dance?"

"Do you always ask strangers to dance?"

"Only the beautiful ones."

She rolls her eyes. "Now that's a line if I've ever heard one."

I shake my head. "Not a line."

"Really?"

"Really."

"Well sorry," she says as she takes her drink from the bartender. "I don't dance."

"What do you mean you don't dance? Who doesn't dance?"

"Me," she says before taking a sip. "Sorry to ruin your night."

She turns back to the bar, but I don't let that stop me. I'm persistent if nothing else.

"I'm Oliver."

I extend my hand to her, because that's what drunk me feels like is the right thing to do at the moment. For a second I think she's just going to walk away. She looks down at my hand, then back up to me. I'm about to pull it back when her hand meets mine. I don't know if it's the Jack or what, but I swear I think I was just electrocuted.

"Nice to meet you Oliver. I'm Izzy. How about another drink?"

Yes, next up in the Rolling Hills crew is Oliver and Izzy in The One I Need, coming August 2023. We all know how much Oliver loves proposing, so it's only going to be fitting for him to end up in an accidental marriage. He is about to go to Vegas after all...

So who's Izzy? You can meet her in Match Maker. If you liked Betsy, then just wait until you meet this bad ass businesswoman. Read Match Maker for free with Kindle Unlimited!

Bonus Scene

Betsy

~~ Seven Months Later ~~

"Good morning, beautiful."

I smile before I even open my eyes. Feeling Wes's lips on my cheek first thing in the morning is always a good reason to smile. But today there's more to it.

Today is Christmas morning.

I roll over to my back, slowly opening my eyes to see Wes leaning over me. "Merry Christmas."

He gives me another kiss, only this time on the lips, and not as deep as I'd like. Probably smart. I know we have a full morning and anything more than that will surely cause us to start Christmas morning late. And that would not go over well with the Taylor children.

"What time is it?" I ask.

"Six."

"In the morning?"

He chuckles. "Yeah. I told you we started early around here."

I sit up, though I really wish I was still buried underneath the softest comforter I've ever slept under. "I thought you were joking."

"No joke. The kids have been up for an hour. I've kept them at bay for as long as I can."

"Fine," I grumble. Though I'm not really mad. I'm just not a morning person. I actually think I'm more excited for this Christmas than the kids. Which is saying something. Hank started making a wishlist in September. "How long do I have before I'm attacked?"

Wes looks to our bedroom door then back to me. "Five seconds."

More like two. As soon as he finishes, the door slams open as all three kids run into our room and jump on the bed. Well, two. Emerson didn't run. But she dutifully followed behind, recording each moment like a pro. She's Magnolia and my producer now. She loves it. And she's damn good at it.

"Merry Christmas Betsy!"

"Thanks you guys," I say, giving a hug to each of the kids. "Thanks for letting me sleep."

"We let you sleep as long as we could," Hank says. "But six is our limit. We're usually done by now."

"Well thanks for that," I say. "But I'm awake. I'm ready. Let's go open some presents."

"You're not ready," Magnolia says, giving me a once over. "You're not in your Christmas day pajamas. Also, we don't go downstairs first. We wait upstairs. You and Daddy go check and make sure Santa came. And when you give us the signal we come down. *That's* how Christmas day works."

"Yes ma'am," I say with a little salute. When did Magnolia become Emerson?

"Come on you two," Emerson says. "Let's go wait in my room while Betsy gets dressed."

The two don't argue. They follow their sister out with no questions asked. And it's not just because it's Christmas morning. This is how it goes in this house. Hank and Magnolia would jump off a cliff for Emerson. They love her so much. And she loves them. They haven't fully realized it yet, but over the past year, they've grown a bond that not many siblings have. And when it comes to Emerson, she's their glue. She's their leader and a damn good one.

And I'm so proud of her for that. I'm even prouder for how she's come into her own since moving to Rolling Hills. She's now in seventh grade, getting straight As, is on student council, and joined the band. She has friends she loves, a style she's grown into, and I must say, is a pretty badass teenager. She even asked us about signing her up for CPR courses so she can become a certified babysitter.

Hell, I didn't even do that when I became the nanny. Probably should have. Whoops.

"Get dressed," Wes says, leaning in for one more kiss. "I'll go downstairs and get the tree lit."

"Sounds good." I smile as I watch him walk out the door, donning this year's matching Christmas set of red and green striped pajamas. They look ridiculous.

I fucking love them.

I jump out of bed and head to the en suite bathroom, quickly doing what I need to do so I don't need to make them wait any longer. I know last year I spent Christmas with them—it's a day I'll never forget—but this year feels like my first real Taylor family Christmas. And I want it to be perfect.

The presents are already set up around the tree. Wes and I stayed up last night until one in the morning making sure everything was perfect. We could have gone to bed after that, but we didn't. Wes held me as we sat and took in the glow of the tree and just relaxed after the hectic day. We didn't say much. I know I was thinking about how far we've come in just a year. I have a feeling he was thinking the same thing too.

It's funny to think about that at this time a year ago, Wes and I were just beginning this. We had no idea what we were in for. We didn't know if this was a good idea. We didn't know how the kids would react. We didn't know anything.

Now looking back, I can't believe we ever had a doubt.

I give my hair a quick brush and throw on the Christmas day jammies as I head out of our bedroom. I peek across the hall to Emerson's room, only to see no one there. Did they go down without me? After Magnolia's emphatic speech?

I check the other rooms only to see no one there. "Where is everyone?"

The house is strangely quiet as I start heading down the stairs. There aren't many lights on, and with it still being dark outside, the only lights I can see are the lights of the tree and I'm guessing a few of the other decorations we have around the living room.

I'm halfway down the stairs when I almost fall the rest of the way. Not because I lose my footing. No. It's because of the sight in front of me.

The three kids are each holding a sign.

Emerson's has two words....

Will you

Next is Hank...

Marry

Then there's Magnolia.

Our Dad?

∼

Wes

As soon as I can tell that she's read all three, I lower myself to one knee and hold the ring up for display. She gasps on the staircase as she takes everything in.

I know she's going to say yes, but that doesn't make me any less nervous doing this. I don't know how Oliver did this so often. I do know this though, this is the last time I'm doing it.

Because Betsy and I? We're for life. That I'm sure of.

Hell, even the kids know it's a sure thing. When I talked to them about marrying Betsy, they not only asked what took me so long, they demanded to be a part of it. And, it was their idea to do it on Christmas morning. As Emerson so eloquently said, this was the day that we became a family. It only made sense for this day to make it official.

I couldn't have said it better myself.

As for the signs, those were my idea. I didn't even need to ask Oliver for help. He was mad at me though because I took Amelia and Whitley with me to shop for engagement rings. That wasn't my fault. He was preoccupied.

That's what happens when you fall in love.

Speaking of love...

Tears are falling down Betsy's cheeks as she makes her way down the rest of the steps. The kids don't move, even though I can tell from the corner of my eye Magnolia is about to jump out of her pajamas. She blows them each a kiss as she walks toward me.

"Merry Christmas, beautiful."

She laughs through the tears. "This is quite the Christmas morning."

I take her hand in mine. "There are not enough ways to say how much I love you. And I don't know if I could even name all the things I love you for. I love the way you love me. I love how you are not just a bonus mom to the kids, but also a friend and a mentor. I love how you love fiercely and unapologetically. I love the way you fight for the ones you love. Sometimes even causing me to have to pay for damages."

This makes everyone laugh. And yes, it might have been a reference to our summer vacation in California when the kids went to visit Cara. Things were fine for the entire trip, until we went to pick them up. Cara said something snarky to Betsy as we were leaving. I wanted to say something back, but Betsy shook her head telling me not to. And she was right. We needed to be the bigger people.

At least that's what I thought she was conveying to me.

No, Betsy decided not to use her words. She just accidentally knocked over a glass vase that, knowing Cara, was more expensive than it needed to be.

She sent me a bill for damages.

It was worth every penny.

"Betsy Sullivan, I love you. When I think of forever, I only think of you. Will you do me the honor of being my wife?"

She doesn't make me wait. "Yes Wes. I'll marry you."

I slide the ring on her finger and stand up, bringing her in for a kiss that normally I don't give around the kids. They don't seem to mind though judging by their applause in the background.

Her hands cup my face, and I can feel the metal of the ring against my cheek. Knowing I'm going to feel that for the rest of my life only doubles down on the love that I feel for this woman.

I wish I could keep kissing her, but I feel a poking at my side—and it's coming from someone with tiny fingers.

"Daddy?"

We chuckle as we pull away. I'm not mad though. The real celebration is going to happen tonight when the kids are spending the night at their grandparents.

"Yeah sweetie?"

"Am I going to be in the wedding?"

I look over to Betsy. "You'd have to ask the bride."

Magnolia turns to Betsy, who is all smiles. "Of course you are," Betsy says. "I couldn't imagine getting married without the three of you in the wedding."

Magnolia lets out a sigh of relief. "Good. Just no green dresses. It's not in my color wheel."

Betsy starts cracking up laughing as I'm left a little perplexed. Magnolia doesn't seem to mind though. She's already in front of the tree, inspecting the presents.

"Color wheel?"

Betsy wraps her arms around my neck, which . "Your daughter is a budding fashion icon. Of course she knows her color wheel."

I just shake my head as I bring her in close to me. "What am I going to do with you?"

"I don't know. But you're stuck with me now."

I lean down and give her one more kiss. "I wouldn't have it any other way."

Also by Chelle Sloan

FULL CHELLE SLOAN READING LIST

All titles available with Kindle Unlimited

NASHVILLE FURY SERIES

Off the Record

Off Track

Off Season

Off Limits

Off the Market at Christmas

LOVE ONLINE SERIES

Thirst Trap

Match Maker

Run Run Rudolph

ROLLING HILLS

The One I Want

The One I Need (Coming August 2023)

THE SALVATION SOCIETY

Reformation: A Salvation Society Novel

Acknowledgments

When I first started my author journey so long ago, I always thought I'd write small town. I'd write about groups of friends and families. It's what I loved reading, and that's what I wanted to write.

Now don't get me wrong, I love that I wrote the Nashville Fury. I can't imagine this world I've created without starting with the Fury. But somehow, I think I was always meant to be here. Because I have never felt so good writing a book in my life.

I loved these characters from the first page. Single dad tropes are my catnip, and Wes is everything I love in a single dad character. And then there's Betsy. She just came alive from the moment I started writing her. I used to think something was wrong with me as an author because others talked about how characters would "speak" to them, and I never really had that.

But with Betsy? Her loud mouth was clear as day.

I love this book with my whole heart and I hope you did too. Because I've found my way to Rolling Hills, and I don't know if I'm leaving anytime soon.

Now, to the thank you...

First and foremost, my parents. As always, you are my biggest cheerleaders even if you still have no idea what I'm doing. You've allowed me to follow my dreams and my path, and for that I am forever grateful.

To my family and friends: Your support has been amazing.

Many of you have no clue how I ended up here, but that doesn't mean the support hasn't been there. I love you all.

Amanda, who would have thought when we met seven years ago that one day we'd be here together? Thank you for keeping my life in order. Thank you for reminding me to drink water. And thank you for being my best friend. I promise I won't fire you this week.

Kelly, you've been with me on this book journey since day one. Not only are you an amazing alpha reader, but you are an amazing friend.

Julia, Georgia, Mae, and Claire: How did I write a book before I met you ladies? All I know is I don't ever want to write one without y'all again. A special shout out to Georgia, who was the idea generator behind the hot tub scene.

Kiezha, thank you for correcting my bad grammar habits and being an amazing editor. Michele and Chloe: Thank you for dotting the Is and crossing the Ts.

Corinne, I'm here because of you. If you wouldn't have given me a chance I wouldn't have started writing. You forever changed my life.

Adriana, thanks for always picking up the phone.

Last but not least: Readers. I love you all. Whether this was your first book by me, or you've been here since Reformation, I'm truly thankful for all of you. There are so many amazing authors you could be reading. I'm humbled that you chose me.

About the Author

Known for her witty sense of humor, Chelle Sloan is a former sports reporter who recently completed her Masters in Journalism, and is now putting that to good use — one happily ever after at a time.

An Ohio native, she's fiercely loyal to Cleveland sports, is the owner of way too many — yet not enough — tumblers and will be a New Kids on the Block fan until the day she dies. She does her best writing at Starbucks, where you can usually find a venti Pink Drink within reach. Oh, and yes, you probably saw her on TikTok.

As for her own happily every after? Maybe one day...

Stay up to date with all things Chelle by joining the VIP Squad!
Reader Group: Chelle Sloan's Book Squad
Website: www.chellesloan.com

www.ingramcontent.com/pod-product-compliance
Lightning Source LLC
Chambersburg PA
CBHW070610300726
48975CB00006B/1775